Isaac Israel Hayes

Cast Away in the Cold

An Old Man's Story of a Young Man's Adventures, as Related by Captain John Hardy

Isaac Israel Hayes

Cast Away in the Cold
An Old Man's Story of a Young Man's Adventures, as Related by Captain John Hardy

ISBN/EAN: 9783337082932

Printed in Europe, USA, Canada, Australia, Japan

Cover: Foto ©Andreas Hilbeck / pixelio.de

More available books at **www.hansebooks.com**

AN OLD MAN'S STORY OF A YOUNG MAN'S ADVENTURES,

AS RELATED BY

CAPTAIN JOHN HARDY, MARINER.

By DR. ISAAC I. HAYES,

AUTHOR OF "AN ARCTIC BOAT JOURNEY," "THE OPEN POLAR SEA," ETC.

BOSTON 1892
LEE AND SHEPARD PUBLISHERS
10 MILK STREET NEXT "THE OLD SOUTH MEETING HOUSE"

CONTENTS.

—•—

CHAPTER I.

CHAPTER II.

CHAPTER III.

CHAPTER IV.

CHAPTER V.

CHAPTER XIII.

CHAPTER XIV.

CHAPTER XV.

CHAPTER XVI.

CHAPTER XVII.

CHAPTER XVIII.

CHAPTER XIX.

CHAPTER XX

CAST AWAY IN THE COLD.

CHAPTER I.

RELATES HOW AN ANCIENT MARINER MET THREE LITTLE PEOPLE AND PROMISED THEM A LITTLE STORY.

A BRIGHT sun shone on the little village of Rockdale; a bright glare was on the little bay close by, as on a silver mirror. Three bright children were descending by a winding path towards the little village; a bright old man was coming up from the little village by the same path, meeting them.

The three children were named William Earnest, Fred Frazer, and Alice. Alice was William Earnest's sister, while Fred Frazer was his cousin. William Earnest was the eldest, and he was something more than eleven and something less than twelve years old. His cousin Fred Frazer was nearly a year younger, while his sister Alice was a little more than two years

I

A

younger still. Fred Frazer was on a holiday visit to his rela-
tives, it being vacation time from school; and the three children were ready for any kind of adventure, and for every sort
of fun.

The children saw the old man before the old man saw the
children; for the children were looking down the hill, while
the old man, coming up the hill, was looking at his footsteps.

As soon as the children saw the old man, the eldest recognized him as a friend; and no sooner had his eyes lighted on
him than, much excited, he shouted loudly, "Hurrah, there
comes the ancient mariner!"

His cousin, much surprised, asked quickly, "Who's the ancient mariner?" And his sister, more surprised, asked tim-
idly, "What's the ancient mariner?"

Then the eldest, much elated, asked derisively, "Why,
don't you know?" And then he said, instructively: "He's
been about here for ever so long a time; but he went away
last year, and I have n't seen him for a great while. He's the
most wonderful man you ever saw, — tells such splendid stories, — all about shipwrecks, pirates, savages, Chinamen, bear-
hunts, bull-fights, and everything else that you can think of.
I call him the 'Ancient Mariner,' but that is n't his right
name. He's Captain Hardy; but he looks like an ancient
mariner, as he is, and I got the name out of a book. Some
of the fellows call him 'Old Father Neptune.'"

"What a funny name!" cried Fred.

"What do they call him Father Neptune for?" inquired
Alice.

"Because," answered William, looking very wise, — "because,
you know, Neptune, he's god of the sea, and Captain Hardy
looks just like the pictures of him in the story-books. That's
why they call him Old Father Neptune."

By this time the old man had come quite near, and William, suddenly leaving his companions, dashed ahead to meet him.

"O Captain Hardy, I'm so glad to see you!" exclaimed the little fellow, as he rushed upon him. "Where did you come from? Where have you been so long? How are you? Quite well, I hope," — and he grasped the old man's hand with both his own, and shook it heartily.

"Well, my lad," replied the old man, kindly, "I'm right glad to see you, and will be right glad to answer all your questions, if you'll let them off easy like, and not all in a broadside"; and as they walked on up the path together, William's questions were answered to his entire satisfaction.

Then they came presently to Fred and Alice, who were introduced by William, very much to the delight of Fred; but Alice was inclined to be a little frightened, until the strange old man spoke to her in such a gentle way that it banished all timidity; and then, taking the hand which he held out to her, she trudged on beside him, happy and pleased as she could be.

The party were not long in reaching the gate leading up to the house of William's father. A large old-fashioned country-house it was, standing among great tall trees, a good way up from the high-road; and William asked his friend to come up with them and see his father, "he will be so delighted"; but the old man said he "would call and see Mr. Earnest some other time; now he must be hurrying home."

"But this isn't your way home, Captain Hardy, — is it?" exclaimed William, much surprised. "Why, I thought you lived away down below the village."

"So I did once," replied the old man; "that is, when I

lived anywhere at all ; but you see I've got a new home now, and a snug one too. Look down there where the smoke curls up among the trees, — that's from my kitchen."

" But," said William, " that's Mother Podger's house where the smoke is."

" So it was once, my lad," answered the old man ; "but it's mine now ; for I've bought it, and paid for it too ; and now I mean to quit roaming about the world, and to settle down there for the remainder of my days. You must all come down and see me ; and, if you do, I'll give you a sail in my boat."

" O, won't that be grand ! " exclaimed William ; and Fred and Alice both said it would be "grand"; and then they all put a bold front on, and asked the old man if he would n't take them to see the boat now, they would like *so* much to see it.

" Certainly I will," answered the old man. " Come along," — and he led the way over the slope down to the little bay where the boat was lying.

" There she is! " exclaimed he, when the boat came in view. " Is n't she a snug craft ? She rides the water just like a duck," — whereupon the children all declared that they had never, in all their lives, seen anything so pretty, and that " a duck could not ride the water half so well." .

It was, indeed, a very beautiful little boat, or rather yacht, with a cosey little cabin in the centre, and space enough behind and outside of it for four persons to sit quite comfortably. The yacht had but one mast, and was painted white, both inside and out, with only the faintest red streak running all the way around its sides, just a little way above the water-line,

Captain Hardy (for that was the old man's proper name and title, and therefore we will give it to him) now drew his little yacht close in to a little wharf that he had made, and the children stepped into it, and ran through the cosey cabin, which was but very little higher than their heads, and had crimson cushions all along its sides to sit down upon. These crimson cushions were the lids of what the Captain called his "lockers," — boxes where he kept his little "traps." In this little cabin there was the daintiest little stove, on which the Captain said they might cook something when they went out sailing.

When they had finished looking at the yacht, they jumped ashore again, and then, after securing the craft of which he was so proud, the Captain took the children to his house. It was a cunning little house, this house of the Captain's. It was only one story high, and it was as white and clean as a new table-cloth, while the window-shutters were as green as the grass that grew around it. Tall trees surrounded it on every side, making shade for the Captain when the sun shone, and music for the Captain when the wind blew. In front there was a quaint porch, all covered over with honeysuckles, smelling sweet, and near by, in a cluster of trees, there was a rustic arbor, completely covered up with vines and flowers. Starting from the front of the house, a path wound among the trees down to the little bay where lay the yacht; and on the left-hand side of this path, as you went down, a spring of pure water gurgled up into the bright air, underneath a rich canopy of ferns and wild-flowers.

William was much surprised to find that this house, which everybody knew as "Mother Podger's house," should now really belong to Captain Hardy; and he said so.

"You'd hardly know it, would you, since I've fixed it up, and made it shipshape like?" said the Captain. "I've done it nearly all myself too. And now what do you think I've called it?"

The children said they could never guess, — to save their lives, they never could.

"I call it 'Mariner's Rest,'" said the Captain.

"O, how beautiful! and so appropriate!" exclaimed William; and Fred and Alice chimed in and said the same.

"And now," went on the Captain, "you must steer your course for the 'Mariner's Rest' again, — right soon, too, and the old man will be glad to see you."

"Thank you, Captain Hardy," answered William, with a bow. "If we get our parents' leave, we'll come to-morrow, if that will not too much trouble you."

"It will not trouble me at all," replied the Captain. "Let it be four o'clock, then, — come at four o'clock. That will suit me perfectly; and it may be that I'll have," continued he, "a bit of a story or two to tell you. Besides, I think I promised something of the kind before to William, when I came home this time twelvemonth ago. Do you remember it, my lad?'"

William said he remembered it well, and his eyes opened wide with pleasure and surprise.

"Now what is it?" inquired the Captain, thoughtfully. "Was it a story about the hot regions, or the cold regions? for you see things don't stick in my memory now as they used to."

"It was about the cold regions, that I'm sure of," replied William; "for you said you would tell me the story you told Bob Benton and Dick Savery, — something, you know, about your being '*cast away in the cold*,' as Dick Savery said you called it."

" Ah, yes, that's it, that's it," exclaimed the old man, as if recalling the occasion when he had made the promise with much pleasure. " I remember it very well. I promised to tell you how I first came to go to sea, and what happened to me when I got there. Eh ? That was it, I think."

" That was exactly it, only you said you were ' cast away in the cold,' " said William.

" No matter for that, my lad," replied the Captain, with a knowing look, — " no matter for that. If you know how a story's going to end, it spoils the telling of it, don't you see ? Consider that I did n't get cast away, in short, that you know nothing of what happened to me, only that I went to sea, and leave the rest to turn up as we go along. And now, good-day to all of you, my dears. Come down to-morrow, and we'll have the story, and maybe a sail, if the wind's fair and weather fine, — at any rate, the story."

The children were probably the happiest children that were ever seen, as they turned about for home, showering thanks upon the Captain with such tremendous earnestness that he was forced in self-defence to cry, " Enough, enough ! run home, and say no more."

CHAPTER II.

CAPTAIN JOHN HARDY, OTHERWISE ANCIENT MARINER, OTHERWISE OLD MAN.

CAPTAIN HARDY, or Captain John Hardy, or Captain Jack Hardy, or plain Captain Jack, or simple Captain, as his neighbors pleased to name him, was a famous character in the village. Everybody knew the captain, and everybody liked him. He was a mysterious sort of person, — here to-day and there to-morrow, —coming and going all the time, until he fairly tired out the public curiosity and people's patience altogether, so that even the greatest gossips in the town had to confess at length that there was no use trying to make anything of Captain Jack, and they prudently gave up inquiring and bothering their heads about him ; but they were glad to see him always, none the less.

The Captain was known as a great talker, and was always, in former years, brimful of stories of adventure to tell to any one he met during his short visits to the village, — any one, indeed, who would listen to him ; and, in truth, everybody was glad to listen, he talked so well. Many and many a summer evening he spent seated on an old bench in front of the village inn, reciting tales of shipwrecks, and stories of the sea and land, to the wondering people. Of late years, however, he was not disposed to talk so much, and was not so often seen at his favorite haunt. "I 'm getting too old," he would say, " to tarry from home after nightfall."

He had now grown to be fifty-nine years old, although he really looked much more aged, for he bore about him the marks of much hardship and privation. His hair was quite white, and fell in long silvery locks over his shoulders, while a heavy snow-white beard covered his breast. There was always something in his appearance denoting the sailor. Perhaps it was that he always wore loose pantaloons, — white in summer, and blue in winter, — and a sort of tarpaulin hat, with long blue ribbons tied around it, the ends flowing off behind like the pennant of a man-of-war.

Captain Hardy was known to everybody as a generous, warm-hearted, and harmless man ; but he was thought to be equally improvident. The poor had a constant friend in him. No beggar ever asked the Captain for a shilling without getting it, if the Captain had a shilling anywhere about him. Sometimes he had plenty of money, yet when at home he always lived in a frugal, homely way. Great was the rejoicing therefore, among his friends (and they were many), when it was known that he had fallen in with a streak of good fortune. Having been instrumental in saving the British bark *Dauntless* from shipwreck, the insurance companies had awarded him a liberal salvage, and it was to secure this that he had gone away on his last voyage. As soon as he came home he went right off and bought the house which we have before described, with the money he brought back ; and for once got the credit of doing a prudent thing.

The old man's happiness seemed now complete. " Here," exclaimed he, " Heaven willing, I will bring the old craft to an anchor, and end my days in peace." But after the excitement of fitting up his house and grounds, and getting his little yacht in order, had passed over, he began to feel a little

1 *

lonely.   He was so far away from the village that he could
not meet his old friends as often as he wished to.   We have
seen that he was a great talker ; and he liked so much to
talk, and thus to :" fight his battles over again," as it were,
and he had so much to talk about, that an audience was quite
necessary to him.   It is not improbable, therefore, that he
looked upon his meeting with William and Fred and Alice as
a fortunate event for him ; and if the children were delighted,
so was he.   He was very fond of children, and these were
children after his own heart.   To them the coming story was
a great event, — how great the reader could scarcely understand, unless he knew how much every boy in Rockdale was
envied by all the other boys, big and little, when he was
known to have been especially picked out by Captain Hardy
to be the listener to some tale of adventure on the sea.

CHAPTER III.

Which shows the Old Man to be a Man of his Word.

AS we may well suppose, the Captain's little friends did not tarry at home next day beyond the appointed time; but true as the hands of the clock to mark the hour and minute on the dial-plate, they set out for Captain Hardy's house as fast as they could go, — as if their very lives depended on their speed. They found the Captain seated in the shady arbor, smoking a long clay pipe. "I'm glad to see you, children," was his greeting to them; and glad enough he was too, — much more glad, maybe, than he would care to own, — as glad, perhaps, as the children were themselves.

"And now, my dears," continued he, "shall we have the story? There is no wind, you see, so we cannot have a sail."

"O, the story! yes, yes, the story," cried the children, all at once.

"Then the story it shall be," replied the old man; "but first you must sit down," — and the children sat down upon the rustic seat, and closed their mouths, and opened wide their ears, prepared to listen; while the Captain knocked the ashes from his long clay pipe, and stuck it in the rafter overhead, and clearing up his throat, prepared to talk.

"Now you must know," began the Captain, "that I cannot finish the story I'm going to tell you all in one day, — indeed, I can only just begin it. It's a very long one, so you must come down to-morrow, and next day, and every bright day after that until we 've done. Does that please you?"

"Yes, yes," was the ready answer, and little Alice laughed loud with joy.

"Will you be sure to remember the name of the place you come to? Will you remember that its name is 'Mariner's Rest'? Will you remember that?"

"Yes, indeed we will."

"And now for the boat we 're to have a sail in by and by; what do you think I 've called that?" asked the Captain.

"Sea-Gull?" guessed William.

"Water-Witch?" guessed Fred.

"White Dove?" guessed Alice.

"All wrong," said the Captain, smiling a smile of the greatest satisfaction. "I 've painted the name on her in bright golden letters, and when you go down again to look at her, you 'll see *Alice* there, and the letters are just the color of some little girl's hair I know of."

"Is that really her name?" shouted both the boys at once, glad as they could be; "how jolly!" But little Alice said never a word, but crept close to the old man's side, and the old man put his great, big arm around the child's small body, and as the soft sunlight came stealing in through the openings in the foliage of the trees, flinging patches of brightness here and there upon the grass around, the Captain began his story.

"Now, my little listeners," spoke the Captain, "you must know that what I am going to tell you occurred to me at a very early period of my life, when I was a mere boy; in fact, the adventures which I shall now relate to you were the first I ever had.

"To begin, then, at the very beginning, I must tell you that I was born quite near Rockdale. So you see I have good reason for always liking to come back here. It is like coming home, you know. The place of my birth is only eleven miles from Rockdale by the public road, which runs off there in a west-nor'westerly direction.

"My mother died when I was six years old, but I remember her as a good and gentle woman. She was taken away, however, too early to have left any distinct impression upon my mind or character. I was thus left to grow up with three brothers and two sisters, all but one of whom were older than myself, without a mother's kindly care and instruction ; and I must here own, that I grew to be a self-willed and obstinate boy ; and this disposition led me into a course of disobedience which, but for the protecting care of a merciful Providence, would have brought my life to a speedy end.

"My father being poor, neither myself nor my brothers and sisters received any other education than what was afforded by the common country school. It was, indeed, as much as my father could do at any time to support so large a family, and, at the end of the year, make both ends meet.

"As for myself, I was altogether a very ungrateful fellow, and appreciated neither the goodness of my father nor any of the other blessings which I had. Of the advantages of a moderate education which were offered to me I did not avail myself, — preferring mischief and idleness to my studies ; and I manifested so little desire to learn, and was so troublesome to the master, that I was at length sent home, and forbidden to come back any more ; whereupon my father, very naturally, grew angry with me, and no doubt thinking it hopeless to try further to make anything of me, he regularly bound me over,

or hired me out, for a period of years, to a neighboring farmer, who compelled me to work very hard ; so I thought myself ill used, whereas, in truth, I did not receive half my
deserts.

"With this farmer I lived three years and a half before he
made the discovery that I was wholly useless to him, and that
I did not do work enough to pay for the food I ate ; so the
farmer complained to my father, and threatened to send me
home. This made me very indignant, as I foolishly thought
myself a greatly abused and injured person, and, in an evil
hour, I resolved to stand it no longer. I would spite the old
farmer, and punish my father for listening to him, by running
away.

"I was now in my eighteenth year, — old enough, as one
would have thought, to have more manliness and self-respect ;
but about this I had not reflected much.

"I set out on my ridiculous journey without one pang of
regret, — so hardened was I in heart and conscience, — carrying with me only a change of clothing, and having in my
pocket only one small piece of bread, and two small pieces of
silver. It was rather a bold adventure, but I thought I should
have no difficulty in reaching New Bedford, where I was fully
resolved to take ship and go to sea.

"The journey to New Bedford was a much more difficult
undertaking than I had counted upon, and, I believe, but for
the wound which it would have caused to my pride, I should
have gone back at the end of the first five miles. I held on,
however, and reached my destination on the second day,
having stopped overnight at a public house or inn, where my
two pieces of silver disappeared in paying for my supper and
lodging and breakfast.

"I arrived at New Bedford near the middle of the afternoon of the second day, very hot and dusty, for I had walked all the way through the broiling sun along the high-road; and I was very tired and hungry, too, for I had tasted no food since morning, having no more money to buy any with, and not liking to beg. So I wandered on through the town towards the place where the masts of ships were to be seen as I looked down the street, — feeling miserable enough, I can assure you.

"Up to this period of my life, I had never been ten miles from home, and had never seen a city, so of course everything was new to me. By this time, however, I had come to reflect seriously on my folly, and this, coupled with hunger and fatigue, so far banished curiosity from my mind that I was not in the least impressed by what I saw. In truth, I very heartily wished myself back on the farm; for if the labor there was not to my liking, it was at least not so hard as what I had performed these past two days, in walking along the dusty road, — and then I was, when on the farm, never without the means to satisfy my hunger.

"What I should have done at this critical stage, had not some one come to my assistance, I cannot imagine. I was afraid to ask any questions of the passers-by, for I did not really know what to ask them, or how to explain my situation; and, seeing that everybody was gaping at me with wonder and curiosity (and many of them were clearly laughing at my absurd appearance), I hurried on, not having the least idea of where I should go or what I should do.

"At length I saw a man with a very red face approaching on the opposite side of the street, and from his general appearance I guessed him to be a sailor; so, driven almost to desperation, I crossed over to him, looking, I am sure, the very picture of despair, and I thus accosted him : 'If you please, sir, can you tell me where I can go and ship for a voyage ? '

"'A voyage !' shouted he, in reply, 'a voyage ! A pretty looking fellow you for a voyage !'— which observation very much confused me. Then he asked me a great many questions, using a great many hard names, the meaning of which I did not at all understand, and the necessity for which I could not exactly see. I noticed that he called me 'landlubber' very frequently, but I had no idea whether he meant to compliment or abuse me, though it seemed more likely to me that it was the latter. After a while, however, he seemed to have grown tired of talking, or had exhausted all his strange words, for he turned short round and bade me follow him, which I did, with very much the feelings a culprit must have when he is going to prison.

"We went down a steep hill, and arrived presently at a low, dingy place, the only peculiar feature of which was that it smelled of tar and had a great many people lounging about in it. It was, as I soon found out, a 'shipping office,'— that is, a place where sailors engage themselves for a voyage. No sooner had we entered than my conductor led me up to a tall desk, and then, addressing himself to a sharp-faced man on the other side of it, he said something which I did not clearly comprehend. Then I was told to sign a paper, which I did without even reading a word of it, and then the red-faced man cried out in a very loud and startling tone of voice, ' Bill !' when somebody at once rolled off a bench, and scrambled to his feet. This was evidently the 'Bill' alluded to.

"When Bill had got upon his feet, he surveyed me for an

instant, as I thought, with a very needlessly firm expression
of countenance, and then started towards the door, saying
to me as he set off, 'This way, you lubber.' I followed after
him with much the same feelings which I had before when I
followed the man with the red face, until we came down to
where the ships were, and then we descended a sort of ladder,
or stairs, at the foot of which I stumbled into a boat, and had
like to have gone overboard into the water. At this, the
people in the boat set up a great laugh at my clumsiness, —
just as if I had ever been in a boat before, and could help
being clumsy. To make the matter worse, I sat down in the
wrong place, where one of the men was to pull an oar ; and
when, after being told to 'get out of that,' with no end of hard
names, I asked what bench I should sit on, they all laughed
louder than before, which still further overwhelmed me with
confusion. I did not then know that what I called a 'bench,'
they called a 'thwart,' or more commonly 'thawt.'

"At length, after much abuse and more laughter, I managed
to get into the forward part of the boat, which was called, as
I found out, 'the bows,' where there was barely room to coil
myself up, and the boat being soon pushed off from the wharf,
the oars were put out, and then I heard an order to 'give way,'
and then the oars splashed in the water, and I felt the boat
moving ; and now, as I realized that I was in truth leaving
my home and native land, perhaps to see them no more forever, my heart sank heavy in my breast ; and it was as much
as I could do to keep the tears from pouring out of my eyes,
as we glided on over the harbor. Indeed, my eyes were so
bedimmed that I scarcely saw anything at all until we came
around under the stern of a ship, when I heard the order 'lay
in your oars.' Then one of the men caught hold of the end

B

of a rope, which was thrown from the ship; and, the boat
being made fast, we all scrambled up the ship's side; and
then I was hustled along to a hole in the forward part of the
deck (having what looked like a box turned upside down over
it), through which, now utterly bewildered, I descended, by

The Romance of the Sea.

means of a ladder, to a dark, damp, mouldy place, which was
filled with the foul smells of tar and bilge-water, and thick
with tobacco-smoke. This, they told me, was the 'fo'casle,'
that is, forecastle, where lived the 'crew,' of which I became

now painfully conscious that I was one. If there had been the slightest chance, I should have run away; but running away from a ship is a very different thing from running away from a farm.

"If I had wished myself back on the farm before, how much more did I wish it now! But too late, too late, for we were all ordered up out of the forecastle even before I had tasted a mouthful of food. In truth, however, it is very likely that I was too sick with the foul odors, tobacco-smoke, and heart-burnings to have eaten anything, even had it been set before me.

"Upon reaching the deck, I was immediately ordered to lay hold of a wooden shaft, about six feet long, which ran through the end of an iron lever; and being joined by some more of the crew, we pushed down and lifted up this lever, just like firemen working an old-fashioned fire-engine. Opposite to us was another party pushing down when we were lifting up, and lifting up when we were pushing down. I soon found out that by this operation we were turning over and over what seemed to be a great log of wood, with iron bands at the ends of it, and having a great chain winding up around it. The chain came in through a round hole in the ship's side, with a loud 'click, click,' and I learned that they called it a 'cable,' while the machine we were working was called a 'windlass.' The cable was of course fast to the anchor, and it was very evident to me that we were going to put to sea immediately. The idea of it was now as dreadful to me as it had before been agreeable, when I had contemplated it from the stand-point of a quiet farm, a good many miles away from the sea. But I could not help myself. No matter what might happen, my fate was sealed, so far as concerned this ship.

"We had not been long engaged at this work of turning
the windlass, before my companions set up a song, keeping
time with the lever which we were pushing up and down, one
of them leading off by reciting a single line, in which something was said about Sallie coming, or having come, or going
to come to 'New York town'; after which they all united in
a dismal chorus, that had not a particle of sense in it, so far
as I could see, from beginning to end. When they had finished off with the chorus, the leader set to screaming again
about 'Sallie' and 'New York town,' and then as before came
the chorus. Having completely exhausted himself on the
subject of Sallie, he began to invent, and his inventive genius
was rewarded with a laugh which interfered with the chorus
through about two turns of the windlass. What he invented
I will recite, that you may see how senseless it was; and I
will drawl it out very slow to imitate them. But first let me
say, when they were through with this chorus, the leader put
in his tongue again, inventing a sentiment to rhyme with
the first, howling it out as if he would split his throat in the
endeavor. This is what it all was: —

> 'We've picked up a lubber in New Bedford town, —
> Come away, away, sto-r-m along, John,
> Get a-long, storm a-long, stor-m 's g-one along,'

> 'Our lubber 's lugger-rigged, and we 'll do him brown, —
> Come away, away, sto-r-m along, John,
> Get a-long, storm a-long, storm 's g-one along.'

The last sentiment about lugger-rigged lubber being done
brown made them all laugh even more than the other, and
caused an interruption of the chorus to the extent of at least
four revolutions of the windlass; but when the laugh was
over, they went at the dismal chorus with double the energy

they had shown before, repeating all they had then said about
'John's getting along,' and 'storming along,' as if they rather
liked John for doing these things. Thus they went on without much variety, until I was sick and tired enough of it.
The 'lubber' part of it was too clearly aimed at me to be
mistaken ; but I could not discover in it anything but nonsense all the way through to the end.

"After a while I heard some one cry out, 'The anchor's
away,' which as I afterwards learned, meant the anchor had
been lifted from the bottom ; and then the sailors all scattered
to obey an order to do something, which I had not the least
idea of, with a sail, and with some ropes, which appeared to
me to be so mixed up that nobody could tell one from the
other, nor make head nor tail of them. In the twinkling of
an eye, however, in spite of the mixed-up ropes, there was a
great flapping of white canvas, and a creaking and rattling
of pulleys. Then the huge white sail was fully spread, the
wind was bulging it out in the middle like a balloon, the ship's
head was turned away from the town, and we were moving
off. Next came an order to 'lay aloft and shake out the top-
sail'; but happily in this order I was not included, but was,
instead, directed to 'lend a hand to get the anchor aboard,'
which operation was quickly accomplished, and the heavy
mass of crooked iron which had held the ship firmly in the
harbor was soon fastened in its proper place on the bow,
to what is called a 'cat-head.' By the time this was done,
every sail was set, and we were flying before the wind out
into the great ocean.

"And now you see my wish was gratified. I was in a ship
and off on the 'world of waters,' with the career of a sailor before me, — a career to my imagination when on the farm full

of romance, and presenting everything that was desirable in life. But was it so in reality when I was brought face to face with it, — when I had exchanged the farm for the forecastle? By no means. Indeed, I was filled with nothing but disgust first, and terror afterwards. The first sight which I had of the ocean was much less satisfactory to me than would have been my father's duck-pond. I soon got miserably sick ; night came on, dark and fearful ; the winds rose ; the waves dashed with great force against the ship's sides, often breaking over the deck, and wetting me to the skin. I was shivering with cold ; I was afraid that I should be washed overboard ; I was afraid that I should be killed by something tumbling on me from aloft, for there was such a great rattling up there in the darkness that I thought everything was broken loose. I could not stand on the deck without support, and was knocked about when I attempted to move ; every time the ship went down into the trough of a sea I thought all my insides were coming up. So, altogether, you see I was in a very bad way. How, indeed, should it be otherwise ? for can you imagine any ills so great as these ?

1st, To have all your clothes wet ;

2d, To have a sick stomach ; and,

3d, To be in a dreadful fright.

Now that was precisely my condition ; and I was already reaping the fruits of my folly in running away from home and exchanging a farm for a forecastle."

The Captain here paused and laughed heartily at the picture he had drawn of himself in his ridiculous *rôle* of "the young sailor-boy," and, after clearing his throat again, was about to proceed with the story, when he perceived that the shades of evening had already begun to fall upon the arbor. Looking out among the trees, he saw the leaves and branches standing sharply out against the golden sky, which showed him that the day was ended and the sun was set. So he told his little friends to hasten home before the dews began to fall upon the grass, and come again next day. This they promised thankfully, and told the Captain that they "never, never, never would forget it."

But the head of William was filled with a bright idea, and he was bound to discharge it before he left the place. "O Captain Hardy," cried the little fellow, "do you know what I was thinking of?"

"How should I, before you tell me?" was the Captain's very natural answer.

"Why, I was thinking how nice it would be to write all this down on paper. It would read just like a printed book."

The Captain said he "liked the idea," but he doubted if William could remember it. But William thought he could remember every word of it, and declared that it was splendid; and Fred and Alice, following after, said that it was splendid too. But whether the story that the Captain told was splendid, or the idea of writing it down was splendid, or exactly what was splendid, was not then and there settled; yet it was fully settled that William was to write the story down the best he could, and ask his father to correct the worst mistakes. And now, when this was done, the happy children said "Good evening" to the Captain, and set out merrily for home, little Alice holding to her brother's hand, as she tripped lightly over the green field, turning every dozen steps to throw back through the tender evening air, from her dainty little finger-tips, a laughing kiss to the ancient mariner, whose face beamed kindly on her from the arbor door.

CHAPTER IV.

THE OLD MAN, HAVING RELATED TO THE LITTLE PEOPLE HOW THE YOUNG
MAN WENT TO SEA, NOW PROCEEDS TO TELL WHAT THE YOUNG MAN DID
THERE.

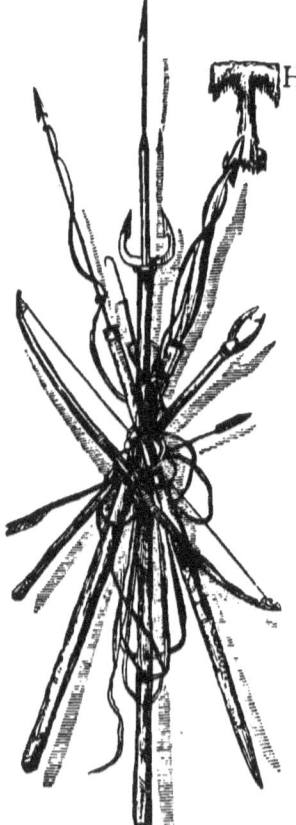

HE two days which the old man
and his young friends had passed
together had so completely broken
down all restraint between them, that
the children almost felt as if they had
known the old man all their lives.
It was therefore quite natural, that,
when they went down next day, they
should feel inclined to give him a surprise. So they concerted a plan of
sneaking quietly around the house
that they might come upon him suddenly, for they saw him working in
his garden, hoeing up the weeds.

"Now let 's astonish him," said
William.

"That 's a jolly idea," said Fred,
while Alice said nothing at all, but
was as pleased as she could be.

The little party crawled noiselessly
along the fence, through the open

gate, and sprang upon the Captain with a yell, like a parcel of wild Indians ; and sure enough they did surprise him, for he jumped behind his hoe, as if preparing to defend himself against an attack of enemies.

"Heyday, my hearties!" exclaimed the Captain, when he saw who was there. "Ain't you ashamed of yourselves to scare the old man that way?" and he joined the laugh that the children raised at his own expense, — enjoying it as much as they did.

"That's a trick of William's, I'll be bound," said he ; "but no matter, I'll forgive you ; and I'm right glad you've come, too, for it's precious hot, and I'm tired hoeing up the weeds ; so now, let us get out of the sun, into the crow's nest."

"The crow's nest!" cried William. "What's that?"

"Why, the arbor, to be sure," said the Captain. "Don't you like the name?"

"Of course I do," answered William. "It's such a cunning name."

It was but a few steps to the "crow's nest," and the happy party once seated, the Captain was ready in an instant to pick up the thread where he had broken it short off when they had parted in the golden evening of the day before, and then to spin on the yarn.

"And now, my lively trickster and genius of the quill," said he to William, "how is it about writing down the story? What does your father say?"

"O," answered William, "I've written down almost every word of what you said, and papa has examined it, and says he likes it. There it is";—and he pulled a roll of paper from his pocket and handed it to the Captain.

The old man took it from William's hand, looking all the

2

while much gratified ; and after pulling out a pair of curious-looking, old-fashioned spectacles from a curious-looking, old-fashioned red-morocco case, which was much the worse for wear, he fixed them on his nose very carefully, and then, after unfolding the sheets of paper, he glanced knowingly over them.

"That's good," said he ; "that's shipshape, and as it ought to be. Why, lad, you're a regular genius, and sure to turn out a second Scott, or Cooper, or some such writing chap."

"I am glad you like it, Captain Hardy," said William, pleased that he had pleased his friend.

"Like it!" exclaimed the Captain. "Like it!! that's just *what* I do ; and now, since I'm to be made famous in this way, I'll be more careful with my speech. And no bad spelling either," ran on the Captain, while he kept turning back the leaves, "as there would have been if you had put it down just as I spoke it. But never mind that now ; take back the papers, lad, and keep them safe ; we'll go on now, if we can only find where the yarn was broken yesterday. Do any of you remember ? "

"I do," said William, laughing. "You had just got out into the great ocean, and were frightened half to death."

"O yes, that's it," went on the Captain, — "frightened half to death ; that's sure enough, and no mistake ; and so would you have been, my lad, if you had been in my place. But I don't think I'll tell you anything more about my miserable life on board that ship. Had n't we better skip that ? "

"O no, no!" cried the children all together, "don't skip anything."

"Well, then," said the obliging Captain, glad enough to see how much his young friends were interested, "if you *will* know what sort of a miserable time young sailors have of it,

I'll tell you; and let me tell you, too, there's many a one of them has just as bad a time as I had.

"In the first place, you see, they gave me such wretched food to eat, all out of a rusty old tin plate, and I was all the time so sick from the motion of the vessel as we went tossing up and down on the rough sea, and from the tobacco-smoke of the forecastle, and all the other bad smells, that I could hardly eat a mouthful, so that I was half ready to die of star-vation; and, as if this was not misery enough, the sailors were all the time, when in the forecastle, quarrelling like so many wild beasts in a cage; and as two of them had pistols, and all of them had knives, I was every minute in dread lest they should take it into their heads to murder each other, and kill me by mistake. So, I can tell you, being a young sailor-boy isn't what it's cracked up to be."

"O, wasn't it dreadful!" said Alice, "to be sick all the time, and nobody there to take care of you."

"Well, I wasn't so sick, maybe, after all," answered the Captain, smiling, — "only *sea-sick*, you know; and then, for the credit of the ship, I'll say that, if you had nice plum-pudding every day for dinner, you would think it horrid stuff if you were sea-sick."

"But don't people die when they are sea-sick?" inquired Alice.

"Not often, child," answered the Captain, playfully; "but they feel all the time as if they were going to, and when they don't feel that way, they feel as if they'd like to.

"However, I was miserable enough in more ways than one; for to these troubles was added a great distress of mind, caused by the sport the sailors made of me, and also by remorse of conscience for having run away from home, and thus got

myself into this great scrape. Then, to make the matter
worse, — as if it was not bad enough already, — a violent
storm set upon us in the dark night. You could never imagine how the ship rolled about over the waves. Sometimes
they swept clear across the ship, as if threatening our lives;
and all the time the creaking of the masts, the roaring of the
wind through the rigging, and the lashing of the seas, filled
my ears with such awful sounds that I was in the greatest
terror, and I thought that every moment would certainly be
my last. Then, as if still further to add to my fears, one of
the sailors told me, right in the midst of the storm, that we
were bound for the Northern seas, to catch whales and seals.
So now, what little scrap of courage I had left took instant
flight, and I fell at once to praying (which I am ashamed to
say I had never in my life done before), fully satisfied as I
was that, if this course did not save me, nothing would. In
truth, I believe I should actually have died of fright had not
the storm come soon to an end ; and indeed it was many days
before I got over thinking that I should, in one way or another, have a speedy passage into the next world, and therefore I did not much concern myself with where we were
going in this. Hence I grew to be very unpopular with the
people in the ship, and learned next to nothing. I was always in somebody's way, was always getting hold of the
wrong rope, and was in truth all the time doing mischief
rather than good. So I was set down as a hopeless idiot, and
was considered proper game for everybody. The sailors tor-
mented me in every possible way.

"One day (knowing how green I was) they set to talking
about fixing up a table in the forecastle, and one of them said,
'What a fine thing it would be if the mate (who turned out to

be the red-faced man I had met in the street, and who took
me to the shipping-office) would only let us have the keelson.'
So this being agreed to in a very serious manner (which I
had n't wit enough to see was all put on), I was sent to carry
their petition. Seeing the mate on the quarter-deck, I approached, and in a very respectful manner thus addressed
him: 'If you please, sir, I come to ask if you will let us have
the keelson for a table?' Whereupon the mate turned
fiercely upon me, and, to my great astonishment, roared out at
the very top of his voice, 'What! what 's that you say? Say
that again, will you?' So I repeated the question as he had
told me to, — feeling all the while as if I should like the deck
to open and swallow me up. I had scarcely finished before I
perceived that the mate was growing more and more angry;
if, indeed, anything could possibly exceed the passion he was
in already. His face was many shades redder than it was
before, — and, indeed, it was so very red that it looked as if it
might shine in the dark. His hat fell off, as it seemed to me,
in consequence of his stiff red hair rising up on end, and he
raised his voice so loud that it sounded more like the howl of
a wild beast than anything I could compare it to. 'You lubber!' he shouted. 'You villain!' he shrieked; 'you, you!' —
and here it seemed as if he was choking with hard words
which he could n't get rid of, — 'you come here to play tricks
on me! You try to fool me! I 'll teach you!' — and, seizing
hold of the first thing he could lay his hands on (I did not
stop to see what it was, but wheeled about greatly terrified),
he let fly at me with such violence that I am sure I must
have been finished off for certain had I not quickly dodged
my head. When I returned to the forecastle, the sailors had
a great laugh at me, and they called me ever afterwards 'Jack

Keelson.' The keelson, you must know, is a great mass of wood down in the very bottom of the ship, running the whole length of it ; but how should I have learned that?

"At another time I was told to go and 'grease the saddle.' Not knowing that this was a block of wood spiked to the mainmast to support the main boom, and thinking this a trick too, I refused to go, and came again near getting my head broken by the red-faced mate. I did not believe there was anything like a 'saddle' in the ship.

"And thus the sailors continued to worry me. Once, when I was very weak with sea-sickness and wanted to keep down a dinner which I had just eaten, they insisted upon it, that, if I would only put into my mouth a piece of fat pork, and *keep it there*, my dinner would stay in its place. The sailors were right enough, for as soon as my dinner began to start up, of course away went the fat pork out ahead of it.

"But by and by I came to my senses, and, upon discovering that the bad usage I received was partly my own fault, I stopped lamenting over my unhappy condition, and began to show more spirit. Would you believe it? I had actually been in the vessel five days before I had curiosity enough to inquire her name. They told me that it was called the *Blackbird;* but what ever possessed anybody to give it such a ridiculous name I never could imagine. If they had called it Black Duck, or Black Diver, there would have been some sense in it, for the ship was driving head foremost into the water pretty much all the time. But I found out that the vessel was not exactly a ship after all, but a sort of half schooner, half brig, — what they call a brigantine, having two masts, a mainmast and a foremast. On the former there was a sail running fore and aft, just like the sail of the little yacht *Alice*, and on the latter there was a foresail, a foretop-sail, a foretop-gallant-sail, and a fore-royal-sail, — all of course square sails, that is, running across the vessel, and fastened to what are called yards. The vessel was painted jet-black on the outside, but inside the bulwarks the color was a dirty sort of green.

"Such, as nearly I can remember, was the brigantine *Blackbird*, three hundred and forty-two tons register. Brigantine is, however, too large a word; so when we pay the *Blackbird* the compliment of mentioning her, we will call her a ship.

"Having picked up the name of the ship, I was tempted to pursue my inquiries further, and it was not long before I had got quite a respectable stock of seaman's knowledge, and hence I grew in favor. I learned to distinguish between a 'halyard,' which is rope for pulling the yards up and letting them down, from a ' brace,' which is used to pull them around so as to ' trim the sails,' and a ' sheet,' which is a rope for keeping the sails in their proper places. I found out that what I called a floor the sailors called a ' deck '; a kitchen they called a ' galley '; a pot, a ' copper '; a pulley was a ' block '; a post was a ' stancheon '; to fall down was to ' heel over '; to climb up was to ' go aloft '; and to walk straight, and keep one's balance when the ship was pitching over the waves, was to ' get your sea legs on.' I found out, too, that everything behind you was 'abaft,' and everything ahead was ' forwards,' or for'ad as the sailors say; that a large rope was a 'hawser,' and that every other rope was a ' line '; to make anything temporarily secure was to ' belay ' it; to make one thing fast to another was to 'bend it on '; and when two things were close together, they were ' chock-a-block.' I learned, also, that the right-hand side of the vessel was the ' starboard ' side, while the left-hand side was the 'port' or 'larboard' side; that the lever which moves the rudder that steers the ship was called the 'helm,' and that to steer the ship was to take 'a trick at the wheel'; .that to 'put the helm up' was to turn it in the direction from which the wind was coming (windward), and to 'put the helm down' was to turn it in the direction the wind was going (leeward). I found out still further, that a ship has a 'waist,' like a woman, a 'forefoot,' like a beast, besides 'bull's eyes' (which are small holes with glass in them to admit light), and 'cat-heads,' and 'monkey-rails,' and 'cross-trees,' as well as 'saddles' and 'bridles' and 'harness,' and many other things which I thought I should never hear anything more of after I left the farm. I might go on and tell you a great many more things that I learned, but I should only tire your patience without doing any good. I only want to show you how John Hardy began his marine education.

"When it was discovered how much I had improved, they proposed immediately to turn it to their own account; for I was at once sent to take 'a trick at the wheel,' from which I came away, after two hours' hard work, with my hands dreadfully blistered, and my legs bruised, and with the recollection of much abusive language from the red-faced mate, who could never see anything right in what I did. I gave him, however, some good reason this time to abuse me, and I was glad of it afterwards, though I was badly enough scared at the time. I steered the ship so badly that a wave which I ought to have avoided by a skilful turn of the wheel, came breaking in right over the quarter deck, wetting the mate from head to foot. He thought I did it on purpose (which you may be sure I did not do). Again his face grew red enough to shine of a dark night, and his mind invented hard words faster than his tongue would let them out of his ugly throat.

"I tell you all this, that you may have some idea of what a ship is, and how sailors live, and what they have to do. You can easily see that they have no easy time of it, and, let me tell you, there is n't a bit of romance about it, except the stories that are cut out of whole cloth to make books and songs of. However, I never could have much sympathy for my shipmates in the *Blackbird;* for if they did treat me a little better when they found that I could do something, especially when I could take a trick at the wheel, I still continued to look upon them as little better than a set of pirates, and I felt satisfied that, if they were not born to be hanged, they would certainly drown."

"I don't think I 'll be a sailor," said Fred.

"Nor I either," said William. "But, Captain," continued the cunning fellow, "if a sailor's life is so miserable, what do you go to sea so much for?"

"Well, now, my lad," replied the Captain, evidently at first a little puzzled, "that 's a question that would require more time to explain than we have to devote to it to-day. Besides" (he was fully recovered now), "you know that going to sea in the cabin is as different from going to sea in the forecastle as you are from a Yahoo Indian. But never mind that, I must get on with my story, or it will never come to an end. I 've hardly begun it yet."

CHAPTER V.

IN WHICH THE ANCIENT MARINER, CONTINUING HIS STORY, BORROWS AN
ILLUSTRATION FROM THE "ANCIENT MARINER" OF SONG, AND THEN
PROCEEDS TO TELL HOW THEY WENT INTO THE COLD, AND WERE CAST
AWAY THERE.

> "'And now there came both mist and snow,
> And it grew wondrous cold :
> And ice mast-high came floating by,
> As green as emerald.'

" I RECITE this from a famous poem because it suits so
well what came of us, for you must understand that, while
all I have been telling you was going on, we were approaching
the northern regions, and were getting into the sea where ice
was to be expected. A man was accordingly kept aloft all
the time to look out for it : for you will remember that we
were going after seals, and it is on the ice that the seals are
found. The weather now became very cold, it being the
month of April.

" At length the man aloft cried out that he saw ice. 'Where
away?' shouted the red-faced mate. 'Off the larboard bow,'
was the answer. So the course of the ship was changed, and
we bore right down upon the ice, and very soon it was in sight
from the deck, and gradually became more and more distinct.
It was a very imposing sight. The sea was covered all over
with it, as far as the eye could reach, — a great plain of whiteness, against the edge of which the waves were breaking and
sending the spray flying high in the air, and sending to our

ears that same dull, heavy roar which the breakers make when beating on the land.

"As we neared this novel scene, I observed that it consisted mostly of flat masses of ice, of various sizes (called by the sealers 'floes') ; some were miles in extent, and others only a few feet. The surface of these ice floes or fields rose only about a foot or so above the surface of the water. Between them there were in many places very broad openings, and when I went aloft and looked ahead, these ice-fields appeared like a great collection of large and small flat white islands, dotted about in the midst of the ocean. Through these openings between the fields the ship was immediately steered, and we were soon surrounded by ice on every side. To the south, whence we had come, there was in an hour or so apparently just as much ice as there was before us to the north, or to the right and left of us, — a vast immeasurable waste of ice it was, looking dreary and frightful enough, I can assure you.

" I have said that the pieces of ice now about us were called 'floes,' or ice-fields ; the whole together was called 'the pack.' We were now in perfectly smooth water, for you will easily understand that the ice which we had passed broke the swell of the sea. But the crew of the ship did not give themselves much concern about the ice itself ; for it was soon discovered that the floes were covered in many places with seals.

"Now you must understand that seals are not fish, but are air-breathing, warm-blooded animals, like horses and cows, and therefore they must always have their heads, or at least their noses, out of water when they breathe. When the weather is cold, they remain in the water all the time, merely putting up their noses now and then (for they can remain a long time under water without breathing) to sniff a little fresh air, and then going quickly down again. In the warm weather, however, they come up bodily out of the sea, and bask and go to sleep in the sun, either on the land or on the ice. Many thousands of them are often seen together.

"As we came farther and farther into the 'pack,' the seals on the ice were observed to be more and more numerous. Most of them appeared to be sound asleep; some of them were wriggling about, or rolling themselves over and over, while none of them seemed to have the least idea that we had come all the way from New Bedford to rob them of their sleek coats and their nice fat blubber.

"We were now fairly into our 'harvest-field,' and when a suitable place was discovered the ship was brought up into the wind, that is, the helm was so turned as to bring the ship's head towards the wind, when of course the sails got 'aback,' and the ship stopped. Then a boat was lowered, and a crew, of which I was one, got into it, with the end of a very long rope, and we pulled away towards the edge of a large ice-field, hauling out the rope after us, of course, from the coil on shipboard. As we approached the ice, the seals near by all became frightened, and floundered into the sea as quickly as they could, with a tremendous splash. In a few minutes they all came up again, putting their cunning-looking heads out of the water, all around the boat, no doubt as curious to see what these singular-looking beings were that had come amongst them, as the Indians were about Columbus and his Spaniards, when they first came to America.

"As soon as we had reached the ice, we sprang out of the boat on to it, and, after digging a hole into it with a long, sharp bar of iron, called an ice-chisel, we put therein one end of a large, heavy, crooked hook, called an ice-anchor, and then to a ring in the other end of this ice-anchor we made fast the end of the rope that we had brought with us. This done, we signalled to the people on board to 'haul in,' which they did on their end of the rope, and in a little while the ship was drawn close up to the ice. Then another rope was run out over the stern of the ship, and, this being made fast to an ice-anchor in the same way as the other, the ship was soon drawn up with her whole broadside close to the ice, as snug as if she were lying alongside of a dock in New Bedford.

"And now began the seal-hunt. It would not interest you to hear all about the preparations we made, first to catch the seals, and then to preserve the skins and try out the oil from the blubber, and put it away in barrels. For this latter duty some of the crew were selected, while others were sent off to kill and bring in the seals. These latter were chosen with a view to their activity, and I, being supposed to be of that sort, was one of the party. I was glad enough, I can assure you, to get off the vessel for once on to something firm and solid, even if it was only ice, and at least for a little while to have done with rocking and rolling about over the waves.

"Each one of the seal-catchers was armed with a short club for killing the seals, and a rope to drag them over the ice to the ship. We scattered in every direction, our object being each by himself to approach a group of seals, and, coming upon them as noiselessly as possible, to kill as many of them as we could before they should all take fright and rush into the sea. In order to do this, we were obliged to steal up between the seals and the water as far as possible.

"My first essay at this novel business was ridiculous enough, and, besides nearly causing my death, overwhelmed me with mortification. It happened thus. I made at a large herd of seals, nearly all of which were lying some distance from the edge of the ice, and before they could get into the water I had managed to intercept about a dozen of them. Thus far I thought myself very lucky ; but, as the poet Burns says,

'The best laid schemes o' mice and men
    Gang aft a-gloy,
And leave us naught but grief and pain
    For promised joy,' —

so it fell out with me. The seals, of course, all rushed towards the water as fast as they could go, the moment they saw me coming. But I got up with them in time, and struck one on the nose, killing it, and was in the act of striking another, when a huge fellow that was big enough to have been the father of the whole flock, too badly frightened to mind where he was going, ran his head between my legs, and, whipping up my heels in an instant, landed me on his back, in which absurd position I was carried into the sea before I could recover myself. Of course I sunk immediately, and dreadfully cold was the water ; but, rising to the surface in a moment, I was preparing to make a vigorous effort to swim back to the ice, when another badly frightened and ill-mannered seal, as I am sure you will all think, plunged into the sea without once looking to see what he was doing, and hit me with the point of his nose fairly in the stomach.

"I thought now for certain that my misfortunes were all over, and that my end was surely come. However, I got my head above the surface once more, and did my best to keep it there ; but my hopes vanished when I perceived that I was at least twenty feet from the edge of the ice. It was as much as I could do to keep my head above water, without swimming forward, so much embarrassed was I by my heavy clothing,

the great cold, and the terrible pains (worse than those of colic) caused by the seal hitting me in the stomach. I am quite

John Hardy takes a Ride without meaning it.

certain that this would have been the last of John Hardy's
adventures, had not one of my companions, seeing me going
overboard on the back of the seal, rushed to my rescue. He
threw me his line for dragging seals (the end of which I had
barely strength to catch and hold on to), and then he drew
me out as one would haul up a large fish.

"I came from the sea in a most sorry condition, as you can
well imagine. My mouth was full of salt water. I was so
prostrated with the cold that I could scarcely stand, and my
pains were so great that I should certainly have screamed had

I not been so full of water that I could not utter a single word. But I managed, after a while, to get all the water spit out, and then, after drawing into my lungs a few good long breaths of air, I felt greatly refreshed. I could still, however, hardly stand, and was shivering with the cold. But I found that I had strength enough to stagger back to the ship, where I was greeted in a manner far from pleasant.

"The sailors looked upon my adventure as a great joke, never once seeming to think how near I was to death's door, and the mate simply cried out 'Overboard, eh ? Pity the sharks did n't catch him !' It was clear enough that this red-faced tyrant would show me no mercy ; and when, pale and cold and pant- ing for breath, I asked him for leave to go below for a while, he cried out, 'Yes, for just five minutes. Be lively, or I 'll warm your back for you with a rope's end.'

"The prospect of a 'back warming' of this description had the effect to make me lively, sure enough, although I was shiv- ering as if I would shake all my teeth out, and tumble all my bones down into a heap. As soon as I reached the deck, the mate cried out again for me to 'be lively,' and when he set after me with an uplifted rope's end, his face glaring at me all the while like a red-hot furnace, you may be sure I was quite as lively as it was possible for me to be, and was over the ship's side in next to no time at all, and off after seals again. After a while I got warmed up with exercise, and this time, being more cautious, I met with no similar misadventure, and soon came in dragging three seals after me. The mate now com- plimented me by exclaiming, 'Why, look at the lubber !'

"We continued at this seal-hunting for a good many days, during which we shifted our position frequently, and made what the sealers called a good 'catch.' But still the barrels in the hold of the ship were not much more than half of them filled with oil, when a great storm set in, and, the ice threatening to close in upon us, we were forced to get everything aboard, to cast loose from the ice-field, and work our way south into clear water again, which we were fortunate enough to do without accident. But some other vessels which had come up while we were fishing, and were very near to us, were not so lucky. Two of them were caught by the moving ice-fields before they could make their escape, and were crushed all to pieces. The crews, however, saved themselves by jumping out on the ice, and were all successful in reaching other vessels, having managed to save their boats before their ships actually went down. It was a very fearful sight, the crushing up of these vessels, — as if they were nothing more than eggshells in the hand.

"This storm lasted, with occasional interruptions, thirteen days, but the breaks in it were of such short duration that we had little opportunity to 'fish' (as seal-catching is called) any more. We approached the ice several times, only to be driven off again before we had fairly succeeded in getting to work, and hence we caught very few seals.

"By the time the storm was over the season for seal-fishing was nearly over too ; so we had no alternative, if we would get a good cargo of oil, but to go in search of whales, which would take us still farther north, and into much heavier ice, and therefore, necessarily, into even greater danger than we had hitherto encountered. Accordingly, the course of the vessel was changed, and I found that we were steering almost due north, avoiding the ice as much as possible, but passing a great deal of it every day. The wind being mostly fair, and the ice not thick enough at any time to obstruct our passage, we hauled in our latitude very fast."

"Excuse me, Captain Hardy," here interrupted William, "what is hauling in latitude?"

"That 's for going farther north," answered the Captain. "Latitude is distance from the equator, either north or south, and what a sailor makes in northing or southing he calls 'hauling in his latitude,' just as making easting or westing is 'hauling in his longitude.'"

"Thank you, Captain," said William, politely, when he had finished.

"Is it all clear now?" inquired the Captain.

"Yes," said William, "clear as mud."

"Clear as mud, eh! Well, that is n't as clear as the pea-soup was they used to give us on board the *Blackbird*, for that was so clear that, if the ocean had been made of it, you might have seen through it all the way down to the bottom; indeed, one of the old sailors said that it was n't soup at all. 'If dat is soup,' growled he, 'den I 's sailed forty tousand mile trough soup,' — which is the number of miles he was supposed to have sailed in his various voyages.

"But no matter for the soup. The days wore on none the less that the soup was thin, and still we kept going on and on, — getting farther and farther north, and into more and more ice. Sometimes our course was much interrupted, and we had to wait several days for the ice to open; then we would get under way again, and push on. At length it seemed to me that we must be very near the North Pole. It was a strange world we had come into. The sun was shining all the time. There was no night at all, — broad daylight constantly. This, of course, favored us; indeed, had there been any darkness, we could not have sailed among the ice at all. As it was, we were obliged to be very cautious, for the ice often closed upon us without giving us a chance to escape, obliging us to get out great long saws, and cut out and float away great blocks of the ice, until we had made a dock for the ship, where she could ride with safety. We had many narrow escapes from being crushed.

" At first, when we concluded to go after whales, there were several vessels in company with us. At one time I counted nine, all in sight at one time ; but we had become separated in thick weather ; and whether they had gone ahead of us, or had fallen behind, we could not tell. However, we kept on and on and on ; where we were, or where we were going, I, of course, had not the least idea ; but I became aware, from day to day, that greater dangers were threatening us, for *icebergs* came in great numbers to add their terrors to those which we had already in the ice-fields. They became at length (and suddenly too) very numerous, and not being able to go around them on account of the field-ice, which was on either side, we entered right amongst them. The atmosphere was somewhat foggy at the time, and it seemed as if the icebergs chilled the very air we breathed. I fairly shuddered as we passed the first opening. The ice was now at least three times as high as our masts, and very likely more than that, and it appeared to cover the sea in every direction. It seemed to me that we were going to certain destruction, and indeed I thought I read a warning written as it were on the bergs themselves. Upon the corner of an iceberg to the left of us there stood a white figure, as plain as anything could possibly be. One hand of this strange, weird-looking figure was resting on the ice beside it, while the other was pointing partly upwards toward heaven, and backwards toward the south whence we had come. I thought I saw the figure move, and, much excited, I called the

attention of one of the sailors to it. ' Why, you lubber,' said
he, ' don't you know that the sun melts the ice into all sorts
of shapes.   Look overhead, if there is n't a man's face ! '   I ,
looked up as the sailor had directed me, and, sure enough,
there was a man's face plainly to be seen in the lines of an immense tongue of ice which was projecting from the side of a
berg on the right, and under which we were about to pass.

"I became now really terrified.   In addition to these
strange spectral objects, the air was filled with loud reports,
and deep, rumbling noises, caused by the icebergs breaking
to pieces, or masses splitting off from their sides and falling
into the sea.   These noises came at first from the icebergs in
front of us ; but when we had got fairly into the wilderness
of ice which covered the sea, they came from every side.   It
struck me that we had passed deliberately into the very jaws
of death, and that from the frightful situation there was no
escape.

"I merely mention this as the feeling which oppressed me,
and which I could not shake off.   Indeed, the feeling grew
upon me rather than decreased.   The fog came on very thick,
settling over us as if it were our funeral shroud.   Some snow
also fell, which made the air still more gloomy.   The noises
were multiplying, and we could no longer tell whence they
came, so thick was the air.   We were groping about like a
traveller who has lost his way in a vast forest, and has been
overtaken by the dark night.

"It seemed to me now that our doom was sealed, — that all
our hope was left behind us when we passed the opening to
this vast wilderness of icebergs; and the more I thought of
it, the more it seemed to me that the figure standing on the
corner of the iceberg where we entered, whether it was ice or

whatever it was, had been put there as a warning. How far my fears were right you shall see presently.

"The fog, as I have said, kept on thickening more and more, until we could scarcely see anything at all. I have never, I think, seen so thick a fog, and it was with the greatest difficulty that the ship was kept from striking the icebergs. Then, after a while, the wind fell away steadily, and finally grew entirely calm. The current was moving us about upon the dead waters; and in order to prevent this current from setting us against the ice, we had to lower the boats, and, making lines fast to the ship and to the boats, pull away with our oars to keep headway on the ship, that she might be steered clear of the dangerous places. Thus was made a slow progress, but it was very hard work. At length the second mate, who was steering the foremost boat, which I was in, cried out, 'Fast ice ahead.' Now 'fast ice' is a belt of ice which is attached firmly to the land, not yet having been broken up or dissolved by the warmth of the summer. This announcement created great joy to everybody in the boats, as we knew that land must be near, and we all supposed that we would be ordered to make a line fast to the ice, that we might hold on there until the fog cleared up and the wind came again. But instead of this we were ordered by the mate to pull away from it. And then, after having got the vessel, as was supposed, into a good, clear, open space of water, — at least, there was not a particle of ice in sight, — we were all ordered, very imprudently, as it appeared to every one of us, to come on board to breakfast.

"We had just finished our breakfast, and were preparing to go on deck, and then into the boats again, when there was a loud cry raised. 'Ice close aboard! Hurry up! Man the

boats!' were the orders which I heard among a great many
other confusing sounds; and when I got on deck, I saw,
standing away up in the fog, its top completely obscured in
the thick cloud, an enormous iceberg. The side nearest to
us hung over from a perpendicular, as the projecting tongue
on which I had before seen the man's face. It was very evident that we were slowly drifting upon this frightful object, —
directly under this overhanging tongue. It was a fearful
sight to behold, for it looked as if it was just ready to crumble
to pieces; and indeed, at every instant, small fragments were
breaking off from it, with loud reports, and falling into the
sea.

"We were but a moment getting into the boats. The boat
which I was in had something the start of the other two.
Just as we were pulling away, the master of the ship came on
deck, and ordered us to do what, had the red-faced mate done
an hour before, would have made it impossible that this
danger should have come upon us. 'Carry your line out
to the fast ice,' was the order we received from the master;
and every one of us, realizing the great danger, pulled as hard
as he could. The 'fast ice' was dimly in sight when we
started, for we had drifted while at breakfast towards it, as
well as towards the berg. Only a few minutes were needed
to reach it. We jumped out and dug a hole, and planted the
ice-anchor. The ship was out of sight, buried in the fog. A
faint voice came from the ship. It was, 'Hurry up! we have
struck.' They evidently could not see us. The line was
fastened to the anchor in an instant, and the second mate
shouted, 'Haul in! haul in!' There was no anwer but 'Hurry
up! we have struck.' 'Haul in! haul in!' shouted the
second mate, but still there was no answer. 'They can't hear

nor see,' said he, hurriedly; and then, turning to me, said, 'Hardy, you watch the anchor that it don't give way. Boys, jump in the boat, and we'll go nearer the ship so they can hear.' The boat was gone quickly into the fog, and I was then alone on the ice by the anchor, — how much and truly alone you shall hear.

"Quick as the lightning flash, sudden as the change of one second to another, there broke upon me a sound that will never leave my ears. It was as if a volcano had burst forth, or an earthquake had instantly tumbled a whole city into ruins. A fearful shock, like a sudden explosion, filled the air. I saw faintly through the thick mists the masts of the ship reeling over, and I saw no more; — vessel and iceberg and the disappearing boat were buried in chaos. The whole side of the berg nearest the vessel had split off, hurling thousands and hundreds of thousands of tons of ice, and thousands of fragments, crashing down upon the doomed ship. Escape the vessel could not, nor her crew, the shock came so suddenly. The spray thrown up into the air completely hid everything from view; but the noise which came from out the gloom told the tale.

"Presently there was a loud rush. Great waves, set in motion by the crumbling iceberg, with white crests that were frightful to look upon, came tearing out of the obscurity, and, perceiving the danger of my situation, I ran from it as fast as I could·run. And I was just in time; for the waves broke up the ice where I had been standing into a hundred fragments, and, crack after crack opened close behind me.

"I had not, however, far to run before I had reached a place of safety, for the force of the waves was soon spent. And when I saw what had happened, I fell down flat upon the ice, crying, 'Saved, but for what? to freeze or starve! O that I had perished with the rest of them!'

"So now you see that I was really and truly *cast away in the cold.* In almost a single instant the ship which had borne me through what had seemed great perils was, so far as appeared to me, swallowed up in the sea, — crushed and broken into fragments by the falling ice, and every one of my companions was swallowed up with it. And there I was on an ice-raft, in the middle of the Arctic Sea, without food or shelter, wrapped in a great black, impenetrable fog, with the prospect of a lingering death staring me in the face."

The Captain here paused as if to take breath, for he had been talking very fast, and had grown somewhat excited as he recalled this terrible scene. The eyes of the children were riveted upon him, so deeply were they interested in the tale of the shipwreck; and it was some time before any one spoke.

"Well!" exclaimed William at last, "that was being cast away in the cold for certain, Captain Hardy. I had no idea it was so frightful."

"Nor I," said Fred, evidently doubting if Captain Hardy was really the shipwrecked boy; but Alice said not a word, for she was lost in wonder.

"I should not have believed it was you, Captain Hardy," continued William, "if you had not been telling the story yourself, this very minute; for I cannot see how you should ever have got out of that scrape. It's ever so much worse than going into the sea on the seal's back."

The Captain smiled at these observations of the boys, and said: "It was a pretty bad scrape to get into, and no mistake;

but through the mercy of Providence I got out of it in the end, as you see ; otherwise I should n't have been here to tell the tale ; but how I saved myself, and what became of the rest of the crew, you shall hear to-morrow, for it is now too late to begin the story. The evening is coming on, and your parents will be looking for you home ; so good by, my dears. To-morrow you · must come down earlier, — the earlier the better, and if there 's any wind we 'll have a sail." And now the children once more took leave of the ancient mariner, with hearts filled with thanks, which they could never get done speaking, and with heads filled with astonishment that the Captain should be alive to tell the tale which they had heard.

CHAPTER VI.

THE OLD MAN MEETS THE LITTLE PEOPLE UNDER PECULIAR CIRCUMSTANCES, AND RELATES TO THEM HOW THE YOUNG MAN, BEING CAST AWAY IN THE COLD, RESCUED A SHIPMATE, AND ALSO OTHER MATTERS, WHICH, IF PUT INTO THIS TITLE, WOULD SPOIL THE STORY ALTOGETHER.

HIS time Captain Hardy was not to be caught napping, as on the previous day. Indeed, he was out looking for his young friends even before the time. "If they don't come soon," said he to himself, "I'll go after them";—and they did not come soon, at least the Captain thought they were a long time in coming, and he started off, if not after them, at least to look after them. When he had reached the brow of the hill from which both the Captain's and Mr. Earnest's houses could be seen, the old man discovered the children coming down one of the winding paths which led through Mr. Earnest's grounds. It was some moments before they saw the Captain, and when they did see him there was much wondering what had happened to bring him up so far on the hill.

"Why, what's the matter with him?" exclaimed William. "Look, he's flinging up his hat!"—and the little people set off upon a rapid run.

Meanwhile the Captain stood on the brow of the hill, whirling round his tarpaulin hat with the long blue ribbons flying wildly in the wind. When the children came nearer, they heard the old man calling loudly to them, "Come, my hearties, you are slow to-day. Be lively, or we'll lose the chance."

"What chance?" asked William, when they had come up with him.

"The wind, the wind,—why, don't you see there's a spankin' breeze? I was afraid we'd lose our sail, so I came to hurry you up."

"Hurrah! hurrah!" shouted both the boys together; and without further ado the Captain hurried the little people along with him down through the woods to the water.

The old man had been down there before, and had everything in readiness. The little yacht was lying close beside the little wharf. "Look sharp now, and be lively," exclaimed the Captain as he helped them one by one aboard; and then he got in himself, and shoved the yacht off from the landing, and with the assistance of a singular-looking boy, whom the Captain called "Main Brace," he spread the sails, and the lively craft was soon skimming over the waters, carrying as lively a party as ever set out on an afternoon frolic. "Jolly" was the only word which seemed at all to express the children's pleasure, and if the boys said "it's jolly" once, they must have said it fifty times at least; while little Alice exhibited her excitement by jumping from one side of the boat to the other, stopping now and then to lean over the side and watch the

little waves gurgling past them, sometimes dipping her deli-
cate hands into the water, and screaming with delight when
the spray flew over her.

The party were seated (when seated at all) in what is called
the "stern sheets," that is, on the seat in the open space
behind the cabin heretofore described, — the good-natured
and kindly Captain in the midst of them, firmly holding the
helm or tiller of his boat, and guiding it with steady hand
wherever he wished it to go, cracking a pleasant joke now and
then, and enjoying in all the fulness of his big, warm heart
the joyous delight of his young guests. And he was in no
hurry to stop the sport, for he ran on clear across the harbor,
and then said he would "'bout ship," and put back again.

"What's 'bout ship?" inquired William.

"That's going about on the other tack," replied the Captain.

"What's going about on the other tack?" asked William,
as wise as he was before.

"I'll show you," said the Captain. "Now see here: first I
give the proper order, as if somebody else was giving it to me,
and I was the man at the wheel: 'Hard-a-lee,' do you observe ; — now look, I put the helm down as far as I can jam
it, — there ; — look now, how that turns the boat and brings her
up into the wind, — you see the sails begin to shiver, — the wind
is blowing right in your faces now ; — now we have turned
nearly round ; the boat, you see, has come up on an even
keel, — level, you know ; — now look out sharp for your heads
there, — the boom is going to jibe over to the other side ; —
there, don't you see we've turned round, — that house over
there near the beach that was almost ahead of us is now behind us. There goes the boom, — bang ! There fills the sail,
see it bulging out, — the jib, you see, shakes a little yet, — but

there she goes now filled out like the other ; and now you see I 've got the helm back where I had it before, in the middle, 'steady,' you know, and there goes the *Alice* off on the starboard tack, and an easy bowline back towards the Mariner's Rest again. Was n't that nicely done ?"

"Splendid! splendid!" cried William ; "I wish I could do it."

" I 'll teach you, — it 's easy learned," answered the Captain ; "but look out there, or you 'll go overboard ; get up to windward, and trim the boat ; you see we are leaning over to the other side now."

And thus the Captain kept on "tacking" across the harbor, going to and fro, for more than an hour, enjoying every minute of it just as much as the children did. When at length, however, the children began to quiet down a little (the sharp edge of novelty being worn off), the Captain ran into shoal water, and brought his boat's head once more up into the wind ; but this time, instead of letting her head "pay" off to starboard, he steered her right into the wind's eye, with the sails shivering all the time, until the boat stopped, when he cried out to Main Brace to "let go the anchor," which Main Brace did promptly, with an "Ay, ay, sir!" and then he "clewed" up the sails, and spread a white and red striped and red-fringed awning over the place where they were seated, and said he was now going on with the story. "Is n't this a tip-top place," said he, "for story-telling?" And the children all said it was "tip-top," and "jolly," and "grand," and made many little speeches about it, which to put down here would make this account so long that everybody would get tired before getting to the end of it.

"Now I call this a much better place than the 'Crow's

Nest,'" went on the Captain; "for, don't you see, when we knocked off yesterday I was standing in the middle of the sea, on a great ice-raft. To be sure we are not exactly in the middle of the sea here, nor on an ice-raft either, but we are on salt water, and that's where I like to be. The air is better for the wits, and the tongue too, for that matter, than on the land there, which is a good enough place to be when there is no wind; but I like to be on the water, and have plenty of sea-room, when the wind blows, especially when it blows a gale, — for on land, at such times, I'm always afraid that the trees will blow over on me, or the house will blow down on my head, or some dreadful accident will happen, whereas on the sea one has no fears at all; and besides, at sea one is always at home, — come rain or shine, he's always his house with him, and never has to go groping about for shelter."

"Only you mustn't be in the forecastle," put in cunning William, who remembered the Captain's fright when he first found himself at sea in the *Blackbird*.

"Never mind that, lad," replied the Captain, "I was only a boy then, and hadn't come to years of discretion. I've made better friends with the sea since that day. But let us go on, or we'll never get through with this story, any more than the Flying Dutchman will get into port, though he keeps on beating up and down forever; and as for to-day, why, we'll leave off just where we began, like thieves in a treadmill, if we don't get started pretty soon.

"Well, you see, as I was saying, you left me standing on an ice-raft in the middle of the Arctic Sea, cast away in a cold and forbidding place, and all alone. My shipmates were all either drowned or killed outright by the falling ice, so far at least as I knew. The prospect ahead was not a pleasing one, for of course, as I think I have said before, the first thought which crossed my mind was, that I should starve or freeze to death very soon. I was greatly astonished by what had happened, and indeed it was hard for me to believe my senses, so suddenly had this great disaster come upon me. I stood staring into the mist, and listening to the terrible sounds which came out of it, as one petrified ; yet after a little time I recovered myself sufficiently to realize my situation. The instinct of life is strong in every living thing, and young sailor-boys are no exception to the rule ; so, after I had stood in the presence of this frightful chaos for I have not the least idea how long, I began to think what I should do to save myself.

"The waves which had been raised after a while began steadily to subside, and, as the sea became more calm, I found that I could approach nearer to where the wreck had happened by jumping over some of the cracks which had been made in the ice, and walking across piece after piece of it. These pieces were all in motion, rolling on the swell of the sea, and, the farther I went, of course the greater the motion became. I had to proceed cautiously, and when I jumped from one fragment of ice to another, I was obliged to look carefully what I was about, for if I missed my footing I should fall into the sea, and be either drowned or ground up by the moving ice.

"Had the iceberg all gone to pieces at once, the sea would soon have become quiet ; but it was evident from the noises which reached me that a considerable part of the berg was still holding together, and was wallowing in the sea in consequence of its equilibrium being disturbed by the first crash, and was still keeping the waters moving. I could indeed vaguely see this remaining fragment, swaying to right and left, and I could also perceive that, with every roll, fresh masses were breaking off, with loud reports, like the crash of artillery. I could, however, discover nothing of the ship nor either of the boats. I was able to detect, even at a considerable distance, some fragments of ice floating and rolling about, when the fog would clear up a little ; and, as I peered into the gloom, I thought at one time that I saw a man standing upon one of them. It was but a moment, for the fog closed upon the ob- ject, whatever it may have been, and it vanished as a spectral figure.

" My eyes were strained to catch a further glimpse of this object, but nothing more was to be seen of it. From this my attention was soon attracted by a dark mass which had drifted upon the edge of the broken ice, not far to the right of the place where I had been standing when the boat left me. I soon made this out to be some part of the wreck of the ship. In a few moments I could clearly see that it was a piece of a mast ; then I could plainly distinguish the 'fore-top.' Each succeeding wave was forcing it higher and higher out of the water, and I discovered, after a few moments, that other tim- bers were attached to it, and that beside these were sails and ropes, making of the whole a considerable mass.

" After observing this fragment of the wreck attentively for some time, I thought I perceived a man moving among the tangled collection of timbers and ropes and sails, endeavor- ing to extricate himself. Whatever it might be, it was some distance above the sea, — so high, indeed, that the waves no longer washed it fairly, — only the spray.

" It soon became clear to me that my suspicions that this was a man were correct ; and being more convinced that one of my shipmates at least was yet alive, I rushed forward to rescue him if possible, without once stopping to give a thought to the risks I would encounter. It was clear that he could not liberate himself.

"You will remember that I was now standing on a fragment of ice which had been broken off from the solid ice-field by the waves. It was one of a number of similar fragments, all lying more or less close together, and between me and the place where I had been standing when the waves began to subside, and the ice ceased to break up. Before me the ice was in the same broken condition as behind me, only, being nearer the open water, the pieces were rolling more, so that there was much greater danger in springing from piece to piece. Without, however, pausing to reflect upon this circumstance, I rushed forward as fast as I could go, jumping with ease over every obstacle in my way, until I was on the piece of ice that held up the end of the tangled wreck. I had evidently arrived in the very nick of time, for the wreck was, instead of coming farther up, now beginning to sink back into the sea.

"What I had taken for a man proved to be one, or, as I soon found out, a boy, — the cabin-boy of the ship, a light, pale-faced lad, and only fourteen years old. The boy was evidently fast in some way among the rigging, and had been trying to free himself. As I came closer, I observed that he was entirely quiet, and had sunk out of view. Quick as thought I mounted up into the wreck, and then I saw the boy with a rope tangled round his leg, and lying quite insensible. Underneath him another man was lying, much mutilated, and evidently quite dead. As I was mounting up, a wave washed in under the wreck, but I escaped with only a little spray flying

3*

over me, which, however, did not wet me much. It was but the work of a moment to whip out my knife, which I carried in a belt, like every other sailor, and cut the rope which bound the boy down, and which he had tried in vain to loosen. After this I had no further difficulty, and, seizing the boy around the waist with one arm (he was very light even for his years),

Rescued from the Wreck.

I clambered out of the wreck to the ice without getting much more water upon me, and, hurrying off, did not stop until I had jumped with my burden across several cracks, and ran across several pieces of ice, reaching a place of present safety on the unbroken or fast ice. Here I laid down my insensible burden, all dripping with the cold water, and in a state of great anxiety I bent over the boy. At first I thought that he was dead, but it was soon clear that this was not the case, for he was breathing, although slowly, yet freely. Out from his wet hair a little blood was oozing, and upon examining the spot I found that there was a bad bruise there, and that the skin was broken, though there was not a serious cut. This was clearly the cause of his present unconsciousness, as his breathing seemed conclusively to show that he had managed to keep his head above water, and had not been brought to his present state by drowning. It occurred to me that the blow had simply stunned him, and that it had come almost at the moment I arrived to rescue him. I could not perceive that the skull was fractured, and I felt convinced that, if the boy could be warmed and allowed to lie at rest, he would after a while come to his senses. To this conclusion I arrived while leaning over the poor fellow, examining his hurt, while he lay on the chilly ice, never once thinking where I was, and all the while calling frantically to him ; but I might as well have called to a stone. When I rose up, fully impressed with the necessity of securing for the lad rest and warmth, and fully realized, for the first time, my powerless situation (that I was even apparently unable to save myself, still less the boy), my heart seemed to give way entirely, and I sank down once more beside him. A prayer to Heaven for succor, which I had no thought could ever come to me, rose to my lips, and at that very moment a ray of hope dawned upon me. The great fog was breaking away, the bright sun was scattering the mists, and land was bursting through it near at hand. Light, fleecy clouds were rolling up above the sea, and, as they floated off before a gentle wind, a blaze of sunshine burst through an opening in them and fell upon myself and the boy whose life I had, at least for the present, saved.

"I could now look out over the sea for a considerable distance. Although there was still much confusion, yet the ice was steadily quieting down, and the waves caused by it were subsiding rapidly. But a change not less marked had taken place in the space between where I stood and the open water. The wreck from which I had rescued the boy had settled back into the sea, and the fragments of ice were separating and floating off. Had I delayed a few minutes longer, I should never have reached the fast ice, but should have drifted off upon the dark waters, as the man had done whom I saw standing in the fog that I have told you of before.

"As the fog cleared up more and more, the land which first appeared stood out boldly, and the sea was visible over a range of many miles. It was dotted all over with fragments of ice and numerous icebergs, many of which reached up into the disappearing mists, looking like white mountains in miniature, with clouds drifting across their summits. The land did not appear to be more than a mile distant from me, and it was evident that I stood upon ice which was fast to it. Indeed, when I was first cast upon this ice, I might have known, had I paused to reflect, that land must be very near, as the name 'fast ice' indicates clearly of itself that simple fact.

"With this lighting up of the air, various thoughts came into my mind. First, could I get to the land and save the boy as well as myself; secondly, could I aid anybody else; and thirdly, could I save anything of the wreck out of the sea. These last two reflections were quickly disposed of, for although I could see many fragments of the wreck, none were within reach, and no other person was in sight, — ship and boats and men were all gone down before the crushing avalanche, and nothing was left but myself and a senseless boy.

"I must here pause to tell you that, although we were in the Arctic regions, and on the ice, the weather was not cold, the time being the middle of the summer. Of course the dense fog made the air damp and chilly, but, as I have said, not exactly cold. My shipmates, before the wreck happened, never dressed in anything warmer than the usual woollen clothing, and seldom wore coats. For some reason, I do not exactly remember why, I had, upon going on deck from breakfast that fatal morning, in addition to my ordinary coat, put on a heavy pilot-cloth overcoat, which had been furnished me by the master of the ship, — the price of it to be deducted from my wages. And it was most fortunate that I had put this coat on, for it now served a good purpose in wrapping up the boy.

"Seeing that there was now nothing to be gained by longer delay on the ice, I picked up the boy in my arms and started for the land. It may strike you as somewhat strange that I should have gone about it so calmly, or indeed that I did not fall down in despair, and at once give up the hope of saving myself when there was so little, or rather no, apparent prospect of it before me. But for this there were some very natural reasons. In the first place, the thought of saving the boy's life kept my mind from dwelling too much upon my own misfortunes; and then, the hope of finding the land which had come in sight out of the fog inhabited, stimulated my courage, and inspired exertion.

"Although the boy was not heavy, yet I found that in the

distance I had to carry him I grew much fatigued ; but the necessity for haste made me strong, and to save the boy's life seemed now much more desirable than to save my own, inasmuch as if the boy died, and I survived him, and could in any way manage to live on, I should be in a worse condition than if dead, as it appeared to me, — being all alone.

"As I approached very near the land, I became much alarmed by discovering that a considerable space of water, partly filled with fragments of ice, intervened between me and the shore ; but, after holding to the right for a little distance, I came at length to a spot where the ice was firmly in contact with the land, and, after climbing over some very rough masses which had been squeezed up along the shore, I got at last upon the rocks, and then on a patch of green grass, where I laid down the insensible boy in the blazing sun.

"What was I now to do ? The boy was yet in very much the same condition that he was when I set out with him for the shore. Meanwhile more than half an hour must have elapsed, during which time the boy was wrapped in his wet clothes, which, to a man in the full possession of his senses, would have been prostrating enough. It seemed to me that he was sinking under the effects of the blow which he had received, and the wet clothes which were on his body. I had, however, the gratification of knowing that I was on firm land, and away from the cold ice. The grass was warm, and the air, as I have said, was scarcely chilly. Under these improved conditions it was clearly better to expose the boy's body wholly to the air than to allow him to remain in his wet clothes. The first thing, therefore, which I did was to divest myself of my own clothing, in order that I might give my warm under-clothing to the boy. This left for myself only my pantaloons and my coat. After buttoning the coat tightly round me, I undressed the boy, and rubbed his body with such parts of the tail of my overcoat as his clothes had not wetted while carrying him, and, this done, I drew on to him my shirt and drawers, and then, pulling up the grass, I heaped that about him, and over this threw my damp overcoat, — the grass preventing it from touching him. All this occupied but a few minutes, for I worked with the energy of despair. I then set to rubbing and pounding his feet and hands which were very cold, to get some circulation back into them.

"I had now done all that it was possible for me to do for the present towards the restoration of my poor companion, who still remained in precisely the same insensible state as before, and I now determined to look about me and ascertain if there were any evidences of human beings living near at hand.

"The scene around me was dreary enough to strike terror into a stouter heart than mine ; and, when I had fully viewed it, I had to confess that it did not seem probable that any living thing, not to mention human beings, could possibly be there. The first thought I had was to shout and halloo again and again at the very top of my voice ; but no answer reached me except the echo of my own words in a deep and dark gorge close by. This echo startled me and made me afraid, though I never could tell why. My loud calling had failed to produce any impression upon the boy whatever, and I felt sure that he was going to die. Without exactly knowing what I did, or what I was doing it for, I now ran to the right over the green grass, and then over rough stones up to a considerable elevation, and commenced hallooing again, when, much to my astonishment, I heard a great fluttering and loud sounds right below and within thirty feet of me. I sprang back as if some terrible enemy had attacked me ; but I recovered myself in an instant, when I observed that the fluttering came from a number of birds which rose from among the rocks. The birds were brown and quite large, and I knew at once that they were eider-ducks, for I had seen them frequently before, while in the ship, and the sailors had told me their name.

"Without having any distinct motive in doing so, I went down to where the birds had risen, when still others rose before me in great numbers. The rapidity of their flight, and the loud noise which they made, startled others still farther away, and thus flock after flock kept on rising from among the rocks, screaming, and flapping their wings in a very loud manner. Several hundreds, perhaps thousands of them, must have thus got upon their wings and commenced sailing overhead.

"You must know that the eider-duck, in order to protect its eggs from the air when it goes off to get for food the little fish that it catches in the sea, plucks from its breast the fine feathers called *down*, in which it buries its eggs very carefully. In each of the nests I found there was a good handful of this down, and the thought at once occurred to me to gather a quantity of it, and cover the boy with it. I went to work immediately, and collected a great armful of it, and, hastening to where the boy was, I deposited it, and then hurried back for more. In a very short time I had accumulated a great pile, and, spreading a thick layer of it out close beside the boy, I drew him over upon it, and then covered him completely, and spread my overcoat as I had done before.

"The value of putting this discovery to prompt use was soon seen. The boy, from being cold almost as a corpse, began to show some symptoms of returning warmth. His breathing seemed to be more rapid and free, and his eyelids began to move a little, though they did not fully open for some time; but it was then only for an instant, and I was not certain whether he recognized me or not. I called to him loudly by name, I rubbed his forehead, I pounded his hands, but he gave no further recognition; yet he was getting more and more warm, and in this circumstance I rested my hope.

"Having accomplished this much, and feeling pretty sure that the boy would recover in the end, my mind very naturally fell back upon the contemplation of my own unhappy condition. I moved a few steps from the boy, and sat down upon a rock overlooking the sea. There was nothing there to inspire me with courage, when this question came uppermost in my mind: 'Suppose the boy does recover from his present stupor, how are we going to live?' Could anybody indeed be in a more sorry state? Let me enumerate: —

"1st. I had been shipwrecked, — a fortune usually considered bad enough under any circumstances.

"2d. I had lost all of my companions except a feeble boy whom I had rescued from death, and who was now helpless on my hands.

"3d. I was cast away on a desert land, I knew not where, but very far towards the North Pole, as was clear enough from the immense quantities of ice which whitened the sea before me.

"4th. I was chilly, and had no fire nor means of making any. Nor had I sufficient clothing to cover me.

"5th. I was hungry, and had no food nor means of obtaining any.

"6th. I was thirsty, and had nothing to drink, nor could I discover anything.

"7th. I was without house or hut to shelter me.

"8th. I was without weapons to defend myself against the attacks of wild beasts, if any there should be to molest me.

"To counteract these evils I had four things, namely : —

"1st. Life.

"2d. The clothes on my back.

"3d. A jack-knife.

"4th. The mercy of Providence.

"And this was all! What chance was there for me?

"Little enough, one would think. And, in truth, there did not seem to be any at all. When I thought of all this, I buried my face in my hands, and moaned aloud, and the big tears began to gather in my eyes."

"O, was n't it awful!" exclaimed William.

"I don't see what you *could* do, Captain Hardy," exclaimed Fred.

"The poor boy," exclaimed Alice, — "I hope he did n't die. Did he, Captain Hardy?" — and the child began to imitate the example set by John Hardy, when he rested on the rock and looked out upon the icy sea and speculated upon the chances of his ever seeing again the home from which he had so foolishly run away.

"Well, I 'll tell you about that some other time," answered the Captain. "You may be sure I did n't die, at any rate, whatever may have happened to the boy ; but just now I can tell you no more, for look there at that cloud coming up out of the sea, appearing, for all the world, as if it meant to pipe a squall after us, by and by ; and now, with your leave, we 'll

slip home while the play's good. So here goes. Up anchor."
"Ay, ay, sir," answered William, as he jumped forward very
unnecessarily to help Main Brace, to whom the order to "up
anchor" was given.

"Halloo!" cried the Captain. "Turned sailor already, eh?"

While Main Brace and William were getting in the anchor,
the Captain was stowing away the awning, and then, the yacht
being free, he spread the sails, and with his helm brought her
to the wind; and there being now a lively breeze, the party
were not long in crossing over to the Captain's anchoring-
ground, where he turned so as to stop her as he had done
before, and then cried out, "Stand by to let go the anchor,"
to which William answered, "Ay, ay, sir!" and when the
boat had stopped, the Captain cried out again, "Let go," and
William answered, "Ay, ay!" again, and let it go. Then, as
soon as the Captain had secured his yacht and stowed away
the sails, the whole party hurried ashore, and up the path to
the Captain's cottage, for already great drops of rain were
beginning to patter on the leaves, and the roaring wind was
heard among the forest trees, giving the first warning cry of
a coming shower.

CHAPTER VII.

In which the Reader will discover, as the Little People did, how a Life was saved, and a Life was begun.

THE Captain and his little friends had barely reached the cottage when the storm came down in earnest. The tall trees bowed their heads beneath the heavy blasts of wind, which shook them to their very roots, and the music of the rustling and sighing leaves was heard until the sounds were drowned by the fierce, dashing rain.

"Now this is a regular blow-hard, and no mistake," exclaimed the Captain, as the party stood in the doorway watching the bending trees and the clouds that rushed so wildly overhead. "Good thing we picked up our anchor when we did, or just as like as not we should have had to lie there all night."

"Why, we could n't have stayed there in such a storm, could we, Captain Hardy?" said Fred, inquiringly.

"To be sure we could," replied the Captain, "and snug enough too. Yes, indeed, the little *Alice* would have ridden out the gale handsomely. Then we might have stowed ourselves away in the cabin as nice as could be, and have been just as dry as we are here."

"And gone without supper," put in William, with a practical eye to the creature comforts.

"Easy there, my lad," answered the Captain. "Do you

think you catch an ancient mariner on the water without 'a shot in his locker'?"

"Would n't it have been jolly, — eating supper in the cabin," exclaimed William ; "and then, Captain Hardy, would you have gone on with the story?"

"To be sure I would," answered the Captain.

"Then I 'm sorry we did n't stay there," replied William.

"Good," said the Captain. "But what says little Alice?"

"I 'd rather hear the story where we are," was the reply. And as the lightning flashed and the thunder rattled more and more, the little girl crept closer to the old man's side.

"Then I 'm glad we came away," replied the captain ; "and we 'll go right on too, for I see you don't like listening to the storm."

"O, I 'm dreadfully afraid!" said Alice.

"Go on, go on! Captain Hardy," exclaimed both the boys together.

"But where was I when we left off to run away, in such a lubberly manner, from the storm?" inquired the Captain. "Let me see," and he put his finger to his nose, looking thoughtful.

"You were just beginning to cry," put in William.

"To be sure I was, that 's it ; and so would you cry, too, my boy, if you had an empty stomach under your belt, and nothing but a jack-knife in it," answered the Captain.

"That I would," exclaimed William, "I should have cried my eyes out. But, Captain Hardy, — if you 'll excuse me, — was the jack-knife in the empty stomach or in the belt?"

"Ah, you little rogue! I 'll not mind *you* any more," said the Captain, laughing ; "what would Fred have done?"

"I think I should have broke my heart," said Fred, promptly.

"That's not so easy done as crying," exclaimed the Captain. "But what says little Alice; what would she have done?"

"I don't know," replied Alice, gently; "but I think I should have gone and tried to get the poor boy to speak to me, and then I would have tried to comfort him."

"That's it, my charming little girl; that's just exactly what I did. But it was n't so easy either, I can tell you; for the boy was still as dull as ever. I tried to rouse him in every way I could think of; but he would not arouse. I spoke to him, I called to him, I shouted to him; but he would not answer me a single word."

"What was his name, Captain Hardy? Won't you tell us his name?" asked Fred.

"Ah! that I should have done before; but I forgot it. His name was Richard Dean. The sailors always called him 'the Dean.' He was a bright, lively boy, and everybody liked him. To see him in such a state made my very heart ache. But he was growing warm under his great load of eider-down, and that I was glad to see; and at last he showed some feeble signs of consciousness. His eyes opened wide, his lips moved. I thought he was saying something, though I could not understand for some time what it was. Then I could make out, after a while, that he was murmuring, 'Mother, mother!' Then he looked at me, wildly like, and then he turned his head away, and then he turned it back and looked at me again. 'Hardy,' said he, in a very low voice, 'is that you?' 'Yes,' I said; 'and I 'm glad you know me,' — which you may be very sure I was.

"But the poor fellow's mind soon wandered away from me again; and I could see that it was disturbed by visions of something dreadful. 'There! there!' he cried, 'it's tumbling on me!—the ice! the ice! it's tumbling on me!' and he tried to spring up from where he lay. 'There's nothing there at all, Dean,' said I, as I pressed him down. 'Come, look up; don't you see me?' He was quiet in an instant; and then, looking up into my face, he said, 'Yes, it's Hardy, I know; but what has happened to us,—anything?' Without pausing to give me time to answer, he closed his eyes and went on,—'O, I've had an awful dream! I thought an iceberg was falling on the ship. I saw it coming, and sprang away! As it fell, the ship went down, and I went down with it,—down, down, down; then I came up, clinging to some pieces of the wreck. Another man was with me; we were drifted with the waves to the land. I kept above the water until I saw somebody running towards me. When he had nearly reached me, I drowned. O, it was an awful dream!—Did you come to call me, Hardy?'—and he opened wide his eyes. 'Is it four bells? Did you come to call me?'— 'No, no, I have n't come to call you, it is n't four bells yet,' I answered, scarcely knowing what I said; 'sleep on, Dean.'— 'I'm glad you did n't come to call me, Hardy. I want to sleep. The dream haunts me. I dreamed that I was fast to something that hurt me, when I tried to get away. It was an awful dream,—awful, awful, awful!'—and his voice died away into the faintest whisper, and then it ceased entirely. 'Sleep, sleep on, poor Dean!' murmured I; and I prayed with all my heart that his reason might not be gone.

"'What could I do?' 'What should I do?' were the questions which soon crossed my mind respecting the Dean. There was, however, one very obvious answer,—'Let him alone'; so I rose up from his side, and saw, as I did so, that he was now sleeping soundly, — a genuine, quiet sleep. He had become quite warm ; and, after some minutes' watching, it appeared to me very likely that he would, after a while, wake up all right, — a conclusion which made me very happy ; that is, as happy as one so situated could be.

"After leaving the Dean I once more considered my condition. It seemed to me that I had grown many years older in these few hours, and I commenced reasoning with myself. Instead of sitting down on the rock, and beginning to cry, as I had done before, I sat down to reflect. And this is the way I reflected : —

" ' 1st,' I said, 'while there is life there is hope ' ; and,

" ' 2d. So long as the land remains unexplored, I have a right to conclude that it is inhabited ' ; and,

" ' 3d. Being inhabited, there is a good chance of our being saved ; for even the worst savages cannot refuse two such helpless creatures food and clothing.'

" Having thus reflected, I arrived at these conclusions respecting what I should do ; namely, —

" ' 1st. I will go at once in search of these inhabitants, and when I find them, I will beg them to come and help me with a sick companion.

" ' 2d. On my way I will make my dinner off raw eggs, of which there are so many hereabout, for I am so frightfully hungry that I can no longer resist the repulsive food.

" ' 3d. I will also hunt on my way for some water, as I am so thirsty that I scarcely know what to do.

" ' 4th. For the rest I will trust to Providence.'

" Having thus resolved, I immediately set out, and in a very few minutes I had eaten a whole dozen raw eggs, — and that, too, without any disgust at all. Then, as I walked on a little farther, I discovered that there were a multitude of small streams dashing over the rocks, the water being quite pure and clear, — coming from great snow-banks on the hill-tops, which were melting away before the sun.

"Being thus refreshed with meat and drink, it occurred to me to climb up to an elevation, and see what more I could discover. The ice was very thick and closely packed together all along the shore; but beyond where the wreck had happened the sea was quite open, only a few straggling bits of field-ice mixed up with a great many icebergs, — indeed, the icebergs were too thick to be counted. I thought I saw a boat turned upside down; but it was so far away that I could not make out distinctly what it was. It was clear enough to me that nobody had been saved from the wreck except the Dean and myself.

"As I looked around, it appeared very evident to me that the land on which I stood was an island.

"After hallooing several times, without any other result than to startle a great number of birds, as I had done before, I set out again, briskly jumping from rock to rock, the birds all the while springing up before me and fluttering away in great flocks. There seemed to be no end to them.

"As I went along, I soon found that I was turning rapidly to the left, and that I was not only on an island, but on a very small one at that. I could not have been more than two hours in going all the way around it, although I had to clamber most of the way over very stony places, stopping frequently to shout at the top of my voice, with the hope of being heard by some human beings; but not a soul was there to answer me, nor could I discover the least sign of anybody ever having been there.

4

"This failure greatly discouraged me, but still I was not so much cast down as you might think. Perhaps it was because I had eaten so many eggs, and was no longer hungry ; for, let me tell you, when one's stomach gets empty, the courage has pretty much all gone out of him.

" Besides this, I had made some discoveries which seemed in some way to forebode good, though I could not exactly say why. I found the birds thicker and thicker as I proceeded. Their nests were in some places so close together that I could hardly walk without treading on their eggs. I also saw several foxes, some of which were white and others were dark gray. As I walked on, they scampered away over the stones ahead of me, and then perched themselves on a tall rock near by, apparently very much astonished to see me. They seemed to look upon me as an intruder, and I thought they would ask, ' What business have you coming here ? ' They had little idea how glad I should have been to be almost anywhere else, — on the farm from which I had run away, for instance, — and leave them in undisputed possession of their miserable island. They seemed to be very sleek and well-contented foxes ; for they were gorging themselves with raw eggs, just as I had been doing, and they were evidently the terror of the birds. I saw one who had managed in some way to capture a duck nearly as large as himself, and was bouncing up the hill — to his den, no doubt — with the poor thing's neck in his mouth, and its body across his shoulder.

"Then, too, I discovered, from the east side of the island, where the ice was solid, a great number of seals lying in the sun, as if asleep, on the ice ; and when I came around on the west side, where the sea was open, great schools of walruses, with their long tusks and· ugly heads, were sporting about in the water as if at play, and an equally large number of the narwhal, with their long horns, were also playing there. Only that they are larger, and have these hideous-looking tusks, walruses are much like seals. The narwhal is a small species of whale, being about twenty feet long, and spotted something like an iron-gray horse. Its great peculiarity is the horn, which grows, like that of a sword-fish, straight out of the nose, and is nearly half as long as the body. Like all the other whales, it must come up to the surface of the water to breathe ; and its breathing is done through a hole in the top of the head, like any other whale's. You know the breathing of a whale is called 'spouting,' or 'blowing,' — that is, when he breathes out it is so called, and when he does this he makes the spray fly up into the air.

"This breathing of the largest whales can be seen several miles ; that is, I should say, the spray thrown up by their breath. So you see the common expression of the whale-fishers, 'There she blows!' is a very good one ; for sometimes, when the whale is very large, the spray looks like a small waterspout in the sea.

"Besides the narwhal, which I have told you about, I saw another kind of whale, even smaller still. This is called the white whale, though it is n't exactly white, but a sort of cream-color. They had no horns, however, like the narwhal ; and they skimmed along through the water in great numbers, and very close together, and when they come to the surface they breathe so quickly that the noise they make is like a sharp hiss.

"Considering the numbers of these animals, — the seals and walruses and narwhals and white whales, — I was not surprised, when I went close down to the beach, to find a great quantity of their bones there, evidently of animals that

had died in the sea and been washed ashore. Indeed, as I
went along a little farther, and had reached nearly to the

John Hardy making Discoveries.

place where I had left the Dean, I found the whole carcass
of a narwhal lying among the rocks, where it had been
thrown by the waves, and very near it I discovered also a
dead seal. About these there were several foxes, which went
scampering away as soon as they saw me. They had evidently come there to get their dinner; for they had torn a
great hole in the side of the dead narwhal, and two of them
had begun on the seal. I thought if I could get some of the
skins of these pretty foxes, they would be nice warm things
to wrap the Dean's hands and feet in, so I began flinging

stones at them as hard as I could ; but the cunning beasts
dodged every one of them, and, running away up the hillside,
chattered in such a lively manner that it seemed as if they
were laughing at me, which provoked me so much that I
went on vowing to get the better of them in one way or
another.

"All this time, you must remember, I had left the poor
Dean by himself, and you may be sure I was very anxious to
get back to him ; but before I tell you anything more about
him, I must stop a minute longer to describe more particularly this island on which I had been cast away. You must
understand there were no trees on it at all ; and, indeed,
there were scarcely any signs of vegetation whatever. On
the south side, where we landed after the wreck, the hillside
was covered for a short distance with thick grass, and above
this green slope there were great tall cliffs like the palisades
of the Hudson River, — which you must all see some time ;
but all the rest of the way around the island I saw scarcely
anything but rough rocks, very sharp and hard to walk over.
In some places, however, where the streams of melted snow
had spread out in the level places, patches of moss had grown,
making a sort of marsh. Here I discovered some flowers in
full bloom, and among them were the buttercup and dande-
lion, just like what we find in the meadows here, only not a
quarter so large ; but my head was too much filled with more
serious thoughts at that time to care about flowers.

"You can hardly imagine anything so dreary as this island
was. Indeed, nothing could be worse except the prospect of
living on it all alone, without any shelter, or fire, or proper
clothing, and without any apparent chance of ever escaping
from it.

"I found, however, a sort of apology for a tree growing among the moss beds. I have learned since that it is called a 'dwarf willow.' The stem of the tree, if such it might be called, was not larger than my little finger; and its branches, which lay flat on the ground, were in no case more than a foot long.

"Besides these willows, I discovered also, growing about the rocks, a trailing plant, with very small stem, and thick, dry leaves. It had a pretty little purple blossom on it, and was the only thing I saw that looked as if it would burn. I can assure you that I wished hard enough that I had some way of proving whether it would burn or not. However, since I had discovered so many other things on this my first journey around the island, I was not without hope that I should light upon some way of starting a fire. So I named the plant at once 'the fire plant;' but I have since been told by a wise doctor that I met down in Boston, that its right name is 'Andromeda.' It is a sort of heather, like the Scotch heather that you have all heard about, only it is as much smaller than the Scotch heather as the dwarf willow I told you of is smaller than the tall willow-tree that grows out there in front of the door.

"Although I had not, as I have said, discovered any natives living on the island, yet I came back from my journey feeling less disappointed than I would have thought. No doubt my anxiety to see how the Dean was so occupied my mind that I did not dwell as much upon my own unhappy condition as I otherwise would have done. In truth, I think the Dean must have saved me from despair and death; for, if I had not felt obliged to exert myself in his behalf, I must have sunk under the heavy load of my misfortunes.

"When I came back to the Dean, I found that the poor boy was still sleeping soundly, — a sort of dead, heavy sleep. At first, I thought to arouse him ; but then, again, since I found he was quite warm, I concluded the best thing was not to disturb him. Some color had come into his face ; indeed, there was quite a flush there, and he seemed to be a little feverish. The only thing I now feared· was that his reason might have left him ; and this thought filled me with a kind of dread of seeing him rouse up, just as every one, when he fears some great calamity, tries to postpone the realization of it as long as possible. So I suffered him to remain sleeping, and satisfied myself with watching his now somewhat heavy breathing for a little while, when, growing chilly (for the sun had by this time gone behind the island, thus leaving us in the shadow of the tall cliffs), I began to move about again. I set to work collecting more of the eider-down, so that, when I should be freed from my anxiety about the Dean, I might roll myself up under this warm covering and get some sleep ; for, although my mind was much excited, yet I was growing sleepy, besides being chilly. I also collected a number of eggs, and ate some more of them ; and, using several of the shells for cups, I brought some water, setting the cups up carefully in the grass, knowing that when the Dean opened his eyes he must needs be thirsty as well as hungry.

"All this being done, I fell to reflecting again, and, as was most natural, my thoughts first ran upon what I should do to make a fire. I had found — or at least I thought I had found — something that would burn, as I have said before ; but what should I do for *the first spark?* True, with my jack-knife for a steel, and a flint-stone, of which there were plenty, I could strike a spark without any difficulty ; but what was

there to strike it into, so that it would catch and make a blaze ?
I knew that in some countries people make a blaze by rubbing
two pieces of dry wood together ; but this I could not do, as
I had not a particle of wood. In other countries, I knew, they
have punk, into which they strike a spark, and the spark will
not go out until the punk is all burned up, so that they have
only to blow it on some inflammable substance until a blaze
comes ; but where was I to get the punk from ? I had also
heard that fire had been made with lenses of glass, which,
being held up to the sun, concentrate the rays and make a
great heat, sufficient to set wood and like combustible things
on fire ; but I had no lens. Of course, I have no need to
tell you that I had no matches, such as we have now-a-days
here.

"Thus the night wore on. I say *night*, but you must bear
in mind, as I told you before, that there was really no night
at all,— the sun being above the horizon all the time ; and the
only difference now in the different periods of the day was,
that when the sun was in the south it shone upon us, while
when it was at the north we were under the shadow of the
cliffs. The sun, you must observe, in the Arctic regions, cir-
cles around during the summer, only a little way above the
horizon, never rising overhead, as it does here, but being always quite low down ; and hence it never gives a very strong
heat, although the air is sometimes warm enough to be very
comfortable.

"I was glad when the shadow of the cliff passed from over
me, and the sun was once more in view.

"I now grew quite warm, though my great fatigue did not
vanish ; but I was so anxious about the Dean that I would
not sleep, and kept myself awake by moving about all the

time, staying always near the Dean. At length, soon after the sun appeared, the boy began to show some restlessness ; and as I approached him, I found that his eyes were wide open. He raised himself a little on one arm, and turned towards me as I came up to him, and looked straight at me, so calmly and intelligently that I saw at once he had come to his senses entirely; and so rejoiced was I, that, without thinking at all about what I was doing, I fell down beside him, and clasped him in my arms, and cried out, 'O Dean, Dean!' over and over a great many times. You cannot imagine how glad I was!

" ' Why, Hardy,' said he, in a very feeble voice, 'where are we ? What 's the matter ? What has happened to us ?' Seeing that it was useless for me to attempt to evade the question, I told him all the circumstances of the shipwreck, and how I had carried him there, and what I had been doing. I thought at first this would disturb him, but it did not seem to in the least. After I had finished, he simply said : 'I thought it was all a dream. It comes back to me now. I remember a frightful crash, of being in the water on the wreck, of seeing some one approaching me, of being held down first by a drowning man and then by a rope, of trying to free myself, and then I must have swooned, for I remember nothing more. I have now a vague remembrance of some one talking to me about a dream I had, but nothing distinct.'

" ' But,' said I, ' Dean, don't talk any more about it just now, it will fatigue you ; tell me how you feel.' ' No,' answered he, ' it does not fatigue me, and I want to collect myself. Things are getting clearer to me. My memory returns to me gradually. I see the terrified crew. It was but an instant. I heard the crash. The great body of the ice fell right amid-

4   F

ships, — right upon the galley. Poor cook! he must have
been killed instantly. Some of the crew jumped overboard ;
I tried to, but got no farther than the bulwarks, and then was
in the water ; I don't know how I got there. When I came
up there was a man under me, and I was tangled among
some rigging, but was lifted up out of the water on some large
mass of wreck. The man I told you of tried to get up too ;
but his feet were caught, and I saw him drowning. I saw
another man holding on to the wreck, but a piece of ice struck
him, and he must have fallen off immediately.'

"'Dean, Dean!' said I, 'do stop! you are feverish ; quiet
yourself, and we'll talk of these things by and by' ; — and
the boy fell back quite exhausted. His skin was very hot,
and his face flushed. 'O my head, my head!' exclaimed
he ; 'it pains me dreadfully! Am I hurt?' and he put his
hand to the side of his head where he had been struck, and,
finding that he was wounded, said : 'I remember it now perfectly. A heavy wave came, and was tossing a piece of tim-
ber over me, and I tried to avoid being struck by it. After
that I remember nothing. It must have struck me. I'm not
much hurt, — am I ?'

"'No, Dean,' I answered, 'not much hurt, only a little
bruised.'

'Have you any water, Hardy?' he asked, 'I am so thirsty!'

"It was fortunate that I had brought some in the egg-shells,
and in a moment I had given him a drink. It did me good to
see him smile, as I handed him the water, and ask where I
got such odd cups from. 'Thanks, thanks!' said he ; 'I'm
better now.' Then after a moment's pause he added, 'I want
to get up and see where we are. I'm very weak ; won't you
help me?' But I told him that I would not do it now, for

the present he must lie quiet. 'Then raise me up and let me look about.' So I raised him up, and he took first a look at the strange pile of eider-down that was upon him, and then at the ice-covered sea, but he spoke not a word. Then he lay down, and after a short time said calmly: 'I see it all now. Hard, — is n't it? But we must do the best we can. I feel that I 'll soon be well, and will not be a trouble to you long. Do you know that until this moment I could hardly get it out of my head that I had been dreaming? We must trust in Heaven, Hardy, and do the best we can.'

"Being now fully satisfied as to the complete recovery of the Dean, I gave myself no further concern about watching him ; but at once, after he had, in his quiet way, asked me if I was not very tired, I buried myself up in the heap of eider-down close beside him, and was soon as deeply buried in a sound sleep."

The Captain, evidently thinking that he had gone far enough for one day, now broke off suddenly. The children had listened to the recital more eagerly than on any previous occasion, — so much so, indeed, that they had wholly disregarded the storm ; and little Alice was so absorbed in learning the fate of the poor shipwrecked Dean, that her fears about the thunder and lightning had been quite forgotten. When the Captain paused, the storm had passed over, the sun had burst through the scattering clouds, and in the last lingering drops his silver rays were melted into gorgeous hues ; for

"A rainbow — thrown brightly
Across the dark sky —
(Soft curving, proud arching
In beauty on high)

> " Had circled the even, —
> A bridal ring, given
> To wed earth with heaven,
> As it smiled 'neath the veil of the glittering rain. "

The little birds had come out of their hiding-places, and were merrily singing,

> " Farewell to the rain, the beautiful rain " ;

and the party of little folks that had been hidden away in the " Mariner's Rest," following their example, were soon gayly hastening across the fresh fields, — the old man carrying laughing Alice in his arms, to keep her tender feet from the wet grass.

CHAPTER VIII.

In which the Mariner's Rest and the Ancient Mariner himself receive particular Attention.

HE next day being Sunday, the Captain's little friends did not go down to see him, and the day after being stormy, they could not. So, when Tuesday came, they were all the more eager for the visit that it had been delayed ; and accordingly they hurried off at a very early hour. Indeed, the old man was only too glad to have them come down at any time, for he had during these past few days become so used to their being with him, and he had taken such a fancy to them, that he felt himself quite lost and lonely when a day passed by without seeing them. He was, as we have already seen, rather afraid they might disturb him if he said, "Come at any hour you please," instead of "Come at four o'clock, or three, or two o'clock," as the case might be ; but he had discovered them to be such well-behaved and gentle children, that he made up his mind they could never trouble or annoy him. So when last they parted, he said to them, " Come in the morning, if you like, and play all day about the grounds, and if I have work to do you must not mind. Nobody will disturb you";—and, in truth, there was nobody there to disturb them, for besides the old man and his boy, Main Brace, there was no living thing about the house, if we except two fine old Newfoundland dogs which the Captain had brought home with him from his last voyage, and which he called " Port " and " Starboard." He had also a flock of handsome chickens, and some foreign ducks. "And now," said he, "when you have seen all these, and Main Brace, and me, you have seen my family, for this is all the family that I have, unless I count the pretty little birds that hop and skip and sing among the trees."

Main Brace did all the work about the house, except what the Captain did himself. He cooked, and set the Captain's table, and kept the Captain's house in order generally. As for the house itself, there was not much of it to keep in order. We have already seen that it was very small and but one story high. There was no hall in it, and only five rooms upon the floor. Let us look into it more particularly.

Entering it from the front through the little porch covered over with honeysuckle vines that are smelling sweet all the summer through, we come at once into the largest of the rooms, where the Captain takes his meals and does many other things. But he never calls it his dining-room. Nothing can induce him to call it anything but his "quarter-deck." On the right-hand side there are two doors, and there are two more on the left-hand side, and directly before us there are two windows, looking out into the Captain's garden, where there are fruits and vegetables of every kind growing in abundance. The first door on the right opens into a little room where Main Brace sleeps. This the Captain calls the "forecastle." The other door on the right opens into the kitchen, which the Captain calls his "galley." The first door on the left is closed, but the second opens into what the Captain calls his "cabin," and this connects with a little room behind the door that is closed, which he calls his "state-room,"—and, in truth, it looks more like a state-room of a ship than a chamber. It has no bed in it, but a narrow berth on one side, just like a state-room berth. All sorts of odd-fashioned clothes are hanging on the walls, which the Captain says he has worn in the different countries where he has travelled. Odd though this state-room is, it is not half so odd as the Captain's cabin.

Let us examine this cabin of the Captain. There is an old table in the centre of it. There are a few old books in an old-fashioned bookcase. There is no carpet to be seen, but the floor is almost covered over with skins of different kinds of animals, among which are a Bengal tiger, a Polar bear, a South American ocelot, a Rocky Mountain wolf, and a Siberian fox. In a great glass case, standing against the wall, there is a variety of stuffed birds. On the very top of this case there is a huge white-headed eagle, with his large wings spread out, and at the bottom of it there is a pelican with no wings at all. On the right-hand side there is an enormous albatross, and on the left-hand side there is a tall red flamingo; while in the very centre a snowy owl stands straight up and looks straight at you out of his great glass eyes. And then there are still other birds,—birds little and birds big, birds bright and birds dingy, all scattered about wherever there is room, each sitting or standing on its separate perch, and looking, for all the world, as if it were alive and would fly away only for the glass.

On the walls of this singular room are hanging all sorts of singular weapons, and many other things which the Captain has picked up in his travels. There is a Turkish scymitar, a Moorish gun, an Italian stiletto, a Japanese "happy despatch," a Norman battle-axe, besides spears and lances and swords of shapes and kinds too numerous to mention. In one corner, on a bracket, there is a model of a ship, in another a Chinese junk, in a third an old Dutch clock, and in the fourth there is a stone idol of the Incas, while above the door there is the figure-head of a small vessel, probably a schooner.

When the children came down, running all the way at a very lively rate, the Captain was in his cabin overhauling all these treasures, and dusting and placing them so that they would show to the very best advantage. Indeed, there were so many "traps," as he called them, hanging and lying about, that the place might well have been called a "curiosity shop" rather than a cabin. In truth, it had nothing of the look of a cabin about it.

When the Captain heard the children coming, he said to himself, "I'll give them a surprise to-day," and he looked out through the open window, and called to them. They answered with a merry laugh, and, running around to the door, rushed into the "quarter-deck," and were with the Captain in a twinkling.

"O, what a jolly place!" exclaimed William; "such a jolly lot of things! Why did n't you show them to us before, Captain Hardy?"

"One thing at a time, my lad; I can't show you everything at once," answered the old man.

" But where did you get them all, Captain Hardy ? "

" As for that, I picked them up all about the world, and I could tell a story about every one of them."

"O, is n't that splendid ? — won't you tell us now ? " inquired William.

"And knock off telling you what the Dean and I were doing up there by the North Pole, on that island without a name ? "

William was a little puzzled to know what reply he should make to that, for he thought the Captain looked as if he did not half like what he had said ; so he satisfied himself with exclaiming, " No, no, no," a great number of times, and then asked, "But won't you tell us all about them when you get out of the North Pole scrape ? "

"Maybe so, my lad, maybe so ; we 'll see about that ; one thing at a time is a good rule in story-telling as well as in other matters. And now you may look at all these things, and when you are satisfied, and I have got done putting them to rights, we 'll go on with the story again."

The children were greatly delighted with everything they saw, and they passed a very happy hour, helping the Captain to put his cabin in " ship-shape order," as he said. Then they all crowded up into one corner, and the Captain, seated on an old camp-stool, which had evidently seen much service in a great number of places, did as he had promised.

What he said, however, deserves a chapter by itself ; and so we 'll turn another leaf and start fresh again.

CHAPTER IX.

CONTAINS A RECOVERY, A DISCOVERY, AND A DISAPPOINTMENT.

"AND now," said the Captain, "what was the young man doing, when we knocked off the other day, after the storm?"

William, whose memory was always as good as his words were ready, said he was "just going to sleep."

"True, that's the thing; and I went to sleep and slept soundly, I can tell you. And this you may well enough believe when you bear in mind how much I had passed through since the last sleep I had on board the ship, — for since then had come the shipwreck, the saving of the Dean and carrying him ashore, the walk around the island, besides all the anxiety and worriment of mind in consequence of my own unhappy situation and the Dean's uncertain fate.

"More than twenty-four hours had elapsed since the shipwreck, and if I tell you that I slept full twelve hours, without once waking up, you must not be at all surprised.

"When I opened my eyes again, we were in the shadow of the cliffs once more; that is, the sun had gone around to the north again. The Dean was already wide awake. When I asked him how he was, he said he felt much better, only his head still pained him greatly, and he was very thirsty and hungry.

"I got up immediately, and assisted the Dean to rise. He was a little dizzy at first, but after sitting down for a few minutes on a rock he recovered himself. Then I brought him some water in an egg-shell to drink. And then I gave him a raw egg, which he swallowed as if it had been the daintiest morsel in the world. 'It's lucky, is n't it,' said he, 'that there are so many eggs about?' After a moment I observed that he was laughing, which very much surprised me, as that would have been about the last thing that ever would have entered into my head to do. 'Do you know,' he asked, 'what a very ridiculous figure we are cutting? Look, we are all covered over with feathers. I have heard of people being tarred and feathered, but never heard of anything like this. Let's pick each other.'

"Sure enough we were literally covered over with the down in which we had been sleeping, and when I saw what a jest the poor Dean, with his sore head, made of the plight we were in, I forgot all my own troubles and joined in the laugh with him.

"We now fell to work picking each other, as the Dean had suggested, and were soon as clean of feathers as any other well-plucked geese.

"By this time the Dean's clothes had become entirely dry; so each dressed himself in the clothes that belonged to him, and then we started over to the ·nearest brook, where we bathed our hands and faces, drying them on an old bandanna handkerchief which I was lucky enough to have in my pocket. I had to support the Dean a little as we went along, for he was very weak ; but in spite of this his spirits were excellent, and when he saw, for the first time, the ducks fly up, he said, 'What a great pair of silly dunces they must take us for, — coming into such a place as this.'

"After we had refreshed ourselves at the brook, and eaten

some more eggs, we very naturally began to talk. I related to the Dean, more particularly than I had done before, the events of the shipwreck and our escape, and what I had discovered on the island, and then made some allusion to the prospect ahead of us. To my great surprise, the Dean was not apparently in the least cast down about it. In truth, he took it much more resignedly, and had a more hopeful eye to the future, than I had. 'If,' said he, 'it is God's will that we shall live, he will furnish us the means; if not, we can but die. I would n't mind it half so much, if my poor mother only knew what was become of me.' This reflection seemed to sadden him for a moment, and I thought I saw a tear in his eye ; but he brightened up instantly as a great flock of ducks went whizzing overhead. ' Well,' exclaimed he, ' there seems to be no lack of something to eat here anyway, and we ought to manage to catch it somehow, and live until a ship comes along and takes us off.'

"The Dean took such a hopeful view of the future that we were soon chatting in a very lively way about everything that concerned our escape, and here I must have dwelt largely upon the satisfaction which I took in rescuing the Dean, for the little fellow said : ' Well, I suppose I ought to thank you very much for saving me ; but the truth is, all the agony of death being over with me when you pulled me out, the chief benefit falls on you, as you seem so much rejoiced about it ; but I 'll be grateful as I can, and show it by not troubling you any more. See, I 'm almost well. I feel better and better every minute, — only I 'm sore here on the head where I got the crack.'

" To tell the truth, in thinking of other things, I had neg- lected, or rather quite forgotten, the Dean's wounded head ;

so now, my attention being called to it, I examined it very carefully, and found that it was nothing more than a bad bruise, with a cut near the centre of it about half an inch long. Having washed it carefully, I bound my bandanna handkerchief about it, and we once more came back to consider what we should do.

"Of course, the first thing we thought of and talked about was how we should go about starting a fire; next in importance to this was that we should have a place to shelter us. So far as concerned our food and drink, our immediate necessities were provided for, as we had the little rivulet close at hand, and any quantity of eggs to be had for the gathering, and we set about collecting a great number of them at once; for in a few days we thought it very likely that most of them would have little ducks in them, as, indeed, many of them had already. Another thing we settled upon was, that we would never both go to sleep at the same time, nor quit our present side of the island together; but one of us would be always on the lookout for a ship, as we both thought that, since our ship had come that way, others would be very likely to, though neither of us had the remotest idea in the world as to where we were, any more than that we were on an island somewhere in the northern sea.

"But the fire which we wanted so much to warm ourselves and cook our food, — what should we do for that? Here was the great question; and fire, fire, fire, was the one leading idea running through both our heads; — we thought of fire when we were gathering eggs, we talked of fire when, later in the day, we sat upon the rocks, resting ourselves, and we dreamed of fire when we fell asleep again, — not this time, however, under the eider-down where we had slept before, but on the green grass of the hillside, in the warm sunshine, under my overcoat, for we had turned night into day, and were determined to sleep when the sun was shining on us at the south, and do what work we had to do when we were in the shade.

"Every method that either of us had ever heard of for making a fire was remembered and talked over; but there was nothing that appeared to suit our case. I found a hard flint, and by striking it on the back of my knife-blade I saw that there was no difficulty in getting any number of sparks, but we had nothing that would catch the sparks when struck; so that we did not seem to be any better off than we were before; and, as I have stated already, we fell asleep again, each in his turn, — 'watch and watch,' as the Dean playfully called it, and as they have it on shipboard, — without having arrived at any other result than that of being much discouraged.

"When we had been again refreshed with sleep, we determined to make a still further exploration of the island; so, after once more eating our fill of raw eggs, we set out. The Dean, being still weak and his head still paining him very much from the hurt, remained at the lookout. He could, however, walk up and down for a few hundred yards without losing sight of the only part of the sea that was free enough of ice to allow a ship to approach the island. After a while he came to where I had discovered the dead seal and narwhal lying on the beach, when upon my first journey round the island. I had told him about them, as indeed I had of everything I had seen, and he was curious to try if he could not catch a fox; but his fortune in that particular was not better than mine.

"For myself, I had a very profitable journey, as I found a

place among the rocks which might, with some labor in fixing it up, give us shelter. I was searching for a cave, but nothing of the sort could I come across; but at the head of a little valley, very near to where I left the Dean, I discovered a place that would, in some measure at least, answer the same purpose. Its situation gave it the still further advantage, that we commanded a perfect view of the sea from the front of it.

"I have said that it was not exactly a cave. It was rather a natural tent, as it were, of solid rocks. At the foot of a very steep slope there were several large masses of rough rocks heaped together, evidently having one day slid down from the cliffs above, and afterwards smaller rocks, being broken off, had piled up behind them. Two of these large rocks had come together in such a manner as to leave an open space between them. I should say this space was ten or twelve feet across at the bottom, and, rising up about ten feet high, joined at the top like the roof of a house. The rocks were pressed against them behind, so as completely to close the outlet in that direction. I climbed into this place, and was convinced that if we had strength to close up the front entrance with a wall, we should have a complete protection from the weather. But then, when I reflected how, if we did seek shelter there, we should keep ourselves warm, I had great misgivings; for then came up the question of all questions, 'What should we do for a fire?'

"Although this place was not a cave, yet I spoke to the Dean about it as such, and by that name we came to know it; so I will now use the term, inappropriate though it is. I also told the Dean about some other birds that I had discovered in great numbers. They were very small, and seemed to

have their nests among the rocks all along the opposite side
of the island, where they were swarming on the hillside, and
flying overhead in even greater flocks than the ducks. I
knew they were called 'little auks,' from descriptions the
sailors had given me of them.

The Dean makes provision for a change of diet.

"'But look here what I 've got,' exclaimed the Dean, with
an air of triumph, as soon as I came up with him. 'See this
big duck!'

"The fellow had actually caught a duck, and in a most
ingenious manner. Seeing the ducks fly off their nests, the
happy idea struck him that, if he could only contrive a trap,
or 'dead-fall,' he might catch them when they came back.

So he selected a nest favorable to his purpose, and then piled up some stones about it, making a solid wall on one side of it; then he put a thin narrow stone on the other side, and on this he supported still another stone that was very heavy. Then he took from his pocket a piece of twine which he was fortunate enough to have, and tied one end of it to the thin narrow stone, and, holding on to the other end, hid himself behind some rocks near by. When the duck came back to her nest, he jerked the thin narrow stone away by a strong pull on the twine string, and down came the heavy stone upon the duck's back. 'You should have heard the old thing quacking,' said he, evidently forgetting everything else but the sport of catching the bird: 'but I soon gave her neck a twist, and here we are ready for a dinner, when we only find a way to cook it. Have you discovered any way to make a fire yet?'

"I had to confess that on the subject of fire I was yet as ignorant as ever.

"'Do you know,' continued he, 'that I have got an idea?'

"'What is it?' said I.

"'Why,' replied he, 'you told me something about people making fire with a lens made of glass. Now, as I was down on the beach and looked at the ice there, I thought, why not make a lens out of ice, — it is as clear as glass?'

"'How ridiculous!' said I; 'but suppose you could, what will you set on fire with it?'

"'In the first place,' he answered, 'the pockets of my coat are made of some sort of cotton stuff, and if we could only set fire to that, could n't we blow a blaze into the fire plant, as you call it? See, I 've gathered a great heap of it.' And sure enough he had, for there was a pile of it nearly as high as his head, looking like a great heap of dry and green leaves.

5 G

"The idea did not seem to me to be worth much, but still, as it was the only one that had been suggested by either of us, it was at least worthy of trial; so we went down to the beach, and, finding a lump of ice about twice as big as my two fists, we began chipping it with my knife into the shape we wanted it, and then we ground it off with a stone, and then rubbed it over with our warm hands until we had worn it down perfectly smooth, and into the shape of a lens. This done, we held it up to the sun, relieving each other as our hands grew cold ; but without any success whatever. We tried for a long time, and with much patience, until the ice became so much melted, that we could do nothing more with it, when we threw it away, and the experiment was abandoned as hopeless.

"Our disappointment at this failure was as great as the Dean's hopes had been high. The Dean felt it most, for he was, at the very outset, perfectly confident of success. Neither of us, however, wished to own how much we felt the failure, so we spoke very little more together, but made, almost in silence, another meal off the raw eggs, and, being now quite worn out and weary with the labors and anxieties of the day, we passed the next twelve hours in watching and sleeping alternately in the bright sunshine, lying as before on the green grass, covered with the overcoat. We did not even dare hope for better fortune on the morrow. We had, however, made up our minds to struggle in the best manner we could against the difficulties which surrounded us, and mutually to sustain each other in the hard battle before us. Whether we should live or die was known but to God alone, and to his gracious protection we once more commended ourselves ; the Dean repeating a prayer which he had learned from a pious and careful mother, who had brought him up in the fear of Heaven, and taught him, at a very early age, to have faith in God's endless watchfulness.

"And now, my children," concluded the Captain, "I have some work to do in my garden, to-day, so we must cut our story short this time. When you come to-morrow, I will tell you what next we did towards raising a fire, besides many other things for our safety and comfort."

So the party scattered from the "cabin," — the Captain to his work, and the children to play for a while with the Captain's dogs, Port and Starboard, out among the trees ; and to talk with Main Brace, whom they found to be the most singular boy they had ever seen ; after which they went to the Captain to say "Good evening" to him, and then ran briskly home, — William eager to write down what he had heard, while it was yet fresh upon his memory, and all of them to relate to their parents, over and over again, what this wonderful old man had been telling them, and what a dear old soul he was.

CHAPTER X.

<small>SHOWS HOW SOME THINGS MAY BE DONE AS WELL AS OTHERS, WITH GOD'S HELP AND WITH MUCH PERSEVERANCE.</small>

HEN the children next went to the "Mariner's Rest," it was unanimously agreed that they should go back again to the Captain's "cabin,"— there were so many things that they had not seen, and which they wished to look at. Alice wanted to see the birds, — the owl with the great, big eyes, and the pelican that had no wings, at least only little stumps that were hardly an apology for wings. Fred wanted to see the Chinese junks and the little ship, while William was bent on having the Moorish gun, the Turkish sword, the Japanese "happy despatch," and all the other weapons, offensive and defensive, taken down, that he might have a better view of them. The old man, at all times very ready and willing to gratify his little friends, was never more so than when he found them so much interested in the contents of his cabin ; for every little curiosity or treasure there had an association with some period of his eventful life, and he was never happier than when any one admired what he admired so much, and thus gave him a chance to talk about it.

"Heyday!" said he, when all the children had spoken and made known their wishes, "I'm glad you take so kindly to the old man's den ; you shall come down there and look at it whenever you like, only you must n't toss the things about too much. Run in now, and make yourselves at home. I'll be with you in a little while."

So the children set off without another word, and were quickly diving among the old man's treasures, while the Captain went back to his garden to finish the hoeing of his cabbages.

When the Captain had completed what he was about, he rejoined the children ; and after a great deal of conversation which there is no need that we should here repeat, the party at length sobered down as if they were bent on business, and the Captain, once more drawing his little friends about him by the open window, again took up the tale.

"Now I told you yesterday," said he, "that the Dean and I had gone asleep again after all our work and trouble and anxiety, without having come any nearer to getting up a fire. You have seen that we had enough to eat and drink, and that I had found a place to shelter us if a storm came on ; but nothing could either of us think of to catch a spark. As soon as the Dean had opened his eyes, he said : 'Why, this is too bad! indeed it is, — I thought I had been making a fire.'

"'What with?' I asked.

"'With matches, to be sure,' answered the Dean. 'I thought I had a great load of them in my pocket.'

"'Then,' said I, 'I'm sure I pity you, to wake up out of such a pleasant dream ; for you'll find no matches here, nor any fire either, nor do I think we shall ever have any.'

"'O, don't say that, Hardy,' replied the Dean, sadly, 'I don't think we are so bad off as to say we never will have any fire. Do you really think we are?'

"'I can't say,' I replied ; 'but what can we do?'

"'Try again,' answered the Dean;—and we were soon once more upon our feet, both very determined to do something, but neither of us knowing exactly what it should be.

"So we set off to inspect the cave which I told you of yesterday. The Dean was much pleased with it, and, seeing nothing better to do, we both went to work at once to build up a wall in front of it, feeling very sad and sorrowful as we worked in silence. But in spite of our gloomy thoughts we made good progress, and had soon a solid foundation laid ; but as we went on, it was plain enough to see that our wall was likely to be of very little account, since we had no way of filling up the cracks between the stones.

"This set us once more to thinking. Down below us in the valley there was plenty of moss, or rather turf; but when we tried to pull it up with our hands, we discovered that we could do nothing with it, and we wished for something to dig with. Then I remembered the bones I had found on the beach ; so I told the Dean about them, and we both agreed that they, might be of use to us. The thing which I first thought of was the dead narwhal with the great long horn ; and I im- agined that, if we could only get that out of his head, we should have all we wanted.

"When the Dean and I went down to the narwhal, we foresaw that our task would be even greater than we had supposed ; for the horn which we were after was so firmly embedded in the skull and flesh that it promised to be a very serious work to get it out.

"First, we had to cut away the flesh and fat from the thick nose, until we exposed the skull, and then we had to break the horn loose by dropping heavy stones upon the socket. At length we were successful. But we had consumed almost the whole day about it, and we found ourselves very much fatigued ; so we sat down upon the green grass, and rested and talked for a while, before going back to work upon the wall again. The horn was very heavy, but it answered our purpose; and we were soon digging up the moss with it, and then we carried the moss up to help make out the wall. This moss was very soft, being full of water ; and it fitted with the stones as nicely as any mason's mortar, so that we had no more trouble in making the wall perfectly tight and solid. Nor did we have any trouble in building up a little fireplace and chimney along with it.

"We had some discussion as to what use there was in taking all this pains, since we had no fire to put in our fireplace. But then, if we should in the end find that we could make a fire, we saw that we would have to tear the wall down again if we did not build the fireplace and chimney up at once ; therefore it was clearly better to take a little extra trouble now, and save it possibly in the end, — an observation that might apply to people who were never cast away in the cold, and did not have to build chimneys without knowing what use to put them to.

"We labored very hard, and were well satisfied with the progress we had made, when we found it necessary to knock off, and eat some more raw eggs, and sleep away our fatigue again.

"By this time we had grown tired enough of these raw eggs, and, in truth, were very sick of them. But we had nothing else to eat unless we should devour the duck which the Dean had caught ; and this we could never, as we thought, bring ourselves to do, uncooked as it was.

"The Dean had by this time grown pretty strong again, but still he was so weak that I should not have allowed him to work had he not insisted upon it ; so, when his turn came to go to sleep, I was glad to be at work by myself, and I much surprised the Dean, when he got up again, with what I had done.

"'Do you know what I was thinking of?' said the Dean, as we paused to rest, after we had again worked awhile together.

"'What's that?' said I ; 'for I dare say it's something clever, as you have a wise head on your young shoulders, Dean.'

"'Thank you,' said the Dean ; 'being cast away in the cold don't stop us from paying compliments, anyway ; but I was thinking that we ought to save all the blubber of that old narwhal down there ; we'll want the oil by and by.'

"'What for?' said I.

"'To burn,' said he.

"'Nonsense !' said I ; 'how are you going to burn it?'

"'That's just what we're going to find out,' said the Dean ; 'we'll get a fire somehow, of that I'm sure.'

"'I should like to know how,' said I. 'Perhaps you have another bright idea.'

"'To be sure I have,' answered the Dean.

"'What is it this time?' said I.

"'Well, I don't know,' said he, 'as there's much in it, but I'm going to try the lens again.'

" ' That 's of no use,' said I.

" ' I 'm not so sure,' said he ; 'you know we made a great deal of heat with our lens the other time, — so much that it almost burned my hand. I think the trouble was in my old pocket, which, having once been in salt water, would n't burn ; now I think I 've found out something that is better.'

" ' What 's that ? ' said I.

" ' Why, some cotton stuff,' said he, ' that I found blowing about among the stones.

" ' Cotton ! ' I exclaimed, in great surprise ; ' there 's no cotton growing here.'

" ' Well, it looks like cotton for all that,' answered the Dean, 'and I 'm sure it will burn. Let me get some of it, and I 'll try it.'

" So the Dean ran off, and soon came back again with a little wad of white stuff, that looked very much like cotton, only much finer in its texture. I remembered it perfectly, for I had seen it, everywhere I went, about the little willow-bushes ; and I had even plucked a willow-blossom to find it covered all over with this tender cotton-like substance, which I blew from it with my breath. But the idea had never once come into my head that it would be of any use.

" ' What are you going to do with this ? ' said I to the Dean, when he had showed it to me.

" ' Why,' said he, with much confidence, ' I 'm going to make another lens of ice, and set fire to it.'

" To set fire to it was something easier said than done, yet the idea seemed to take root in my mind ; and how or why it ever came about I can no more tell than I can fly, but somehow or other, it matters not what was my impulse or idea or expectation, the truth is, without saying a single word,

5 *

"Striking fire under difficulties."

I pulled out my knife and the bit of flint which I had found and carefully preserved the day before, and then struck one upon the other (as if it were quite mechanical) above the Dean's little bit of cotton stuff, which lay upon the grass. A great shower of sparks was thrown off with each fresh stroke, and these told of the fineness of the steel and the hardness of the flint. I went on pounding and pounding away, as if resolved on something. And if I was resolved, my resolution was rewarded ; for at length the Dean threw up his hands as suddenly as if a shot had struck him in the heart, and he shouted out, 'A spark, a spark !'

"The Dean's little bit of cotton stuff had taken fire, and

the daintiest little streak of smoke was curling upward from it.

"Without pausing an instant, quick as the hawk to swoop down upon its prey, quick as the lightning-flash, quick as thought itself, I threw away my knife and flint, and caught up the spark. The Dean drew instantly from his pocket the bit of cotton cloth which we had tried to light with the lens the day before, and thrust it in my hand. I put the spark upon it, and then blew.

"The first breath drove all the Dean's light cotton stuff away, and the spark was gone.

"But we were now no longer where we were before. The spark had been made once, and it could be made again; and our hearts were bounding with delight. 'Hurrah! hurrah!' shouted the Dean, 'we're all right now!'

"But our troubles about the fire were very far from ended. We had no difficulty in getting another spark to catch in another piece of this strange sort of tinder, of which we found great plenty near at hand. But it would not blaze. With the slightest breath it vanished almost as a flash of powder; and it was long before we hit upon anything that would do us any further good. We tried all the pieces of cotton cloth that we had about our clothes, picking it into shreds, and, putting the lighted tinder among these shreds, tried to make them blaze. But no blaze could we get. Once only did we raise a little flash, but it was gone in a single instant. We tried the dry leaves of the fire-plant (*Andromeda*), the dry grass, — everything, indeed, we could think of that was within our reach, — but still no blaze, no blaze.

"With sore fingers and wearied patience, and with wits as well as bodies quite exhausted, we fell once more asleep, with

mingling thoughts of triumph and disappointment, and with
prayerful hopes for what the morrow might bring forth running through our minds.

"When the morrow came, a chance seemed to open for us ;
and we resolved to go about our work with caution, determined, since we had gone thus far, that we would in the end
succeed. I don't know whether it was the Dean or I that first
suggested it, but we made up our minds that the *moss* which
we had turned up with the narwhal horn, when we were building at the hut, some of which had dried, would burn. We
picked to pieces some of the long fibres of this moss, and laid
upon them, loosely, some fragments of the tinder. A spark
was struck as before, and upon blowing this a bright blaze
flashed up, and then died out again as quickly as it had come.

"'I have it now!' shouted the Dean, 'we're sure of it next
time !' and without saying another word he darted off towards
the beach. When he came back again, he held in one hand
a chunk of blubber from the narwhal, out of which we
squeezed some drops of oil, and soaked in them some fibres of
the moss.

"Another piece of tinder and another piece of moss were
placed as they had been before ; another spark was struck,
another blaze was blown, and when this came, the Dean was
holding in it his fibres of oil-soaked moss, and we soon had a
lighted torch. 'Hurrah, hurrah!' we might well shout now,
for the thing was done. 'Praised be Heaven ! we have got a
fire at last!'

"Then we added fresh moss to the flaming torch, which
was scarcely larger than a match, and then a few more drops
of oil were added, and so on, oil and moss, and moss and oil,
little by little, gently, gently all the time, until we had secured
at length a good and solid flame.

"Then we laid the burning moss upon a flat stone, and then, as before, moss and oil, and oil and moss, were added, each time in larger and larger quantities, — no longer gently, gently, but with a careless hand, and in less, perhaps, than half an hour we had a great, smoking, fluttering blaze ; and then we threw on some of the driest leaves and twigs of the Andromeda, and some dead willow-stems and dry grass, and then we had a roaring, sputtering, red-hot fire.

"And how we danced, and skipped, and shouted round the fire, like happy children round some new-found toy !

"The next thing was, of course, to turn the fire to some account. On two sides of the blaze we placed large square stones, and over these we put another that was thin and flat ; and then we skinned the duck which the Dean had caught, and cut the rich flesh into little pieces and placed them on the flat stone above the blaze ; and then, to keep the smoke and ashes from the cooking food, we put another light, thin stone upon the flesh, and then we watched and waited for the coming meal. To help the fire along, and make it burn more quickly, we threw into it some little chunks of blubber, and then, in a little while, the duck was cooked.

"O what a royal meal we had ! — we half-famished, shipwrecked boys, — the first hot food we had tasted during all these long, weary, dreary days ; and, not satisfied with the duck, we next broiled some eggs upon the heated stone, and ate and ate away until we were as full as we could hold.

"All this had consumed many hours, and all the time we had been so much excited that we found ourselves quite exhausted when the meal was over, and we could do no more work that day ; so we lay down again upon the grass, to talk and rest and sleep. When we came to sleep, however, we had now another motive, besides watching for a ship, to make us sleep one only at a time ; for we must keep this fire going, which we had got with so much trouble. This was easily done, since we only had to add, from time to time, some branches of the Andromeda, and these kept up a smouldering fire.

"Before either of us went to sleep, we had seen that the first thing now was to catch more ducks ; and this we could either of us do, besides watching the sea for ships, and the fire that it did not go out. Accordingly, as soon as the Dean had fallen asleep, I went about this work, fully resolved upon a plan as to how I should proceed. The knowledge of seals which I had acquired when in the Blackbird had perhaps something to do with it.

"I knew, from the thickness of the seal's skin, that lines could be made out of it very well. You will remember the dead seal that I told you of the other day, lying down on the beach, where it had been thrown up out of the sea by the waves. I forgot to mention, in addition, that we found several other seals, or rather, I should say, parts of them, for most of them had been eaten up by the foxes, or had gone to pieces by decay. So I at once went down, as I was going to say, to the seal that I had first discovered, and, taking out my knife, I made a cut around his neck, close behind the ears. It was a very large seal, and I found it not an easy matter to lift him up so that I could get my knife all the way around him ; but I managed to do it notwithstanding, and made not only one cut but a great many of them, — or rather, I should say, one continuous cut around and around the body of the dead animal ; so you will easily understand that, in this way, by keeping my knife about an eighth of an inch from where it had gone before when it passed around, I obtained at last a long string, or rather one might say a thong, very strong and very pliable. It must have been at least a hundred feet in length when I stopped cutting it, and I divided it into three parts. Having done this, I next went back to where the ducks were thickest, when, of course, the birds flew off their nests. Then I fixed four traps, just as the Dean had done, tying to three of them the seal-skin strings which I had made, and to the fourth I tied the Dean's bit of twine; then I hid myself among the rocks, and waited for the birds to come back.

"I had not long to wait, for in a few minutes two of them returned, and, without appearing to mind at all the trap that I had set for them, crawled upon their nests so quickly that it seemed as if they were mightily afraid their eggs would get cold. Seeing a third one coming, I waited for her too, and the fourth one came soon afterwards; and indeed, by this time, nearly all the birds that had their nests near by had come back to them. As soon as all was quiet, I pulled my strings one after another as quickly as I could, and three of the birds were caught; but the last one was too smart for me, as the noise made by the others had startled her, and the heavy stone only struck her tail as she went squalling and fluttering away, frightening off all the other ducks that were anywhere near.

"I was not long, as you may be sure, in securing my three prizes; and I carried them at once up to the fire near which the Dean was lying under my overcoat in the sun. Soon after this the Dean awoke, and, when he saw what I had done, seemed to be much amused, as he declared that I had stolen his patent; but when he saw what kind of a line I had

made, he was filled with admiration, saying : 'Well, who would
ever have thought of that ?   I 'm sure I never should.'

"Being now very tired, I lay down while the Dean took his
'turn'; and by the time my eyes were opened again he had
caught seven birds, so that we had now in all ten, — enough,
probably, to last us as many days.   This, of course, gave us
a great deal of satisfaction, especially as we soon had one of
them nicely cooked, and thus got a good breakfast.

"We had now been, you see, several days on the island,
and we felt that we had done pretty well already towards
providing for ourselves.   The Dean, as I ought to have mentioned before, had grown in strength very rapidly during the
last forty-eight hours ; and except that his head was still sore
from the cut and bruise, he was entirely well.

"We felt now that, whatever else might happen to us, we
could not want for food, as, besides the eggs, we could have
as many ducks as we pleased to catch.   We had succeeded in
making a fire, and had abundant means to keep it burning.
There were only two things that seriously troubled us.   One
was our lack of shelter, if a storm should come ; and the
other, our lack of proper clothing, if the weather should grow
cold.   But, having succeeded so well thus far, we were very
hopeful for the future.   Heaven had kindly favored us.   The
temperature had been very mild all the time.   There had
been no wind, and scarcely a cloud to obscure the sky.   As
for shelter, we felt that we could manage in two days to en-
close the cave ; and as to the other trouble, although we were
not very clear in our minds about it, yet we did not lose confidence that a ship would come along and take us off before
winter should set in.   So we resolved not to abandon our vigi-
lance, but to keep up a constant watch, as we had done before.

Now that we had made a fire, we knew the smoke would be a great help to us in drawing the attention of the people on board any ship that might come near.

"With these agreeable reflections we went to work much more cheerfully than we had done before."

The captain here "hove to," as he said, observing, that, the day being far spent, he would drop the story for the present. "To-morrow, when you come, I will tell you how we fixed up the cave, and made ourselves more comfortable in many ways. Meanwhile you can reflect upon what I have told you, and you can answer me then whether you think John Hardy and Richard Dean were an enviable pair of boys."

"I can answer that now," said William.

"Well, what is the answer?" asked the Captain, in great good-humor.

"Why, their pluck and courage everybody would envy, or at least they ought to; but, for the rest, I would rather stay at home."

"Well, well," said the Captain, smiling pleasantly, "each to his taste. I rather think I should prefer being in the 'Mariner's Rest' myself"; — saying which he led the way into the grounds in front of the cottage which he loved so well, where he took leave of his little friends once more, making them promise over and over again (for which there was no need at all) that they would come next day and hear about the cave, and how they there built themselves a shelter from the Arctic storms.

CHAPTER XI.

In which the little People are convinced of the Goodness of Providence, as the Reader ought to be, — seeing that to be cast away is not to be forsaken.

WE have now for some time followed the old man through the recital of the wonderful adventures which befell himself and the Dean on the lonely little island in the Arctic Sea ; and we have watched the children going and coming from day to day. And we have seen, too, how happy the children were when listening to the story, and how delighted they were with every little scrap they got of it, and how they remembered every word of it, and how William wrote it down in black and white, and had it safe and sound for future use, — little dreaming, at the time of doing it, that the record he was keeping would find its way at last into a book, and thus give other children than himself and Fred and Alice a chance to make the acquaintance of the good old Captain and the brave and handsome little Dean.

And William Earnest kept his record regularly, and he kept it well, as we have seen before ; and up to this point of time everything was set down with day and date. But now a change had clearly come over the habits of our little party. At first, as has been hitherto related, the old Captain was a little shy of the children, though he so much liked them ; but now all formality was gone between them, and so down the children came to the Captain's cottage whenever they had a mind. The Captain was always glad to see them, be it morning, noon, or evening ; and never were the children, in all their lives before, so happy as when romping through the Captain's grounds, or cooling themselves upon the grass beneath the Captain's trees, or looking at the Captain's " traps " or joking with that oddest boy that was ever seen, Main Brace, or playing with the Captain's dogs, — the biggest dogs that ever bore the odd names of Port and Starboard.

The Captain now said, " Make yourselves at home, my dears, — quite at home " ; and the children did it ; and the Captain always went about whatever he had to do until he was ready once more to begin his story-telling ; and then they would all rush off to the yacht, or to the " Crow's Nest," or the " cabin," or the " quarter-deck," or some other pleasant place ; and as the Captain related something more and more extraordinary, as it seemed to them, each time,

> " the wonder grew
> That one small head should carry all he knew " ;

while, as for the old man himself, he might well exclaim, with the lover in the play, " I were but little happy if I could say how much."

Thus it came about, as we have good reason to suppose, that days and dates were lost in William's journal ; and thus it was that the young and truthful chronicler of this veritable history simply wrote down, from time to time, what the Captain said, without mentioning much about when it was that the Captain said it. Sometimes he wrote with lead pencil, sometimes with pen and ink, and often, as is plain to see from the manuscript itself, at considerable intervals of time ; but always, as there is no doubt, with accuracy ; for William's mind, touching the Captain's adventures, was like the susceptible heart of the Count in the Venetian story, "wax to receive and marble to retain."

So now, after this long explanation, the reader will perceive that we can do nothing else than report the Captain's story, without always saying where the little party were seated at the time the Captain told it. And, in truth, it matters little ; at least so William thought, for he wrote one day upon the page, —

"Where's the use, I 'd like to know, putting in what Fred and me and Alice did, and where we went with the 'ancient mariner' ; I have n't time to write so much, and I 'll only write what the Captain said." ; and so right away he set down what follows.

"Now you see," resumed the Captain, "when we had done all I told you of before, — having slept, you know, and got well rested, — we went about our work very hopefully. But as we were going along, meditating on our plans, the Dean stopped suddenly, and said he to me : 'Hardy, do you know what day it is ?'

"'No,' said I, 'upon my word I don't, and never once thought about it !'

"The Dean looked very sad all at once, and, not being able to see why that should be, I asked what difference it made to us what day it was.

"'Why, a great deal of difference,' said the Dean.

"'How?' said I.

"'Why,' said the Dean, 'when shall we know when Sunday comes?'

"To be sure, how should we know when Sunday came! I had not thought of that before; but the Dean was differently brought up from me; for, while I had not been taught to care much about such matters, the Dean had, and he looked upon Sunday as a day when nobody should do any sort of work. I believe the Dean had an idea in his head, that, if it was Sunday, and he was frozen half to death already, or starved about as badly, and should refuse to work to save himself from death outright, he would do a virtuous thing in sacrificing himself, and would go straight up to heaven for certain. So I became anxious too, and for the Dean's sake, if not for my own, I tried hard to recall what day it was."

"How very queer," said William, "to forget what day it was! How did it happen? Won't you tell us that, Captain Hardy?"

"To be sure," said the obliging Captain, — "as well as I can, that is. Now, do you remember what I told you the other day about the sun shining all the time, — do you remember that, my lad?"

"Yes," answered William, "of course I do. Goes round and round, that way," and he whirled his hat about his head.

"Just so," went on the Captain, — "just so, exactly. Goes round and round, and never sets until the winter comes, and then it goes down, and there it stays all the winter through, and there is constant darkness where the daylight always was before."

"What, all the time?" asked William.

"Yes," replied the Captain ; "dark all the time."

"How dark ?" asked Fred.

"Dark as dark can be.   Dark at morning and at evening.
Dark at noon, and dark at midnight.   Dark all the time, as I
have said.   Dark all the winter through.   Dark for months
and months."

"How dreadful !" exclaimed Fred.

"Dreadful enough, as I can assure you, with no light, all
the whole winter-time, except the moon and stars.   A dreadful thing to live along for days and days, and weeks and
weeks, and months and months, without the blessed light of
day, — without once seeing the sun come up and brighten
everything and make us glad, and the pretty flowers to unfold
themselves, and all the living world praise the Lord for remembering it.   That 's what you never see in all the Arctic
winter, — no sunshine ever streaming up above the hills and
making all the rainbow colors in the clouds.   That 's what
you never see at all, no more than if you were blind and
could n't see.

"But never mind just now about the winter.   We have n't
done with the summer yet, nor with Sunday either, for that
matter.

"As I have said before, the loss of Sunday much grieved
the Dean.   So, you see, we had nothing else to do but make
one on our own account."

"What, make a Sunday !" exclaimed William.   "I 've heard
of people making almost everything, even building castles in
the air ; but I never heard before of anybody putting up a
Sunday."

"Well, you see, we did the best we could.   It is not at all
surprising that we should have lost our reckoning in this way,

seeing that the sun was shining, as I have told you, all the time ; and we worked and slept without much regard to whether the hours of night or day were on us. So we had good reason for a little mixing up of dates. In fact we could neither of us very well recall the day of the month that we were cast away. It was somewhere near the end of June, that we knew ; but the exact day we could not tell for certain. We remembered the day of the week well enough, and it was Tuesday ; but more than this we could not get into our heads ; and so it seemed that there was nothing for us but to sink all days into the one long day of the Arctic summer, and nevermore know whether it was Sunday, or Monday, or Friday, or what day it was of any month ; and if it should be Heaven's will that we should live on upon the island until the New Year came round, and still other years should come and go, we should never know New Year's day.

"But, as I was saying, about making a Sunday for ourselves. I did everything I could to refresh my memory about it. I counted up the number of times we had slept, and the number of times we had worked, and recalled the day when I first walked around the island ; and I tried my best to connect all those events together in such a way as to prove how often the sun had passed behind the cliffs, and how often it had shone upon us; and thus I made out that the very day I am telling you about proved to be Sunday, — at least I so convinced the Dean, and he was satisfied. And that's the way we made a Sunday for ourselves.

"So we resolved to do no work that day; and this was well, for we were very weary and needed rest.

"I need not tell you that we passed the time in talking over our plans for the future, and in discussing the prospects ahead of us, and arranging what we should do. You see we had settled about Sunday, so that was off our minds; and after recalling many things which had happened to us, and things which had been done on the *Blackbird*, we finally concluded that we had found out the day of the month, and so we called the day 'Sunday, the second of July,' and this we marked, as I will show you, thus: On the top of a large flat rock near by I placed a small white stone, and this we called our 'Sunday stone'; and then, in a row with this stone, we placed six other stones, which we called by the other days of the week. Then I moved the white stone out of line a little, which was to show that Sunday had passed, and afterwards, when the next day had gone, we did the same with the Monday stone, and so on until the stones were all on a line again, when we knew that it was once more Sunday. Of course we knew when the day was gone, by the sun being around on the north side of the island, throwing the shadow of the cliffs upon us.

"For noting the days of the month we made a similar arrangement to that which we had made for the days of the week; and thus you see we had now got an almanac among other things.

"'And now,' said the Dean, 'let us put all this down for fear we forget it.' So away the little fellow ran and gathered a great quantity of small pebbles, and these we arranged on the top of the rock so as to form letters; and the letters that we thus made spelled out

'JOHN HARDY AND RICHARD DEAN,
CAST AWAY IN THE COLD,
TUESDAY, JUNE 27, 1824.'

" Now, when we came to look ahead, and to speculate upon

what was likely to befall us, we saw that we had two months of summer still remaining ; and, as midsummer had hardly come yet, we knew that we were likely to have it warmer than before, and we had now no further fears about being able to live through that period. In these two months it was plain that one of two things must happen, — a ship must come along and take us off, or we must be prepared for the dark time that must follow after the sun should go down for the winter ; otherwise a third thing would certainly happen, that is, we should both die, — an event which did not, in any case, seem at all unlikely ; so we pledged ourselves to stand by each other through every fortune, each helping the other all he could. At any rate, we would not lose hope, and never despair of being saved, through the mercy of Providence, somehow or other.

"Having reached this resigned state of mind, we were ready to consider rationally what we had to do. It was clear enough that, if we only looked out for a ship to save us, and that chance should in the end fail, we would be ill prepared for the winter if we were left on the island to encounter its perils. Therefore it was necessary to be ready for the worst, and accordingly, after a little deliberation, we concluded to proceed as follows : —

"1st. We would construct a place to shelter ourselves from the cold and storms. (In this we had made some satisfactory progress already.)

"2d. We would collect all the food we could while there was opportunity.

"3d. We would gather fuel, of which, as had been already proved, there was Andromeda (or fire-plant) and moss and blubber to depend upon. Of this latter the dead narwhal and

6

seal would furnish us a moderate supply; but for the rest we must rely upon our own skill to capture some other animals from the sea; though, as to how this was to be done, we had to own ourselves completely at fault.

"4th. We would in some manner secure for ourselves warmer clothing, otherwise we would certainly freeze; and here we were completely at fault too.

"5th. We would contrive in some way to make for ourselves a lamp, as we could never live in our cave in darkness; and here was a difficulty apparently even more insurmountable than the others, — as much so as appeared the making of a fire in the first instance, — for while we had a general idea that we might capture some seals, and get thus a good supply of oil, and that we might also get plenty of fox-skins for clothing, yet neither of us could think of any way to make a lamp.

"When we came thus to bring ourselves to view the situation, the prospect might have caused stouter hearts than ours to fear; but, as we had seen before, nothing was to be gained by lamentation, so we put a bold front on, firmly resolved to make the best fight we could."

"A poor chance for you, I should think," said Fred, "and I don't see how you ever lived through so many troubles," — while little Alice declared her opinion that "the poor Dean must have died anyway."

"A very bad prospect, indeed, my dears," continued the Captain, — "very bad, I can assure you; but as it is a poor rule to read the last page of a book before you read the rest of it, so we will go right on to the end with our story, and then you will find out what became of the Dean, as well as what happened to myself.

"Well, as I was going to say, when Monday came, we set about our work, not exactly in the order which I have named, but as we found most convenient; and as day after day followed each other through the week, and as one week followed after another week, we found ourselves at one time building up the wall in front of the cave, then catching ducks and gathering eggs, then collecting the fire-plant, and then throwing moss up on the rocks to dry, and then cutting off the blubber and skins of the dead seal and narwhal.

"All of these things were carefully secured; and in a sort of cave, much like the one we were preparing for our abode, only larger, we stowed away all the fire-plant and dried moss that we could get. Then we looked about us to see what we should do for a place to put our blubber in, — that is, you know, the fat we got off the dead narwhal and the seal, and also any other blubber that we might get afterwards.

"When we had cut all the blubber off the seal and narwhal, we found that we had an enormous heap of it, — as much, at least, in quantity, as five good barrels full, — and, since the sun was very warm, there was great danger, not only that it would spoil, but that much of it would melt and run away. Fortunately, very near our hut there was a small glacier hanging on the hillside, coming down a narrow valley from a greater mass of ice which lay above. From the face of this glacier a great many lumps of ice had broken off, and there were also deep banks of snow which the summer's sun had not melted.

"In the midst of this accumulation of ice and snow we had little difficulty in making, partly by excavating and partly by building up, a sort of cave, large enough to hold twice as much blubber as we had to put into it. Here we deposited our treasure, which was our only reliance for light in case we invented a lamp, and our chief reliance for fire if the winter should come and find us still upon the island.

"After we had thus secured, in this snow-and-ice cave, our stock of blubber, we constructed another much like it near by for our food, and into this we had soon gathered a pretty large stock of ducks and eggs.

John Hardy and the Dean provide for the Future.

"When we contemplated all that we had done in this particular, you may be sure our spirits rose very much."

"Odd, was n't it?" said Fred, "having a storehouse made of ice and snow. But, Captain Hardy, if you'll excuse me for interrupting you, what did this glacier that you spoke about look like? and what was it anyway?"

"A glacier is nothing more," replied the Captain, "than a stream of ice made out of snow partly melted and then frozen again, and which, forming, as I have said before, high up on the tops of the hills, runs down a valley and breaks off at its end and melts away. Sometimes it is very large, — miles across, — and goes all the way down to the sea; and the pieces that break off from it are of immense size, and are called *icebergs*. Sometimes the glaciers are very small, especially on small islands such as ours was. This little glacier I tell you of lay in a narrow valley, as I said before; and, as the cliffs were very high on either side, it was almost always in shadow, and the air was very cold there; so you see how fortunate it was that we thought of fixing upon that place for our storehouses. Then another great advantage to us was, that it was so near our hut, — being within sight, and only a few steps across some rough rocks; but among these rocks we contrived, in course of time, to make, by filling in with small stones, a pretty smooth walk.

"As we caught and put away the ducks in our storehouse, we began at length to preserve their skins. At first we could see no value in them, and threw them away; but we imagined at length that, in case we could not catch the foxes, they would serve to make us some sort of clothing, while out of the seal-skin which I mentioned before we could make boots, if we only had anything to sew with.

"Thus one difficulty after another continued to beset us; but this last one was soon partly overcome, for the Dean, on the very first day of our landing, discovered that he had in his pocket his palm and needle, carrying it always about him when on shipboard, like any other good sailor ; but we lacked thread."

"What is a palm and needle, Captain Hardy ? " inquired William.

" A palm," answered the Captain, " is a band of leather go-ing around the hand, with a thimble fitted into it where it comes across the root of the thumb. The sailor's needle differs only from the common one in being longer and three-cornered, instead of round. It is used for sewing sails and other coarse work on shipboard. The needle is held between the thumb and forefinger, and is pushed through with the thimble in the palm of the hand, and hence the name.

" To come back to our story (having, as I hope, made the palm and needle question clear to you), let me ask you to re-member that I told you, when I landed on the island, I had four things, — that is : —

" 1st. My life ;

" 2d. The clothes on my back ;

" 3d. A jack-knife ; and

" 4th. The mercy of Providence.

" But now, you see, I had added a fifth article to that list, in the Dean's needle ; and I might also say that I had a sixth one, too, in the Dean himself, which I did not dare enumerate in the list at first, as I felt pretty sure that the Dean was going to die, or at least wake up crazy.

" But you see a sailor's palm and needle could be of very lit-tle use unless we had some thread, of which we did not possess a single particle, except the small piece that was in the needle, and by which it was tied to the palm. It was a good while before we obtained anything to make thread of, so we will pass that subject by for the present, and come back to what we had more immediately in hand. This was the preparation of our cave, or rather, as we had better say, hut, — that being more nearly what it was.

" The building of our hut, then, was indeed a very difficult task, as the solid wall we had to construct in front was much higher than our heads, and in this wall we had, of course, to leave a door-way and a window, besides a sort of chimney, or outlet, for the smoke from the fireplace, which was beside the door.

" We must have been at least two weeks making this wall, for we had not only to construct the wall itself, but when it got so high that we could no longer reach up to the top, we had to build steps, that we might climb there. We left a window above the door-way, not thinking, of course, to find any glass to put in it, but leaving it rather as a ventilator than a window. It was very small, not more than a foot square, and was easily shut up at any time, if we should not need it. For a door, we used a piece of the narwhal skin. This skin was fastened above the door-way with pegs, which we made of bones, driving them into the cracks between the stones, thus letting the skin fall down over the door-way like a curtain.

" In making the wall, we were greatly helped by the bones which I had found down on the beach, as they were much lighter than the stones, and aided in holding the moss in its place, so that we were able to use much more of that material than we otherwise should have been. When the wall was completed, we were gratified to see how tight it was, and how perfectly we had made it fit the rocks by means of the moss.

" Having completed the wall, our next concern was to ar-

range the interior ; but about this we had no need to be in so
great a hurry as with the wall, for we had now a place to shelter us from any storm that might come, and we could hope to
make ourselves somewhat comfortable there, even although
the inside was not well fitted up ; for we had a fireplace, and
could do our cooking without going outside. When we found
how perfect was the draft through the outlet, or chimney, you
may be very sure we were greatly delighted.

" As it fell out, we had secured this shelter in the very nick
of time, for in two days afterwards a violent storm arose, — a
heavy wind with hail and gusts of snow, — a strange kind of
weather, you will think, for the middle of July. This storm
made havoc with the ice on the east side of the island, breaking it up, and driving it out over the sea to the westward, filling the sea up so much in that direction, that there was no use,
for the present at least, in looking for ships, as none could come
near us. The storm made a very wild and fearful spectacle of
the sea, as the waves went dashing over the pieces of ice and
against the icebergs. When I looked out upon this scene, and
listened to the noises made by the waves and the crushing ice,
and heard the roaring wind, I wondered more than ever what ·
could possess anybody to go to such a sea in a ship, for it
seemed to me that the largest possible gains would not be a
sufficient reward for the dangers to be encountered.

" But so it always was, and always will be, I suppose. Whenever there is a little money to be made, men will encounter
any kind of hazard in order to get it. Thus the risks in going after whales and seals for their blubber, which is very
valuable, are great ; but then, if the ship makes a good voyage, the profits are very large, and when the sailors receive
their 'lay,' that is, their share of the profits on the oil and

whalebone which have been taken, it sometimes amounts to quite a handsome sum of money to each, and they consider themselves well rewarded for all their privations and hardships. And it must be owned that the whalers and sealers are a very brave sort of men, especially the whalers who go among the ice ; for besides the dangers to the vessel, and the danger always encountered in approaching a whale to harpoon him (for, as you must know, he sometimes knocks the boat to pieces with his monstrous tail, and spills all the crew out in the water), he may, while swimming off with the harpoon in him, and dragging the boat by the line which is fast to it, take it into his head to rush beneath the ice, and thus destroy the boat and drown the people.

"But this is too long a falling to 'leeward' of our story, as the sailors would call it ; so we will come right back into the wind again.

"When the weather cleared off after the storm, we went to work as before. But everything about looked gloomy enough. The cliffs were besprinkled with snow, and about the rocks the snow had drifted, and it lay in streaks where it had been carried by the wind. The sea was still very rough, and, as there were many immense pieces of ice upon the water, when the waves rose and fell, the pounding of it on the rocks made a most fearful sound.

"The sun coming out warm, however, soon melted the snow, and, getting heated up with work, we got on bravely. Indeed, we soon became not less surprised at the rapid progress we were making than at the facility with which we accommodated ourselves to our strange condition of life, and even grew cheerful under what would seem a state of the greatest possible distress. Thus you observe how perfectly we may recon-

6 *   I

cile ourselves to any fate, if we have but a resolute will, and the fear of God in our hearts. I do not mean to boast about the Dean and myself: but I think it must be owned that we kept up our courage pretty well, all things considered, — now, don't *you* think so, my dears ?"

"To be sure we do," replied William. "And if anybody dares to doubt it, I will go, like Count Robert, to the cross-road, and give battle for a week to all comers, just as he did."

"Poking fun at the ancient mariner again, — are you?" said the Captain, trying hard to look serious. "And so I'll punish you, my boy, by knocking off just where we are, and saying not another word this blessed day."

CHAPTER XII.

RELATES HOW A DESERT ISLAND BECAME A ROCK OF GOOD HOPE, AND OTHER HOPEFUL MATTERS WHICH TO BE UNDERSTOOD MUST BE READ OF.

"YOU now see," went on the Captain, when the story was again resumed, "that the Dean and myself had by this time fallen into a regular course of life. 'What cannot be helped,' said the Dean, 'we must make the best of.'

"Being thus obliged to make the best of it, we became resigned ; and here let me say that even now I feel much surprised at the ease with which we dropped into ways suitable to our new life. You have seen already how one difficulty after another vanished before our patient efforts ; and now that we had a fire to warm us, and a hut to shelter us, we felt as if we could overcome almost anything. So we gained great courage, and were fast settling down to business, like any other people, feeling that our lives were at least in no present danger.

"The Dean and I had a conversation about this time, which I will try to repeat as nearly as I can. We were seated on the hillside overlooking the sea to the west, attracted by what we at first took for a ship under full sail, steering right in towards the island ; but you can imagine how great was our disappointment when we found that what we had taken for a ship was nothing more than an iceberg looming up above the sea in a misty atmosphere. This was the third time we had been deceived in that manner. Once the Dean had come rushing towards me, shouting at the top of his voice, 'The

fleet! the fleet!' meaning the whale-ships; but he might just
as well have saved himself all that trouble, for 'the fleet'
proved to be only a great group of icebergs; but when I told
him so he would hardly believe it, until he became at last convinced that they were not moving.

"You must know that these icebergs assume all sorts of
shapes, and it was very natural, since we were always on the
lookout for ships, that our imaginations should be excited and
disturbed, and ready to see at any time what we most wanted
to see; nor were we at all peculiar in this, as many people
might tell you who were never cast away in the cold.

"So it is not surprising that we should cry out very frequently 'A sail, a sail!' when there was not a sail perhaps
within many hundred miles of us.

"Well, as I was going to say, the Dean and I sat upon the
hillside overlooking the sea, thinking the icebergs were ships,
or hoping so at least, until hope died away, and then it was
that we fell to talking.

"'Do you think, Hardy,' asked the Dean, 'that any other
ship than ours ever did come this way or ever will?'

"'I'm afraid not,' said I; and I must have looked very
despondent about it, as in truth I was, — much more so than
I would have liked to own.

"I had not considered what the Dean was about, for he was
despondent enough himself, and no doubt wished very hard
that I might say something to cheer him up a bit; but, instead of doing that, I only made him worse, whereupon he
seemed to grow angry, and in a rather snappish way he inquired of me if I knew what I was.

"'No,' said I, quite taken aback. 'What do you mean?'

"'Mean!' exclaimed the Dean. 'Why, I mean to say,' —

and he spoke in a positive way that was not usual with him,
— 'I mean to say,' said he, 'that you are a regular Job's comforter, and no mistake.'

"I had not the least idea at that period of my life as to what kind of a thing a Job's comforter was. I had a vague notion that it was something to go round the neck, and I protested that I was nothing of the sort.

"'Yes, you are, and you know you are,' went on the Dean, — 'a regular Job's comforter, — croaking all the time, and never seeing any way out of our troubles at all.'

"'I should like to know,' said I, — and I thought I had him there, — 'how I can see any way out of our troubles when there is n't any!'

"'Well, you can think there is, if there is n't, — can't you?' and the Dean was ten times more snappish than he was before; and, having thus delivered himself, he snapped himself up and snapped himself off in a great hurry; but, as the little fellow turned to go away, I thought I saw great big tears stealing down his cheeks. I thought that his voice trembled over the last words; and when he went behind a rock and hid himself, I knew that he had gone away to cry, and that he had been ashamed to cry where I could see him.

"After a while I went to him. He was lying on his side, with his head upon his arm. His cap had fallen off, and the light wind was playing gently with his curly hair. The sun was shining brightly in his face, and, sunburnt and weather-beaten though it was, his rosy cheeks were the same as ever. But bitter, scalding tears had left their traces there, for the poor boy had cried himself to sleep.

"His sleep was troubled, for he was calling out, and his hands and feet were twitching now and then, and cruel dreams were weighing on his sleeping, even more heavily, perhaps, than they had been upon his waking thoughts. So I awoke him. He sprang up instantly, looking very wild, and sat upon the rock. 'Where am I? What's the matter? Is that you, Hardy?' were the questions with which he greeted me so quickly that I could not answer one of them. Then he smiled in his natural way, and said, 'After all, it was only a dream.'

"'What was it?' I asked. 'Tell me, Dean, what it was.'

"'O, it was not much, but you see it put me in a dreadful fright. I thought a ship was steering close in by the land; I thought I saw you spring upon the deck and sail away; and as you sailed away upon the silvery sea, I thought you turned and mocked me, and I cursed you as I stood upon the beach, until some foul fiend, in punishment for my wicked words, caught me by the neck, and dragged me through the sea, and tied me fast to the vessel's keel, and there I was with his last words ringing in my ears, with the gurgling waters, "Follow him to your doom," when you awoke me. "Follow him 'to your doom!" I seem to hear the demon shrieking even now, though I 'm wide enough awake.'

"'I don't wonder at your fright, and I'm glad I woke you!' said I, not knowing what else to say.

"'It all comes,' went on the little fellow, 'of my being angry with you, Hardy'; and so he asked me to forgive him, and not think badly of him, and said he would not be so ungrateful any more, and many such things, which it pained me very much to have him say; and so I made him stop, and then somehow or other we got our arms around each other's neck, and we kissed each other's cheeks, and great cataracts of tears came tearing from each other's eyes; and the first and last unkindness that had come between us was passed and gone forever.

"'But do you really think,' said the Dean, when he got his voice again, — 'do you really think that, if a ship don't come along and take us off, we can live here on this wretched little island, — that is, when the summer goes, and all the birds have flown away, and the darkness and the cold are on us all the time?'

"'To be sure we can,' I answered; but, to tell the truth, I had very great doubts about it, only I thought that this would strengthen up the Dean; and as I had, by this time, made for myself a better definition to Job's comforter than a something to go around the neck, I had no idea of being called by that name any more.

"'I'm glad to hear you say that!' exclaimed the Dean. 'Indeed I am!'

"There was no need to give me such very strong assurance that he was 'glad to hear it,' for his face showed as plain as could be that he was glad to hear me say anything that had the least hope in it.

"After this the Dean grew quite cheerful. Suddenly he asked, 'Do you know, Hardy, if this island has a name?'

"Of course I did not know, and told him so.

"'Then I'll give it one right off,' said he; 'I'll call it from this minute the Rock of Good Hope, and here we'll make our start in life. It's as good a place, perhaps, to make a start in life as any other; for nobody is likely to dispute our title to our lands, or molest us in our fortune-making, which is more than could be said if our lot were cast in any other place.'

"This vein of conversation brightened me up a little. Indeed, it was hard to be very long despondent in the presence of the Dean's hopeful disposition. There was much more said of the same nature, which it is not necessary to repeat. It is enough for me to tell you that the upshot of the whole matter was that we came in the end to regard ourselves as settled on the island, if not for the remainder of our lives, at least for an indefinite time, and we made up our minds that there was no use in being gloomy and cast down about it. So from that time forward we were mostly cheerful, and, though you may think it very strange, were generally contented.

"This was a great step gained, and when we now came to make an inventory of our possessions, we did it just as a farmer or merchant would do. Being the undisputed owners of this Rock of Good Hope, we considered ourselves none the less owners of all the foxes, ducks, eggs, eider-down, dead beasts, dry bones, and whatsoever else there might be upon it ; and, besides this, we had a lien upon all the seals and walruses and whales of every kind that lived in the sea, — that is, if we could catch them.

"We now worked with even a better spirit than we had done before, for the idea of being settled on the island for life seemed to imply that we had need to look ahead farther than when our hopes of rescue had been strong.

"And first we finished the hut in which we were to live, — doing it not as if we were putting up a tent for temporary use, but as a man who has just come into possession of a large property puts up a fine house on it, that he may be comfortable for the remainder of his days.

"I have told you our hut was about twelve feet square, and that we had, after much hard labor, succeeded in closing it up perfectly, and in making it tight. Along the peak of it, where the two rocks came together, there was a crack which gave us much trouble ; but at length we succeeded in pounding down into it, with the but-end of our narwhal horn, a great quantity of moss or turf, and thus closed it tight.

"I must tell you here, while we are on the subject of moss, and since I have spoken about it so often, that the moss grew on our island, as it does in all Arctic countries, with a richness that you never see here, — moss being, in truth, the characteristic vegetation of the Arctic regions. In the valley fronting us there was a bed of it several feet thick. Its fibres were very long, — as much, in some places, as four inches, — all of a single year's growth ; and as it had gone on growing year after year, you will understand that there was layer after layer of it. In one place, at the side of the valley to the right as we went down towards the beach, it seemed to have died out after growing for many years ; and when we discovered this, we were more rejoiced than we had been at any time since starting the fire ; for the moss, being dead, had become dry and hard, and burned almost like peat, as we found when we came to try it in our fireplace ; and when we added to it a little of our blubber, it made such a heat that we could not have desired anything better. Indeed, it made our hut so warm that we could leave the door and window both open until the weather became colder.

"One thing which gave us great satisfaction was the immense quantity of the dead moss which was in this bed, — so much, indeed, that, no matter how long we should live there, we could never burn up the hundredth part of it. At first there had not appeared to be much of it, but it developed more and more, like a coal mine, as we dug farther and farther into it.

"Our fireplace was therefore, as you see, a great success ; but we were, after a few days, most unexpectedly troubled with it. Thus far the wind had been blowing only in one direction; but afterwards it shifted to the opposite quarter, driving the smoke all down into the hut, and smothering us out. Neither of us being a skilful mason, we could not imagine what was the matter; but finally it occurred to us, after much useless labor had been spent in tearing part of it down and building it up again, that it was too low, being just on a level with the top of the hut; so we ran it up as much higher as we could lift the stones, which was about four feet, and after that we had no more trouble with it.

"Having succeeded so well with our arrangements towards keeping up a fire, we next fitted up a bed, as the storms now began to trouble us, and we found, when we were driven away from the grass, and were obliged to sleep inside of the hut, that it was a very hard place to sleep, being nothing but rough stones, which made us very sore, and made our bones ache.

"The first thing we did now was to build a wall about as high as our knees right across the middle of the hut, from side to side; then, across the space thus enclosed in the back part of the hut, we built up another wall about three feet high, — thus, you see, making two divisions of it.

"One of these divisions we used as a sort of store-room or closet, levelling the bottom of it with flat stone, of which we had no difficulty in getting all we wanted. We also covered the front part of the hut with stones of the same description, thus making quite a smooth floor. It was not large enough, as you will see, to give us much trouble in keeping it clean. Of the second division, in the back part, we made our bed, by first filling it up with moss, then covering the moss over with dry grass.

"Having given up all hope of a ship coming after us, we

now gave up watching for one ; and we went to sleep together on our new bed, lying on the dry grass, and, as before, covering ourselves over with my large overcoat. We found it to be more comfortable than you would think, and altogether better than anything we had yet had to sleep on. But we came near losing our fire by it, as the last embers were just dying out when we awoke from this our first sleep in the hut.

"But this bed did not exactly suit our fancy, and, seeing the necessity for some better kind of bedclothes, our wits were once more set to working, in order to discover something with which to fasten together the duck-skins that we had been saving and drying, and of which we had now almost a hundred. We had spread them out upon the rocks, and dried them in the sun ; for we had seen that, if we could only find something with which to sew them together, we might make all the clothing that we wanted.

"The eider-duck skin is very warm, having, besides its thick coat of feathers, a heavy underlayer of soft warm down, which, as I told you before, the ducks pick off to line their nests with. The skins are also very strong, as well as warm.

"Now, however, as at other times since we had been cast away, good fortune came to us ; and we had scarcely begun seriously to feel the need of sewing materials before they were thrown in our way, as if providentially. It happened thus : —

"In cutting the blubber from the dead narwhal, we had quite exposed the strong sinews of the tail, without, however, for a moment imagining that we were preparing the way to a most important and useful discovery. After a while this sinew had become partially dried in the sun, and one day, while busy with some one of our now quite numerous occupa-

tions, I was much surprised to see the Dean running towards
me from the beach, and was still more surprised when I heard
him crying out, 'I have it, I have it!'

"It seemed to me that the Dean was always having something, and I was more than ever curious to know what it was
this time.

"He had been down to the beach, and, observing some of
the dried sinew, had begun to tear it to pieces ; and in this
way he found out that he could make threads of it, and he immediately set off to tell me about it. We at once went together down to the beach, and, cutting off all that we could
get of this strong sinew, we spread it upon the rocks, that
it might dry more thoroughly.

"In a few days the sun had completely dried and hardened
a great quantity of this stuff ; and we found that, when we
came to pick it to pieces, we could make, if we chose, very
fine threads of it, — as fine and as strong as ordinary silk.
This was a great discovery truly, as it was the only thing
now wanting, except some cooking utensils, to complete our
domestic furniture. As for the latter, it was some time before
we invented anything ; but thus far we had been occupied
with what seemed to be more important concerns. Over on
the opposite side of the island I found some stones of very
soft texture ; and, upon trying them with my knife, I discovered that they were precisely the same kind of stones that I
had often found at home, and which we there called soapstone.
Upon making further search there proved to be quite an ex-
tensive vein of it ; and since I knew that in civilized countries
griddles are made out of soapstone, I concluded at once that
other kinds of cooking utensils might be made as well. Accordingly I carried to our hut several pieces of it, and there

they lay for a good while, until I could find leisure to carve some pots and other things out of them.

"Thus you see we were getting along very well, steadily collecting those things which were necessary as well for our comfort as our safety. If the island on which we had been cast away was barren and inhospitable, it was none the less capable, like almost every other land, in whatever region of the earth, of furnishing subsistence to men.

"When we saw what we could do with the sinew of the narwhal, we immediately set about preparing some bedclothes for ourselves. This we did by squaring off the duck-skins with my knife, and then sewing them tightly together. Thus we obtained, not only a soft bed to lie upon, but a good warm quilt to cover us.

"This done, we went back to the cooking utensils, which you may be sure we were very much in need of. Out of a good large block of soapstone, by careful digging with the knife, we soon made quite a good-sized pot, which was found to answer perfectly. We could now change our diet a little, — at least, I should say, the manner of cooking it ; for while we could before only fry our ducks and eggs on flat stones, when we got the pot we could boil them. This gave us great pleasure, as we were getting very tired of having but one style of food ; still I cannot say that there was so very much occasion for being over-glad, as at best it was only ducks and eggs, and eggs and ducks, like the boy you have heard of in the story, who had first mush and milk, and then, for variety, milk and mush.

"So one day the Dean said to me, ' Hardy, can't we catch some of these little birds, — auks you call them ?' ' How ?' said I. ' I don't know,' said he ; so we were just as well off as

we had been before. But this set us to thinking again ; and
the birds being very tame, and flying low, it occurred to us
that we might make a net, and fasten it to the end of our narwhal horn, which we had thus far only used while making our
hut. Luckily for us, the Dean — who, I need hardly say, was
a very clever boy in every sense — had learned from one of
the sailors the art of net-making ; and out of some of the narwhal sinew he contrived, in two days, to construct quite a
good-sized net. And now the difficulty was to stretch it ; but

Changing the Diet again.

by this time our inventive faculties had been pretty well sharp-
ened, and we were not long in finding that we could make a

perfect hoop by lashing together three seal ribs which we picked up on the beach ; and, having fastened this hoop securely to the narwhal horn, we sallied forth to the north side of the island, where the auks were most abundant.

"Hiding ourselves away among the rocks, we waited until a flock of the birds flew over us. They flew very low, — not more than five feet above our heads. When they were least expecting it, I threw up the net, and three of them flew bang into it. They were so much stunned by the blow, that only one of them could flutter out before I had drawn in the net ; and the Dean was quick enough to seize the remaining two before they could escape. This, being the first experiment, gave us great encouragement, as it was more successful than we had ventured to hope. We went on with the work, without pausing, for several hours, looking upon it as great sport, as indeed it was ; and since it was the first thing we had done on the island that seemed like sport, the day was always remembered by us with delight.

"So now you see we had begun to mingle a little pleasure with our life ; and this was a very important matter, for you know the old saying, 'All work and no play makes Jack a dull boy.'"

CHAPTER XIII.

THE ANCIENT MARINER TAKES THE LITTLE PEOPLE ON A LITTLE VOYAGE;
AND THE LITTLE PEOPLE BECOME CONVINCED THAT AN ARCTIC WINTER,
AN AURORA BOREALIS, AND AN ANCIENT MARINER, ARE VERY WONDER-
FUL THINGS.

A LIVELY breeze was blowing over the little village of Rockdale, and in a lively way the tall trees were bending down their heads, and swinging to and fro as if they liked it ; for the leaves were beating time, and were singing joyously, and appeared to be saying all the while how glad they would be to keep beating time and singing on forever, if the wind would only please to be so good as to help them on in the joyous business ; and the tall grass and grain were shining in the sun, and rolling round in a very reckless manner, as if they meant to show off their great billows of green and gold, and make the staid and sober little waves that were ruffling up the surface of the bright blue waters of the bay quite ashamed.

"Ha, ha!" laughed our ancient friend, the Captain, when he saw what a day it was. "Ha, ha! what a day indeed!" and right away he began to call loudly for his boy, Main Brace, —

"Main Brace, Main Brace, come here ! Come, bear a hand, and be lively there, you plum-duff, chuckle-headed young land-lubber, and waddle along aft here on your sausage legs."

A feeble voice is heard to answer from the galley, — "Ay, ay, sir ; comin', sir, comin'" ; and the plum-duff head and the sausage legs follow feebly in after the voice, looking surprised.

"Main Brace," — begins the Captain.

" Ay, ay, sir," responds Main Brace ; and the plum-duff head lets fall its lower jaw, and looks amazed, the Captain is so much in earnest.

" Some bait, Main Brace! Do you hear, my lad? Be lively, boy, and get some bait ; and then overhaul the *Alice*, and stand by to be ready when I come down. We 'll go a-fishing to-day, — do you hear, my boy? And we 'll have a jolly time, — do you hear that? So be lively now, and be off with your plum-duff head and your sausage legs. I tell you, away, away! for we 'll go a-fishin'. Away, away! for we 'll go a-sailin', a-sailin', a-sailin'. Away, away! for we 'll go a-sailin', — a-sailin' on the sea."

Without another word the sausage legs made off with the plum-duff head, which had no sooner got outside the door than it began to let out in dislocated fragments, from a mouth that gradually expanded until it reached from ear to ear, " Away, away! we 'll go a-fishin', a-fishin', a-fishin' ; away, away! we 'll go a-sailin', a-sailin', a-sailin' ; away, away! we 'll all be jolly, jolly, jolly, — we 'll all be jolly" ; and so on until the sausage legs had carried the plum-duff head and the refrain together so far down among the trees, towards the water, that all the other "jollys" and the sailin's and the "fishin's," and the rest of it, were blown clean away by the wind.

And off went the Captain, too, hurrying up to the top of the hill behind the cottage, as if the cosey little thing was all afire, and the dear old soul was running up for help ; and when he reached the top of the hill, he began swinging round his old tarpaulin hat, making the long blue ribbons fairly whistle and speak, as if they would say, " Old man, old man, stop a bit, and take breath! — can't you now? and say, what 's this all about, for goodness' sake!"

7   J

The Ancient Mariner becomes excited, and Main Brace makes an effort.

But the old man knew well enough himself what it was all about; for he was signalling his little friends; and every circle of his big arm, and every shake of his long gray beard, and every swing of his old tarpaulin hat, seemed to sing out, "Hurrah, hurrah, for a jolly day! hurrah, hurrah, my children gay! hurrah, hurrah, let's up and away, upon the bright blue waters!"

By and by the children caught sight of the old tarpaulin hat and the blue ribbons and the Captain himself, all in this state of violent excitement; and down they bore at once upon the ancient mariner, as if he were a regular bluff-bowed old East Indiaman, full of golden ingots, and they were clipper-built, copper-fastened, rakish fore-and-afters of the piratical pattern.

"Heyday!" (the old man never thought he had begun until he had thrown off a heyday or so), "heyday, my hearties!" said the ancient mariner, as the children came up to him, — "heyday, my dears! keep on that same course before the wind, and you'll fetch up in the right port"; and so, without further ado, he hurried "my hearties" down to the beach, and aboard the yacht; and then very soon Main Brace (whose mouth had never left off expanding at the prospect of "a fishin'" and "a sailin'" and "a jolly day" generally) had the anchor away; and then the Captain spread the white sails to the lively breeze; and there never was, since the world began, a merrier little party, in a merrier little craft, afloat upon blue water on a merrier day. Indeed, the day was so merry, and the craft was so merry, and the waves were so merry as they came leaping round the yacht, and the wind was so merry as it bulged out the sail and went whistling through the rigging, and the little party in the yacht were so merry, and everything and everybody was so merry, that it would be strange indeed if the fish were not merry too; and the finny creatures played round the pretty hooks, too merry by half to touch them; and then they came merrily up, and poked their heads out close to the top of the water, and stared at the merry-makers in the yacht, and they seemed to be whispering to one another, "O, what a jolly lot of coves they are, to be sure! O, don't they wish they may catch us? — don't they though?" and then they dropped down again to look at the pretty hooks; but only the sober-sided ones that had no idea of being merry went near enough to bite, and these were surely bitten in return; for, if the hook once got into their red gills, they found themselves jerked up before they could say Lobster, and heard merry voices shouting round them, to their great astonishment.

And of these sober-sided fishes who were so unfortunate as to have no idea of being merry, the Captain and his little friends caught as many as they wanted; and then the Captain said to his little friends, "Put away your fishing-tackle now, and come down below into the little cabin, and I'll surprise you." And, sure enough, he did surprise them, — quite as much, perhaps, as if some fairy queen had come, and called them to a fairy banquet; as much indeed, perhaps, as if they had themselves suddenly been turned to fairies, and were doing something that was never even dreamed of by mortal child before; for, while they had been fishing, Main Brace had, by direction of the Captain, been building up a fire in the little stove, and in the very centre of the cabin he had set out a little table, and upon the little table there was spread the whitest little cloth, and on the cloth were set all round the daintiest little plates and knives and forks, and the neatest little napkins, and the cunningest little cups, that were ever seen.

"And now," spoke up the Captain, laughing all the while to see his little friends so much surprised, "fall to, fall to! for we're going to have a jolly feast, or my name is n't Ancient Mariner, nor John Hardy either." And the Captain poured out some fresh foaming milk into the cunning little cups, from a big stone jug; and he brought some fresh white rolls and some golden butter from a little locker; and soon afterward he drew from the little stove some dainty little fish, and dropped one, all crisp and hissing hot, upon each dainty little plate; and now for half an hour there was busy work enough for the dainty little knives and forks. The Captain's little stove proved to be everything that one could wish for in that line; and the Captain's style of cooking showed plainly enough, as William said, that "the Captain had not travelled round the world, and been an ancient mariner, for nothing."

When the meal was over, and everything was cleared away, and the little cabin was once more in ship-shape order, William proposed the Captain's health, — tossing back his head, and drinking a great quantity of imaginary wine from an imaginary glass. "Here's to the health of Captain Hardy, ancient mariner, and other things too numerous to mention, — the jolliest Jack Tar that ever reefed a sail, or walked on the windward side of a quarter-deck! May Davy Jones be a long while waiting for him; and when he does go into Davy's locker, may he go an Admiral!" And then the children all together "Hip, hip, hurrahed" the Captain, until the old man had nearly split himself with laughing at their childish merriment.

"And now for the story," said the Captain, when the laugh was ended. "What do you say to that?"

"The story, — yes, yes, the story," shouted all the children, merrier than ever.

"Down here, or up on deck?"

"Down here, just where we are; it's such a splendid place!"

"Then down here it shall be," went on the Captain, right

well pleased. "Down here it shall be, my dears, if I can only pick up the yarn again where I broke it off. Let me see "; and the old man put a finger to his nose, as he always did when he was thoughtful.

"Aha!" cried he, at length, "I've got my bearings now, as neat as a light-house in a fog. You know, my dears, when we left off last time, we had gone so far along with the story that you could see the Dean and I had got ourselves in soundings, as it were. We had seen the light-ship off the harbor, and were steering for it, so to speak. We had, by working very hard, and by persevering very much, and by using our wits as best we could, gathered about us everything that was needed to insure our present safety, and some things to make us comfortable. We had a hut to shelter us, and clothes to keep us warm, and fire to cook our food.

"But the winter was now coming on very fast, and we knew well enough what that was likely to be. The grass and moss and flowers were dead or dying ; the ice was forming on the little pools, and here and there upon the sea ; little spurts of snow were coming now and then ; the winds were getting to be more fierce and angry, and every day was growing colder and more dark. We knew that the long winter was close upon us, and that the shadow of the night would soon be resting on us all the time. The birds had hatched their young, and quitted their nests, and were flying off to the sunny south, where we so longed to go, and so longed to send a message by them to the loved ones far away. It made us sad — O, how very, very sad! — to see the birds so happy on the wing, and sailing off and leaving us upon the island all alone. Alone, — all, all alone ! Alone upon a desert island in the Frozen Sea ! Alone in cold and darkness ! All, all alone !

"We made ourselves warm coats and stockings out of the skins of the birds that we had caught; and we made caps, too, out of them, — plucking off the feathers, and leaving only the soft, warm, mouse-colored down upon the skin. And out of the seal's skin we made mittens and nice soft boots, or rather, as I might call them, moccasons.

"The birds began to go away about the middle of August, as nearly as we could tell, but it was more than a month after that before they had all left the island. Meanwhile we had caught a great number of them, — two hundred and sixty-six in all; and we had collected, besides, ninety dozen of their eggs. These birds and eggs were all carefully stowed away in our storehouses of ice and rocks near the glacier.

"In the matter of food, we had, therefore, done very well; but we felt the need of some more blubber for our fire, and some warmer clothing than the birds' skins. To supply this latter want, we tried very hard to catch some foxes; but it was a long time before we were successful; for not until all the ducks had gone away would the foxes trouble themselves to go inside our traps. These traps were made of stones, and in building them I had derived the only benefit which had ever resulted to me from my indolent life on the farm. I was always fond of shirking away from my duties, and going into the woods to set rabbit-traps; and, remembering how I made them of wood, I easily contrived a stone one of the same pattern, and it was found afterwards to answer perfectly; for when there were no longer eggs and ducks for them to eat, the foxes went into our traps, which we baited with flesh from the dead narwhal. The pelts of these foxes were thick and warm; and, by the time the weather got very cold, we had obtained a good number, and of them we made suits of clothes at our leisure. There were two kinds of foxes; one was a sort of blue gray, and the other was quite white.

"As the weather grew colder, the little streams which had thus far supplied us with water all froze up ; and we had now nothing to depend upon but the freshly fallen snow, which we had, of course, to melt. Thus you see how important it was that I should have found the soapstone in season, and made a pot of it, else we should not only have been obliged to go without boiled food, but likewise without water. As for fuel, we were for the present relieved from all anxiety by a dead walrus and a small white whale which drifted in upon the beach during a westerly gale. The waves being very strong, they were landed so high up on the beach that there was little fear of their being washed away again.

"It was no easy matter to cut these animals up with our one jack-knife, since, before we could get it done, they had frozen quite hard. The temperature had gone down until it was already below freezing all the time ; and very soon a great deal of snow fell, and was drifted into heaps by the wind. The sea, soon after this, became frozen over quite solid all about the island, although we could still see plenty of clear, open water in the distance. There was one satisfaction, at least, in this freezing up of the sea : we could walk out upon it, and go all around the island without having to clamber over the rough rocks.

"You have now seen pretty much what our life was on the island, and how we were prepared for the winter. Well, the winter came by and by in good earnest, I can tell you. The sunlight all went away, and then, soon afterward, the autumn twilight went away ; and then came the darkness that I told

you is constant, in the winter, up towards the North Pole, for the winter there is but one long night, you know."

Here William, who was, as we have seen, of an inquiring turn of mind, interrupted the Captain to ask if he would not be so good as to mention again how dark it was in this polar winter.

" Dark as midnight," replied the Captain, promptly.

" Dark all the time, did you say, Captain Hardy ? "

" Yes, dark all the time, my lad, — dark in the morning, dark in the evening, dark at midnight, dark at noon, dark, all the time, as any night you ever saw ; only, everything being white with snow, of course makes the night lighter than it does here, where the trees and the houses, and other dark objects, help along the blackness and make it more gloomy, — absorbing the light, you see, while the snow reflects it."

" But what," asked William, " did you do for light in this dark time, since you did not have a lamp ? "

" Easy there, my lad," replied the Captain ; " I 'm just coming to that, you see. Somebody has said that ' necessity is the mother of invention,' or words to that effect ; and darkness, I think, may be considered a ' mother ' of that description. First we made an open dish of soapstone, and put some oil in it ; and then we made a wick out of the dry moss, and set fire to it ; but this was found to make so much smoke that it drove us out of the hut, and it was given up. But we did not throw away the dish, and after a while it occurred to us to powder the dry moss by rubbing it between the hands, and with this powdered moss we lined our soapstone dish all over on the inside with a layer a quarter of an inch thick. After smoothing this down all around the edge (this dish, which we called a lamp, was much like a saucer, only rougher and much lar-

7 *

ger), we filled it half full of oil, and again set fire to it all around the edge ; and this time it worked beautifully, — smoking very little, and giving us plenty of light."

" How cunning ! " exclaimed the children, all at once.

" Rather so," replied the Captain, " but hardly more so than the two little drinking-cups we carved out of the same kind of soapstone that we made the lamp and pot of."

" It must have felt very queer, Captain Hardy," said Fred, inquiringly, " to be in darkness all the time.   I can't imagine such a thing as the winter being all the time dark, — can you, Will ? "

" No, I can't," replied William, — " can you, Sister Alice ? "

" Yes, I think I can," said Alice, quickly.

" Why, how 's that, my little dear ? " asked the Captain, greatly interested.

" O," said Alice, in her gentle way, " I 've only to think of poor blind Jo going round with his little dog, begging from door to door, and never seeing anything in all the world, — no sun, no moon, no stars, no any light to him at all.   Poor Jo's bright summer went out long ago ; and both light and warmth were gone, never to come back again, when old Martha died ! and all 's night to Jo, — and that 's how I know what it is to be in darkness all the time " ; and as little Alice made this little speech about poor blind Jo, the beggar-man, her lovely face looked thoughtful beyond its years ; and, as she finished, the Captain saw a tear stealing from her soft blue eye for poor Jo's sake ; and he caught her in his arms right off, without stopping to think at all what he was doing, and he kissed away the tear ; and, as he did it, a much bigger one came tearing out of his own great hazel eye, and hurried down into his shaggy beard to hide, as if it were quite frightened at what it had been doing with itself.

"Spoken like the little lady that you are, my dear," broke out the Captain; "always thinking of the unfortunate. And you are very right, my child. Poor blind Jo's darkness is much worse than ours ever was, up in the Frozen Sea, upon the lonely island, — far worse indeed, poor man! for you must know that the stars were shining brightly there upon us all the time; and then the moon came every month; and when it came, it came for good and all, and never set for several days; and then sometimes the aurora borealis would flash across the heavens, and clear away the darkness for a little while, as if it were a huge broom sweeping cobwebs from the skies, and letting in the light of day beneath the stars. O, what a splendid sight it was!"

"O, tell us all about it, Captain Hardy, won't you?" asked all the children, with one voice.

"Of course, I will," replied the Captain, "only I can do no sort of justice to that species of natural scenery, don't you see? That's a touch beyond John Hardy's powers of description, as I can well assure you."

The children all declared that they never could think anything beyond John Hardy's powers, and they believed it too.

"Well, well! Now let me see, my dears, what I can do for you. First, you know the scientific chaps, especially my friend the Doctor, down in Boston, say that the aurora borealis is electricity broke loose, and tearing through the air, from pole to pole, for some purpose of its own. It can't be caught, nor bottled up, as Franklin bottled up the lightning, nor analyzed; — in short, nothing can be done with it; and so it goes tearing through the skies, as I have said before, from pole to pole, just where it likes.

"Now this is what it is, so far as one can see. When you go away beyond the Arctic Circle, you see great fiery streams start up from a fiery arch that stretches right across the sky before you ; and from this fiery arch the fiery streams of light shoot up, and then fall back again, — sometimes lasting for a little while, and waving in the sky, to and fro, like a silken curtain of many colors fluttering in the wind; and then again seeming to be phantom things playing hide-and-seek among the stars ; sometimes like wicked spirits of the night, bent on mischief; sometimes like tongues of flame from some great fire in some great world beyond the earth, making one almost afraid that the heavens will break out presently in a roaring blaze, and rain a shower of living coals and ashes on his head.

"And O, how grand the colors are sometimes ! The great arch of light that spans the sky is often bright with all the colors of the rainbow, — changing every instant. And from these flickering belts of light the fiery streams fly up with lightning speed, — green, and orange, and blue, and purple, and bright crimson, — all mingling here and there and everywhere above, while down beneath comes out in bold relief before the eye the broad, white plain of ice and snow upon the ocean, the great icebergs that lie here and there upon it, the tall white mountains of the land, and the dark islands in the sea ; and then the flood of light dies away, and the dark islands in the sea, and the tall white mountains, and the icebergs, and the white plain around, all vanish from the sight, and the mind retains only an impression that the icebergs, with all these bright hues reflected on them from above, had come from space and darkness, like the meteors, then to vanish, and leave the darkness more profound.

"And thus the auroral light and color keep pulsating in the air, up and down, up and down ; and thus the icebergs seem to come and go ; and the very stars above seem to be rushing out with a bold bright glare, and going back again as quickly, singed and withered, as it were, into puny sparks, and, utterly disheartened with the effort to keep their places in the face of such a flood of brightness, are at length resolved no more to try to twinkle, twinkle through the night.

"And that is all I can tell you about the aurora borealis, for that is all I know about it."

"O, is n't he a great one?" whispered William to Fred, who sat close beside him on the locker, — "is n't he, indeed? — to say he can't describe an aurora borealis, when he has blood, thunder, fire, and all creation on his tongue."

"But," went on the Captain, "in spite of this auroral light and the moonlight, the winter was dreary enough. At first we wanted to sleep all the time ; and we had much trouble to keep ourselves from giving way to this desire. If we had done so, it would have made us very unhealthy and altogether miserable. We had to keep up our spirits, whatever else we did ; and after a while, to help us with this, we got into regular habits ; and we set a great clock up in the sky to tell us the time of day."

"A clock up in the sky !" exclaimed both the boys ; "why, Captain Hardy, how was that?"

"Why, don't you see, my lads, the 'Great Bear' and all the other constellations of the north go round and round the Pole-star, which is right above your head ; and it so happened that I knew the 'Great Bear,' and the two stars in its side called 'the Pointers' because they point to the Pole-star. Now these two 'Pointers,' going around once in the four-and-twenty

hours, pointed up from the south at one time, and up from the
north at another time, and up from the east and from the west
in the same way ; and thus you see we had a clock up in the
sky to tell us the time of day, for we had an iceberg picked
out all around for every hour, and when 'the Pointers' stood
over that particular berg we knew what time it was.

" We should have got along through the winter much more
comfortably if we had had some books, or some paper to write
on, and pen and ink to write with ; but these things were quite
beyond the reach of our ingenuity. So our life was very mo-
notonous ; doing our daily duties, — that is, whatever we might
find to do, — and, after wading through the deep snow in
doing it, we came back again to our little hut to get warm, and
to eat and talk and sleep.

" And much talking we did, as I can assure you, about each
other, and each other's life, and what great things we would
do when we got away from the island, hopeless though that
seemed. Thus we came gradually to know each other's history, and thus there came to be greater sympathy between us,
and more indulgence of each other's whims and fancies, as we
got better and better acquainted.

" The Dean had quite a story to relate of himself. He told
me that he was born in the great city of New York. His
father died before he could remember, and his mother was
very poor ; but so long as she kept her health she managed,
in one way or another, to live along from day to day by sewing ; and she managed, too, to send the Dean to school. She
loved her bright-haired little boy so very, very much that she
would have spent the last cent she could ever earn, could she
only give her darling Dean a little knowledge that might help
him on in the world when he grew to be a man. And so she

stinted herself and saved, all unknown to her darling Dean;
and she had not clothing or fire enough to keep her warm in
the bleak winter, when the Dean was out, though she had a
fine fire when the Dean came back. All would have been
well enough if the poor woman had not, with her hard work
and her efforts to save, become thin and weak, and then grown
sick with fever; and now there was nothing for her but the
hospital, for there was no money to pay for medicines, or doctor's bills, to say nothing of rent and fire and clothes.

"And now for the first time the Dean began to realize the
situation; and a vague impression crossed his mind, that the
poor, pale woman, now restless with pain on a narrow bed in a
great long ward of a dreary hospital, — his own dear mother,
suffering here with strange hands only to comfort her, — had
been brought to this for his sake; and when she grew better,
after a long, long time, but was still far from well, he thought
and thought, and cried and cried, and prayed and prayed, and
wished that he might do something to show his gratitude, and
make amends.

"By and by he got into a factory, and worked there early
and late, until he too grew sick, and was carried to the hospital, and was laid beside his poor sick mother, on a narrow bed.
But he soon got well again, though his mother did not, and
then (he could do nothing else) he went to sea as cabin-boy of
a ship sailing to Havana; and he came back too; and, with a
proud heart beating in his little breast, he carried a little purse
of gold and silver coins that the captain gave him to his poor
sick mother; and then he went away again on the same ship,
and came back once more with another purse of money, twice
as big as the first; but the good captain that had been so kind
to him, and rewarded him so well, fell sick, and died of yellow

fever on the passage home, and the mate, who got command
of the ship, being a different sort of man, disliked the Dean,
and told him not to come back any more. And so the poor
Dean did n't know what to do ; until one of his old shipmates
met him in the street, and took him off to New Bedford, and
shipped him as cabin-boy of the Blackbird. 'And now here I
am,' said the poor little Dean, 'and all the rest you know,
— cast away in the cold, in this awful place, while my poor
sick mother has no money and no friends in all the world, and
is thinking all the time what a wretch I am to run away and
desert her, when, God knows, I meant to do nothing of the
sort!' and so the Dean burst out crying, and, to tell you the
truth, I could not help crying a little too.

"But the Dean was a right plucky little fellow, I can tell
you ; and so full of hope and ambition was he, that nothing
could keep him down very long ; and nothing, I believe, could
ever make him despond for a single minute but thinking of
his mother, sick and far away, without friends or money, lying
on a narrow bed, all through the weary, dreary days and
nights, in the dreary ward of a crowded hospital. Poor Dean!
he had something to make him cry, and something always to
make him sad, if he had a mind to be ; but what had I in
comparison ? — I who had gone away from home with no good
motive like the Dean's.

"After the recital of this story of the Dean's, we were both
very sad, until the Dean suddenly roused himself, and said,
'Let's go and look at our traps, Hardy'; and so we sallied
out into the moonlight, and waded through the snow, to see if
there were any foxes for us. To get outside our hut was not
so easy a matter now as it was when we first built it ; for, in
order to keep the cold winds away, we had made a long, low,

narrow passage, with a crook in it, through which we crawled on our hands and knees, before we reached the door.

" We walked all the way around the island, and visited all our traps, of which we had seventeen, but only two of them had foxes in them ; the others were either filled with snow, or were completely covered over with it, for the wind had been blowing very hard the day before.

" As we got farther and farther into the winter, we met with some very strange adventures, — altogether different from anything I have told you of before ; but you see the sun will soon be going down behind the trees, and we are a good long way from the ' Mariner's Rest,' so ' up anchor ' 's the word now, my dears, and ' under way ' again."

The merry little yacht was not long in carrying the merry little party over to the Captain's favorite anchorage ; and then they were all soon ashore, and after many merry and many pleasant speeches, our little friends parted from the ancient mariner once more, leaving him standing in the shadow of the great tall trees, with a string of fish in one hand ; while Fred and William, with Main Brace to help them, and with merry Alice running on ahead, each carried off a string for their next day's breakfast,— a trophy to be proud of, as they thought.

K

CHAPTER XIV.

PROVES THE INGENUITY OF SEALS, AND SHOWS THAT THE GREAT POLAR
BEAR IS NO RESPECTER OF PERSONS.

"WHEN we were last time cruising in the Alice, I think
I told you all about the Arctic winter, — did I not?"
said the ancient mariner to his little friends, when they were
met once more.

"Yes," answered William (who was always ready to act as
spokesman for the party), — "yes, Captain Hardy, all about
the Arctic winter, and the aurora borealis, and the wonderful
moonlight, and the darkness, and how you and the handsome
little Dean lived through it, and what you talked about, and
how you passed the time, and what a doleful life you led, and
what a dreadful thing it was, and how it made you shiver now
to think of it ; and — all that, and a great deal more."

"Certainly," replied the Captain, "certainly, that's it, — all
told off nicely, my lad, just as if you were boxing the compass
or repeating the multiplication table ; — all about how we
protected ourselves from cold, and kept ourselves from hunger,
and prepared a home for ourselves on the Rock of Good Hope.
And this seemed likely to be our home for life too, — so far,
at least, as we could see ; for it appeared clear enough to us
that our condition would never change except with death,
which we, like everybody else, whether they have ever been
cast away or not, wanted to put off as long as possible, having
no wish at all to die, and not liking either to freeze or starve :
so you see we had good motives for energy and patience."

Here little Alice, in her quiet way, interrupted the Captain to say that the aurora borealis had troubled her dreams all night, and that she would like to know, if the Captain pleased, why anything should have such a strange name.

"That I will tell you with pleasure, my dear," answered the Captain ; "I 'll tell you all about it, — of course I will. Aurora borealis, — that means northern light ; and the name comes from a pagan goddess called Aurora, who was supposed to have rosy fingers, and to ride in a rosy chariot, and who opened the gates of the East every morning, and brought in the light of day ; and thus, in course of time, any great flush of light in the heavens got to be called Aurora. And then there was a pagan god called Boreas, who was the North Wind, and had long wings and white hair, and made himself generally disagreeable. So you see Boreas, from being the pagan name for north wind, got to mean the north ; and Borealis, from that, became Northern, and Aurora Borealis became Northern Light."

"Thank you, Captain Hardy," said little Alice ; and Fred and William said "Thank you" too ; while, as for the Captain, he looked very wise and solemn, like other great philosophers, appearing as if he would say, "Don't be surprised, for that 's nothing to what I could do if I had a mind," every word of which the children would have believed, you may well be sure. However, the Captain hastened on with the story (which is more to our present purpose) without giving any further proof of his learning.

"When the winter had fairly set in," said he, "our field of operations was much enlarged ; and, although the birds had all flown away, we were hardly worse off than before, as you shall see ; for all through the summer we had been kept close prisoners on the island ; but now, when the ice was solid all over the sea, we could walk out upon it, and this we did as soon as it would bear. Once the Dean broke through, being a little careless of where he was stepping ; but I got him out, with no more harm coming to him than a cold bath and a fright.

"Soon after this we made a valuable discovery. Some of the seals have a habit, when the sea is frozen over, of cutting holes through the ice with their sharp claws, in order that they may get their heads above the water to breathe, — the seals not being able, as I have told you before, to breathe under water, like fish. They can keep their heads under water about an hour, by closing up their nostrils, so that not a drop can get in ; and, during that time, they do not breathe at all ; but at last they must find the open sea, or a crack in the ice, or else dig a hole through the ice from below, and thus get their heads to the surface in some way, or they would drown.

"As we did not then know anything about the habits of the seals in this respect, I was very much surprised one day, while walking over ice that was everywhere apparently very solid, to find one of my feet suddenly break through. I was carrying, at the time, our great narwhal horn, which had already been used for so many purposes; and when I had got my foot, as quickly as possible, out of the water, I pounded with the heavy horn all about the place, and found that there was a large round hole there that had evidently been made by some animal ; and I could think of nothing else as likely to have made it but a seal. The reason why I had not seen it was because the snow had drifted over it in a hard crust, and through this crust the seal kept open with his nose a small orifice for breathing, that was not larger round than a silver dollar.

"This discovery made us very glad and very curious, — for, having concluded what it was, we concluded also that there must be more like it, and we went in search of them immediately. Our search was soon rewarded, for these seal-holes were very numerous.

"How to catch a seal was the question which now most occupied our thoughts. The difficulty was very great, for we had no weapons of any sort for such a purpose. Once more, however, we fell back upon our narwhal horn. To this horn we had already become much attached, and, as if to express our gratitude, we had bestowed upon it several names, — as, for instance, 'Life-preserver,' 'Crumply Crowbar,' 'The Castaway's Friend,' and the like of that ; but the title which finally stuck to it was 'Old Crumply,' — not that it was exactly a crumply horn, like the one that grew on the head of the cow that tossed the dog, that worried the cat, that killed the rat, that ate the malt, that lay in the house that Jack built, — for it was not crumply at all in that sense, but, on the contrary, was as straight as an arrow, and was no further crumply than crumply means wrinkled and twisted ; and, indeed, the old horn looked as if it might have been once red-hot, and had been twisted several times around before it had cooled off.

"Besides this 'Old Crumply,' we made another weapon, in quite an ingenious way, as we thought, though at a great expense of time and labor. This was called by several names, like the other ; but generally I called it the 'Dean's Delight,' for it was made after the Dean's idea, and he used to flourish it about at a great rate, and was very proud of it. It was simply a kind of spear made by lashing together (after carefully cutting with our knife, and fitting and overlapping) a great many pieces of bones. The lashing was the same string or thong we had before used for the duck-traps. It was very strong, though not half so heavy as ' Old Crumply.'

" But though we had ' Old Crumply,' and the ' Dean's Delight,' we were apparently just as far off as ever from catching a seal. The ' Delight ' was tipped with hard ivory (a piece of walrus tusk carved into proper shape with the jack-knife), and ' Crumply' was of the very best kind of ivory throughout, yet we could not sharpen either of them so as to be of much use. But, remembering the general shape of the harpoon-heads used in whale-ships, I managed to cut one of that pattern out of walrus ivory, and this I set on the end of the ' Dean's Delight,' and then, making a hole in the centre of it, I fastened it to the end of one of our long lines. And thus I had obtained all that was needed, in name at least, for catching a seal ; but only in name, as was soon proved ; for the Dean and I set out at once to try our fortunes in this new line of adventure, and, discovering a seal-hole, we stood near it (on the leeward side, that the seal might not scent us) until the animal appeared, which was not for a long time, and not until we had grown very cold. The seal had evidently been off breathing in another hole. When he did come up, we knew it by a little puff he gave, which threw some spray up through the little orifice in the snow-crust. Quick as thought I plunged the ' Dean's Delight ' down into the very centre of the hole, and struck the animal ; but the ivory harpoon-head that was on the end of it only glanced off, without penetrating the skin ; and the seal, no doubt very much astonished, got off as quickly as he could, more frightened, probably, than hurt ; at least, we heard of him

no more. He never came back to the hole, for it was all froz-
en over next day, and so it remained. We afterwards discovered that when a seal-hole has been once touched, the seal
will never go back to it.

"I was now more puzzled than ever to know what to do;
but I did not give up trying, determined to succeed, one way
or another. Presently it occurred to me that almost anything
that was hard would answer to sharpen the edge and point of
the ivory harpoon-head, and, since I could not get any kind
of metal to make a whole harpoon-head out of, I had to try
some other plan. As good luck would have it, I now thought
of the brass buttons on my coat. Some of these I quickly
tore off. Then I hacked my knife with a sharp flint stone until I had made a saw of it, and with this saw I cut a little
groove along the tapering point of the ivory harpoon-head;
and into this groove, which was about a quarter of an inch
deep, I set the buttons, which I had squared with the knife,
and then wedged them firmly. I had now only to grind all
these bits of brass down even, and to sharpen the whole with
a stone, and my work was done. And a most tedious work
it had been too. The next thing was to put it to the test,
which we quickly did. A seal-hole being soon found, we had
not long to wait before the seal came into it, with a little
puff, as before; and, as soon as the noise was heard, I let fly
with my harpoon, and, striking through the snow-crust, hit the
seal fairly in the neck, and drove the harpoon into him.

"Down sank the seal through the hole, taking the harpoon
along with him, and spinning out the line which was attached
to it at a furious rate. Before the seal was struck, and while
I was watching for him, the Dean had quietly tied the end of
the line that was not fast to the harpoon around the middle of

'Old Crumply,' and when the seal descended into the sea, 'Old Crumply' was whipped along over the snow until it lodged right across the hole, and there the seal was, — 'brought up with a round turn,' as the sailors say.

"And now was anybody ever so rejoiced as we? The Dean fairly shouted with delight, and danced around the hole as if he were crazy, crying 'Bravo, bravo!' and 'Hurrah for Crumply!' and 'Hurrah for Old Crumply!' and hurrah for this, and hurrah for that, until he was fairly hoarse. Meanwhile the seal was trying his best to get away. He darted from side to side, and up and down, without any other result than to tire himself out; for the harpoon held firmly in his body, and the line held firmly to 'Old Crumply,' and 'Old Crumply' lay squarely across the hole.

"By and by the seal was forced to come up to breathe; and, since there was no other place for him, he had to return to the hole where he had been struck. But he did not stay more than a second or so, going down as quickly as he had done before. As soon as the line was loosened, however, we drew in the slack, and wound it around 'Old Crumply,' so that the seal did not have so much of it now to play with. Nor did he remain under so long the second time. When he came up again, we got in all the slack of the line that we could, as before.

"It was now clear enough that we should be sure of the seal, if we could only get something to kill him with; and so the quick-witted Dean ran off at once to the hut, and brought a walrus tusk that we had saved. This was driven into the hard snow not far from the hole, and, while the Dean held it there firmly, I got the line made fast around it. As soon as I saw that this was secure, and that the Dean was holding on bravely, I unfastened the line from 'Old Crumply,' and, when the seal came next time, I gave him a heavy thrust with the sharp end of it. But this did not kill him by any means, nor

Ingenuity is rewarded, and "Old Crumply" distinguished.

did he give me another chance for some time. Then, however, he was almost dead with bleeding, and fright, and hard struggling to get away, to say nothing of holding his breath so long; but I wanted him too badly to have any mercy on him,

8

so I worked away as hard as I could to get in all the line, so that the seal could not sink down through the hole any more.

"At last I was successful, and the seal was fast in the hole, and with all his struggling he could not get away. With the aid of ' Old Crumply,' I now quickly made an end of him. As soon as he was dead, we drew him out on the ice, and rejoiced over him. Such shouting never was before known, at least in that part of the world. If anybody could have heard and seen us, we should have surely been taken up for insane peo ple, especially the Dean, whose joy knew no bounds.

"Having no sledge, we had to drag the dead seal over the ice and snow, for which purpose we made the line fast through his nose. It was no easy task to get him to the hut ; and, when we did at last succeed, we found that the seal was partly frozen, so that we were obliged to draw it inside the hut, and then thaw it, before we could get the skin off, which made the hut very disagreeable. After the skin and blubber were re-moved, we cut off some of the flesh, and made for ourselves a good hot supper, — first cooking a stew in our soapstone pot, and then frying some steaks on a flat stone ; and if anything was before wanting to make us perfectly happy over the cap-ture of so great a prize, we had it now, when we discovered what excellent food it was, and what a quantity there was of it.

"When we had finished butchering the seal, we prepared the skin for making boots ; and we put the blubber and flesh away in our storehouses for future use, — the flesh for food, and the blubber for our fire and lamp. Then we slept, and the very next day we set out to catch more seals, without, however, the same success, for we were unfortunate in every attempt ; and it was, indeed, almost a week, I think, before we

ma!e a second capture. Some time afterward we caught a
third, and then a fourth, and by great good fortune on the
very same day a fifth ; and not long after that we caught
another, which made the sixth.

"But it would have been well had we been content with
five, without coveting a sixth, as this last had like to have been
the ruin of us ; for as we were going slowly back to the hut,
dragging the seal after us, and all unsuspicious of harm, we
were set upon by a great white beast, the like of which we
had never seen before, but which we knew must be one of
those savage animals called polar bears. He was not coming
rapidly, but was rather crawling along cautiously, with mouth
wide open, looking very fierce. As soon as we discovered
him, we dropped the line with which we were dragging the
seal, and ran as fast as our legs would carry us, never stopping
until we had reached the hut and crawled into it, — not once
having had the courage to look back, for at every step we expected that the bear would be atop of us.

" We had left 'Old Crumply' and 'Dean's Delight' where
we captured the seal, intending to go for them the next day ;
and, having no weapon of any kind, we were in the greatest
terror, expecting every moment to hear the bear coming to
tear the hut down, and drag us out, and eat us up.

" But, finding that we were not disturbed, we at length fell
asleep. Upon awaking the next day, and finding that we had
been suffered to go undisturbed thus long, we began to wonder
whether we had not been needlessly alarmed, and finally we
set to wondering whether we had really seen a bear after all,
and at length we grew to feel quite ashamed of ourselves. So
we put on a little bravado, like the boy that whistled in the
dark to keep his courage up, and went out, cautiously ap-

proaching the spot where we had left the seal. Arriving there, we had positive proof enough, if any were wanting, that we had certainly seen a bear. The bones of the seal were all strewn about over the snow, picked as clean as could be. Some foxes were gnawing at them, as we came up ; but they all scampered off when they saw us coming.

"Hurrying on, we picked up 'Old Crumply' and 'Dean's Delight,' and then hastened back to the hut, which we reached without any furthei adventure ; but on the day following, upon going out to visit our fox-traps, we came across the bear's tracks, from which it was evident to us that the wild beast was prowling round the island, where he had already obtained one good meal, and was in hopes, no doubt, of getting another ; and, as we did not know how soon he might feel disposed to begin upon us, we ran back to the hut with all speed, imagining, as we went along, that every rock and snow-drift that we passed was a bear.

"We had now even greater fears than before that we should be attacked and eaten up by the wild beast. It did not once occur to us that the bear would be much more likely to prefer the contents of our storehouses to ourselves, if he came that way, but we thought only of our own safety ; and this was perhaps not unnatural, for boys and men alike are everywhere liable to magnify their own importance, even in the eyes of a bear.

"We had not been in the hut more than a couple of hours, I should say, before we heard the tramp of our enemy. We knew it must be the footsteps of the bear, because it could be nothing else. Our fears were now even greater than ever.

"The bear appeared from the sound of his footsteps, crunching in the snow, to be making directly for us, sniffing the air as he came along, apparently enjoying in advance a supper that he felt quite sure of. He seemed to halt at every step or so, as if greatly relishing the prospect.

"At last he came very near, and we expected at every instant to see his head appear at the window. Resolved to sell our lives as dearly as possible, we grasped our weapons firmly, the Dean his 'Delight' and I 'Old Crumply,' to the end of which I had firmly lashed the jack-knife, after grinding it very sharp on a stone, and giving it a good point. As the knife-blade was quite long, I had strong hopes of giving the bear such a wound, when he appeared at the window, as might be the death of him, or, at any rate, frighten him so badly that he would be glad to run away, and not come back any more.

"Nearer and nearer came the bear, and greater grew our alarm. Our hearts beat violently in our breasts; our faces were pale as death; we held our breath, as if fearful of making the least noise to give the bear encouragement. At length our enemy gave a sudden start. It seemed to us as if he had now made a dash at the window, so we both rose to our feet, with our weapons ready to meet him; but, to our great joy and relief, the sound of his footsteps showed that the beast was retreating, rather than advancing, and was moving more rapidly. A moment afterward we heard the rattle of stones, and now, from fear for ourselves, we passed instantly to fear for our stores; for we knew that it was our stores, and not us, that he was after, and that he must be tearing down one of our principal storehouses. And now, what if he should tear them all down, and eat up all our food and fuel? It was a fearful thought.

"How often do we pass almost insensibly from the greatest terror to the greatest courage! Relieved now from all imme-

diate personal apprehension, we felt at once inspired to protect our property, on the safety of which our lives depended.
We ceased at once to feel like standing passively on the defensive, but immediately crawled out of the hut to do something,
— exactly what, we did not know. Our thoughts had, indeed,
hardly time to take shape in our minds, so quickly had the
change come in the situation and in our feelings.

"The bear was plainly in sight as soon as we got outside,
tearing down our storehouse; but he appeared not to be
thinking of us at all. Without reflecting in the least what I
was about, but filled only with alarm at the prospect of losing
our food and fuel, I set up a loud shout, in which the Dean
joined; and, to our great surprise, the huge beast, that had
caused us so much terror, took fright himself, and without
looking round, or stopping a moment, he made a great bound,
and tore away over the rocks, plunging through the snow-
drifts, and rolling down the hill into the valley, where we had
dug the turf, in a most ridiculous manner.

"We passed now from a state of terror to a feeling of perfect safety, and in such an unexpected manner, too, that we
laughed outright, and we thought that we had been very fool-
ish to be so frightened, and looked upon our enemy as a great
coward. So we concluded that an animal who was so easily
scared as that would never attack us, and therefore, getting
our weapons, we followed after him, hoping to drive him from
the island. The jumps that he had made were quite immense,
showing clearly the state of his mind.

"Following the tracks of the bear, we came very soon in
full view of the beach where the carcass of the narwhal was
lying, half buried in ice and snow. The tracks led in that
direction, and finally pointed straight to the spot. He had in

his flight evidently smelled the old narwhal, and, remembering only that he was hungry, had stopped there ; for presently we caught sight of him, tearing away at the narwhal with as much energy as he had before wasted upon our storehouse.

"We had come quite near to the bear before we saw him ; and now our spirits underwent another sudden change, and our minds were once more filled with such feelings of respect for the bear, that we turned about immediately, and beat a hasty retreat ; and, when once more under the shelter of the hut, prepared again to stand on the defensive.

"All we could now do was to watch the bear closely. So long as the old narwhal lasted, we felt that we were safe enough, even after he had apparently satisfied himself with a good meal, and had gone away, as seemed likely, to sleep. He would certainly, however, come back to the narwhal again when he got hungry ; but now, worse than ever, when he did come back, there were two other bears with him, and all three of them were making a meal off the carcass of the dead narwhal. These last two were quite small ones, — the smaller not being larger than a big Newfoundland dog.

"With this discovery all our newly found courage took rapid flight, and we were overtaken with even greater alarm than before. That the narwhal would soon all be gone seemed plain enough, with three bears feeding upon it ; and then, when this feeding was over, this first bear, knowing where our storehouse was, and forgetting his fright, and having two bears, and perhaps by that time even more, to help him, we were sure he would soon come back again. It seemed as if a great crisis had now come in our fortunes, and what to do we did not know, and what was to become of us we could not imagine. We were in great trouble."

"I don't wonder," exclaimed William, — "the horrid brutes!"

"I should have been scared to death," cried Fred ; while little Alice thought it was too dreadful to think of ; but, "The poor bears, how cold and hungry they must have been!" said she.

CHAPTER XV.

SHOWS, AMONG OTHER CURIOUS MATTERS, THAT TWO BOYS ARE BETTER THAN
ONE, AND THAT PLUCK IS A GOOD THING, ESPECIALLY WHEN POLAR BEARS
ARE AROUND.

THE next record we have of the doings of the ancient
mariner and his little friends reads thus : —

"You will tell us to-day what you did with the bears, —
won't you, Captain Hardy ?" inquired William.

"Well," replied the Captain, laughing in his free-and-easy
way, like a jolly old sailor as he was, taking his long pipe out
of his mouth that he might do it all the better, " I think it
was pretty near being what the bears did with us, my hearties !
yes, that would be quite as near the mark, I 'm thinking."

"No matter, then," said William, — " no matter, Captain
Hardy ; we ain't particular, — any way you like. I 'll put
the question t' other way, then, — what did the bears do with
you ?"

The Captain was in great good-humor to-day, and he kept
on laughing till his pipe went out ; and, while he laughed, he
said, "Why, to be sure, they frightened us !"

"Tit for tat," exclaimed William ; "you frightened them, —
that 's fair."

"That 's so," replied the Captain, — "that 's so, sure enough ;
only they would n't stay frightened, while we did, you see."

"What ! did they find you out ?"

"That they did, my lad, just as soon as they had finished

8*   L the old narwhal. We were sound asleep when they came ; and they soon woke us up with the great noise they made close to the hut.

"But stop a bit !" exclaimed the Captain, reflectively ; "my story's got ahead of me, or I've got ahead of the story, — one or the other ; so I must go back a little," — and he paused, not with his finger to his nose this time, as usual, but to his forehead, as if feeling in his brain for the end of the "yarn," as he always called the story.

In a moment the old man appeared to have quite satisfied himself about the matter, for he started off as fast as he could go : —

"I did n't tell you anything about the fort we built, nor the time we had provisioning it, — did I ?" said he.

"No," answered William, "nothing about a fort."

"Then there's the broken end of the yarn at last," and the old man took his finger from his forehead and stopped feeling for it.

"Well, it was a good long time," continued the Captain, "before the bears finished the old narwhal ; but, finding how much they were occupied in that quarter, we went to our storehouses, and brought all our stores away, and stowed them close to the mouth of the hut, thinking that, if they were dis-covered, we should there be better able to protect them.

"First of all, however, we built up two solid snow-walls, about three feet apart, and as high as our heads, directly on a line with the entrance to our hut, so that when we went outside we walked right between them. Then, behind these walls, we pilled all the birds, seal-flesh and eggs that we had for food, and all the blubber (now frozen quite hard) that we had for fuel, — the former on the right-hand side (going out), and the latter on the left. Having done this, we covered the whole over with snow several feet deep ; and, as a still further protection against our enemies the bears, we built up a great wall all around in front of the hut where there were no high rocks. Through this wall we left only one small hole to crawl through when we went out ; and, when we came inside, we carefully closed it up with some large blocks of snow. But we did not go outside much, being afraid ; and at length, when one of the bears was discovered prowling about very near the hut, we drew within our fortification, closed the opening in the wall as tightly as possible, and were prepared for a siege.

" At first we did not sleep much, being all the time fearful of attack ; but gaining courage as we found, day after day, that the bears did not come to molest us, we at length fell asleep both together ; and it was while we were thus asleep that the bears discovered us. Before either of us awoke, they had actually scaled the wall of our snow-fort, and advanced to where our food and fuel were stowed, close to the mouth of the hut, and were tearing through the snow to get at it.

" We were, naturally enough, much alarmed, not so much on our own immediate account, as on account of our stores, for the bears would, we knew very well, not be likely to trouble us so long as there was anything else to eat ; but then they might just as well eat us first, and the stores afterward, as to eat the stores first ; for then we must surely starve and freeze, which would be quite as bad.

" Fully sensible of our unhappy condition, and the first feeling of alarm having passed over, we began seriously to speculate upon what we should do ; for something had to be done, and that very quickly.

"I looked out through the window, and there were the bears all crowded together in the narrow passage ; and one of them had already got among the frozen ducks, which were tumbling in the snow about his feet, and he had one in his mouth, crunching away at it in such a manner as to leave no doubt that he was either very hungry or was in a violent hurry ; growling all the while, — 'Ung, ung, ung,' — with each crunch he gave, to keep away the other two bears. This bear was much the largest of the three ; the smallest one was not, as I said before, larger than a Newfoundland dog, — not larger than Port or Starboard. Thus you see not only what a destructive, but what a selfish, beast he was.

"From alarm we now got to be angry, as we observed the liberties these bears were taking with our food, and the little ceremony they made of eating up, in this wholesale manner, what had cost us so much hard labor to get, and upon which our very lives now depended.

"I seized 'Old Crumply' in very desperation, and asked the Dean if he would follow me. 'What!' exclaimed he, 'you don't mean to attack them ?' 'That's just what I am going to do,' said I ; 'and, if you can do anything with "The Delight," now's your chance.' 'I'll stand by you,' said the Dean, grasping his weapon ; 'better to be killed outright by the bears than to let them starve us to death, and then very likely kill us afterwards.'

"Desperate as was our condition, I could not help being amused by the Dean's way of putting the matter, — 'first starved to death, and then killed'; and I think this little speech, turned in that happy way, did a great deal to stiffen up my courage.

"I crawled out through the doorway of the hut (which I

have told you was not high enough for us to stand upright in), and, upon coming near the end of it, there was the bear within three feet of me. His head was turned away, and his nose was all buried up in the snow ; for he had just swallowed a duck, and was getting a fresh one, so that he did not see me. My heart seemed to be in my mouth, — so close to the dreadful monster, — so ferocious and fearful did he appear as I looked up at him. Had I been alone, I think I should have retreated ; but here was the Dean behind me, and I was ashamed to back out, having gone thus far. Summoning all my courage, therefore, I brought forward my spear, grasped it with both hands, and plunged it with all my force into the animal's neck, just behind the lower jaw and below the ear.

" It was a fortunate stroke. I had evidently, by chance, cut some great blood-vessel, for the blood spouted from the wound in a regular stream. The bear dropped his duck very quickly, I can tell you. He was probably never so much astonished in all his life before. I had come upon him so stealthily, and he was so absorbed in what he was about, that he had never once suspected the presence of an enemy, but thought himself, no doubt, a very lucky bear to find such a dinner ready caught for him, and was quite as little concerned about who the owner might be as most people would be if they found a bag of gold.

" But I caused him to sing another tune than to be constantly going ' Ung, ung, ung,' to frighten off the little bears, for he roared with terror, so that you might have heard him half a mile ; and, finding that he could not wheel around as quickly as he wanted to, he roared again, louder than before, which sounded so dreadful that I drew back into the hut quite instinctively, and thus lost the opportunity to give him another thrust, which I might very well have done, in the side. When he had got wheeled round, he rolled over the other two bears, and the three together, all roaring in a dreadful way, rolled against the snow-wall of our fort, and broke it down ; and now, as soon as they could scramble to their legs again, they hurried away through the snow down into the valley, — the smallest one trying hard to keep up, and whining piteously all the while, as if he were afraid something terrible was coming to catch him ; and now, just as we had done before, when we had, with our shouts, frightened the bears away when they had first come to disturb us, we ran after them, little thinking of danger, in the excitement of the moment.

" We found that the bear I had wounded held straight down the valley, as was easily told by the red streak he left behind him on the snow. The other two turned to the right, and ran over in the direction of the old narwhal.

" Following the red streak, we came soon down to the beach ; and then climbing over the rough ice which the tide had piled up, we were quickly upon the frozen sea, hurrying on as fast as we could go. Indeed, no feeling of fear ever crossed our minds ; for the great quantity of blood that the bear left behind him somehow or other went to convince us, without much reflection, that the bear must be dead, and that we should presently come upon him.

" While hurrying on at this rate, our spirits received as sudden a check as they had on a previous occasion ; for we did at length come upon the bear, sure enough, and, forgetting all our courage immediately, we wheeled about in great alarm, and ran back towards the hut as fast as we could go.

" Finding, however, that we were not pursued, we turned about again ; and, proceeding more cautiously this time, we came, in a little while, in sight of the bear again, very near

where he was before ; but now he was clearly by no means a
formidable enemy ; for he was going along very slowly, and
making a crooked track, as if he was drunk. Directly he fell
over ; and, in a little while afterwards, we went up to him, and
found him dead, — having bled to death from the wound I had
given him.

"You may easily imagine how rejoiced we were ; for now
we had an enormous supply of food, and a fine bear-skin besides ; so I lost no time in unlashing the knife-blade from the
end of 'Old Crumply,' and with this we began to butcher him.
It was a very cold and tedious operation ; but we got through
with it at last, and then, burying all of the flesh in the snow
except a small piece that we wanted for supper, we returned
to the hut, dragging the skin after us, the Dean whistling, all
the way, 'Bonaparte crossing the Alps,' which he had picked
up, as he told me, from a Frenchman in Havana.

"While we were coming up the valley towards the hut, in
this lively state of mind, the Dean stopped suddenly, and said :
'Suppose, Hardy, the other two bears have taken a notion to
come back' ; and he was right ; for we came presently in
sight of one of them, very near the hut, and making directly
for it. As soon as he saw us, however, he ran away. So
we took a good laugh at his expense, and, thinking the other
one must be near him, though not in sight, we proceeded on
our way. Fortunately, however, before seeing the bear, we
halted long enough to secure the knife-blade again on the
end of 'Old Crumply' ; and it was well that we did this, for,
when we arrived at the broken wall where the bears had made
their way out, much to our surprise, we came right upon the
other bear, close up to the mouth of the hut, busy swallowing
a duck. This was the smallest of the three bears, and he could

not have been more than a year or so old. No sooner did he hear us than he, like the other one, became alarmed ; but, seeing us in the road by which he had entered, he did not try to escape in that way, nor did he appear to have the least idea that he had only to charge upon us to see how quickly he would clear the passage ; for, instead of doing this, he instantly rushed forward, and plunged into our hut, no doubt thinking that would lead to a place of safety.

"I do not exactly know by what motive I was impelled, but I suppose the same that governed me on several other occasions ; that is, a general one belonging to almost all human beings, and, indeed, to most animals, that is, to chase whatever runs away, and to run away from whatever chases.

"At any rate, I rushed up to the doorway of the hut, I believe without any idea at all in my head, and without giving much thought about it, and had like to have got into a great scrape ; for the bear, having found that the hut gave him no chance of escape, had turned about, and was coming out again. I was wholly unprepared for him, so hasty had I been. I could not run, and therefore, quite mechanically, I hit him in the face with the sharp point of 'Old Crumply,' which sent him back into the hut again, and made him roar in an awful manner, as if he were half killed. I knew I must have hit him on some tender spot, — the eye, it proved to be afterwards, so he was half blind as well as half dead.

"It was very unfortunate that I had not let him go, or killed him outright ; for we could now hear him tearing everything to pieces in our hut, trying to find a place of escape. The wall between our sleeping-place and our closet was first knocked over, as he scrambled about ; and there was no doubt that our pots and lamps were all broken to pieces. It was like a great roaring bull in a china shop, and we wished many times that he was only out and off; and, if he had only known our minds upon the subject, a compromise would have been speedily made, and the beast might have gone scot-free on condition of his doing no further mischief.

"The bear was not long in discovering the window. Now, the window being very small, it was evident that, if he attempted it, he would do us a great damage, for he could only pass through by knocking down some part of the wall. No sooner, therefore, had his head appeared in that quarter, than the Dean charged him most gallantly with the 'Delight,' and gave him such a tremendous blow on the nose that he was glad enough to draw his head in again, which he did with a great cry. Then he became quiet for a while, as if meditating what course it was best for him now to pursue.

"Availing myself of this little pause, I exchanged weapons with the Dean, and, fixing the harpoon-head on the end of the 'Delight,' I tied the other end of the line which was fast to it around a large stone that lay across the doorway of the hut. This I did because I thought there might be a possible chance of catching the bear; and that, if we could only get him to run out, I might harpoon him as he passed, and the stone would hold him until we could find some way of despatching him.

"No sooner had these preparations been made than the bear was again in motion; and now he gave a roar that seemed loud enough to have rattled the whole hut down about his ears. This time he had clearly tried the chimney, and had not only scattered the burning moss and fat all about the hut, but had set himself on fire into the bargain; for a great volume of smoke came out through the window, which smelled of burning hair.

"The screams of the bear were now pitiful to hear, and in very desperation he once more tried the window, when the Dean quickly gave him a crack with ' Old Crumply,' which sent him back again.

"Grown now utterly reckless, he bolted right through the door. I was ready for him, standing on the top of the passage-way and on the stone to which the harpoon line was made fast. As the bear came under me, I let drive with the harpoon, and stuck him in the back. And then away he dashed like, a fiery demon, plunging through the snow, smoking and blazing all over. He had evidently rolled all about in our burning fat and moss, as bits of burning moss were sticking to him, setting his hair all on fire, and no doubt scorching his skin to a degree that must have made a dive into the snow very comfortable indeed.

"As soon as he had run out all the line, the stone under my feet, instead of holding fast, gave way, pitching me after the bear, and turning me quite upside down. I landed head-fore-most in a snow-bank. The burning bear went rushing and roaring away, dragging the big stone after him ; but not far, however, for he fell over and died directly, — no doubt partly from fright, but chiefly, perhaps, from his wounds and his severe burns.

"Having got rid of the bear, we gave him no further thought for the present, but rushed into the hut to see what mischief he had done there. The smoke was at first so thick that we were almost smothered by it. Our cloth coats and part of our fur bedding were all mixed up with the burning moss upon the floor, and were being rapidly destroyed. As we had feared, the pots and lamps were all broken ; and, in short, the inside of the hut was in a most sorry state.

"It was a long time before we fully repaired all the damage the bear had done, and we suffered much inconvenience and discomfort before we replaced our pots, cups, and lamps. When we had, however, at last done all this, we were not sorry that the bears had come to disturb us, but on the other hand were rather rejoiced ; for we were now in all respects just as comfortable as ever, and had besides a great warm bear-skin to sleep on, and one more variety of food added to our list, and that, too, in such large quantity that there was no fear of our coming to want very soon."

Seeing that the ancient mariner showed signs of breaking off at this stage of the story, Fred spoke up, and wanted to know more about the bear that had set fire to himself.

"O, it don't much matter about him," replied the Captain. "When we had looked after the hut, and had got the fire put out, and found leisure then to go after the bear, he was dead enough, as I said before ; but much of the hair was singed off him as nicely almost, in some places, as if he had been shaved, so that the skin was of little use to us, and we only used the flesh, which we soon grew very fond of ; for this bear, as I have said before, was a young one, and his flesh was tender."

"What became of the other bear ?" asked William, curious to reach the end of the bear story.

"We never saw anything more of him, nor heard anything more of him either," answered the Captain ; "and indeed we were never troubled any more with bears at all in that way, but thereafter lived in peace.

"That is to say, we lived in peace so far as the bears were concerned ; but the cold and the darkness were now at their greatest, and the winds blew sometimes with such violence that we were often greatly terrified. Indeed, the storms at one time were so constant and so fearful that we could scarcely stir out of doors. Up to this period the weather had been mostly calm and very favorable to our course of life ; but, as the winter began to turn towards the spring, all this was changed.

" Yet we could not but feel thankful for the great privilege of good weather with which Providence had so far blessed us. Had the storms raged in the autumn and early winter as they did now, we should have been quite unable to provide for our wants, and we must have starved. But now our needs were abundantly supplied, and we had little occasion for going abroad unless we wanted to and the weather was favorable. Once only did we experience any serious danger from the weather ; and this, like most evils that befall all human beings, was due to our own imprudence.

" There being a bright moon, and the air being nearly calm and not unusually cold, we were tempted to take a long walk ; and, attracted by one object after another that was upon the frozen sea over which we were walking, — here an iceberg of peculiar formation or remarkable size, there a snow-drift of singular form, — we found ourselves at last several miles away from our hut.

" When we turned about at length to retrace our steps, we discovered that the northern sky, which we now faced (for we had walked out in a southerly direction), showed stormy symptoms, and very quickly afterward a severe gale of wind broke over the island and the desolate sea, and we found ourselves overwhelmed with drifting snow.

" The sky was for the most part cloudless, and no snow fell

from the heavens, but the light snow that lay upon the ice was picked up, as it were, by the wind, and whirled through the air in a manner as beautiful as it was terrible; for the drift coming in streams, with the rushing wind, lashed our faces, torturing us in a terrible manner, chilling us through and through, and almost overpowering us. Then an aurora borealis burst out before us, as if the heavens were on fire, — and from the top of our little island the snow came whirling above our heads in constant streams, that went circling about in a most fantastic way.

"You cannot imagine how grand this storm scene was, — the wind howling around us, the snow-drifts whirling about and spinning over the icy plain, the moon gleaming brightly upon the snow and the icebergs and the island, and every now and then a great blaze of many colors that were reflected on everything about us, would start up from the auroral arch, until the light became almost as great for a few moments as if it were broad day. It was very fearful, and you may be sure that we hastened on to the hut as fast as we could, though we were not in such a great hurry as to be wholly insensible to the magnificence of the scene.

"After we had reached the hut, the Dean repeated some verses which he had picked up somewhere; and when I recite them for you, you will see how appropriate they were to what I have been describing, and how strange seemed to us our situation when we found ourselves in the very place where the poet had imagined the Northwest wind to have a beginning.

"The Nor'west wind is a spirit brave,
        And he cometh from afar;
    He is cradled far down in the depths that yawn
        Beneath the polar star.

"Where no mortal foot hath been, he maketh
　　His track o'er the snowy plain ;
And listens the tread of phantoms dread,
　　With banner and spear and flame.

" Where the billows are booming on frozen shore,
　　O there right kingly is he !
His pinnacled throne the iceberg lone,
　　His empire the boundless sea.

" He rideth aloft on the mountain-tops, —
　　Rare sport doth he meet with there ;
He spinneth the snow in lightning flow,
　　Till it gleams like a witch's hair."

" O the Nor'west wind is a spirit brave,
　　A conquering hero is he ;
And his fierce battle song, as he marcheth along,
　　Is the shout of victory."

"O, how beautiful and appropriate !" exclaimed the children.

"But," said William, "how did you get to the island?"

"Without any other accident," replied the Captain, "than with two frozen noses, which were sore for a long time afterwards. But, after it was all over, we would not have missed the sight for anything, it was so grand ; yet, had we been caught out on the sea a little farther from the hut, we should never have got back, but both of us must have perished.

"Thus you see how Providence continued to watch over the two poor castaways."

CHAPTER XVI.

COVERS A LONG PERIOD OF TIME, AND SHOWS, AMONG OTHER THINGS, HOW A RACE MAY BE LOST AT BOTH ENDS.

 MUST now tell you," continued the Captain, " that, while all these adventures were happening, the winter was passing steadily away; and, from what I have before told you about the Arctic seasons, you will know that when the winter came finally to an end the darkness came to an end too, — that is, to be more particular, first there was a little flush of light at noon, to see which made us very glad, you may be sure ; after this, from day to day, the light grew brighter and brighter, until it was almost broad daylight, as it is here just before the sun has risen in the morning ; then the sun came up a few days afterward only a little way above the horizon (of course right in the south) ; and then, next day, it was a little higher, and the next day a little higher still ; and then, by and by, it was (as it had been in the summer-time before) circling round and round us, shining all the while ; and now our hut was at midnight in the shadow of the cliff ; at noon the sun was blazing down upon us, softening the snow, and making our hearts, O, how happy and thankful ! — more so than I can tell you.

"I thought that never in all my life had I seen anything so

splendid as the sun's bright face when he appeared for the first time after this long dark winter. For you must know we were about one hundred and twenty days without once setting eyes upon the sun at all; and now, when he did rise, after this long interval, what could we do but take off our caps and whirl them round and round our heads, in very joy and gladness? and this I can assure you we did with many a good round cheer.

"The summer now came on steadily, and the temperature became warmer every day. The spring glided into summer, and early in the month of June the snow began to melt in good earnest, and by July great streams were dashing and roaring over the cliffs, and through the gorges, to the sea. Then the sea soon began to show the influence of the summer heat. The ice grew rotten, and, from being white, it got to be quite dark; and we could no longer go out upon it with any safety, except in one particular direction, towards the east, where it was much thicker than in any other place. Then strong winds came, and the rotten ice was broken up, and after that it went drifting here and there to right and left, up and down upon the sea, whichever way the winds were blowing.

"And now once more we kept a sharp lookout for ships, hoping all the time that 'this day will be the day of our deliverance.' But we lived on as we had done before, — every day adding one more disappointment to the list, — for no ship came. Thus watching, waiting, hoping on, we grew restless with anxiety, and were more unhappy than we had ever been in the gloomy winter that had passed away.

"But the summer brought some pleasure to us. As soon as the snow had gone, the grass grew green upon the hillside, and the tiny little plants put out their leaves, and then the tiny little flowers were blooming brightly, and turning up their pleasant faces to the ever-smiling sun.

"And then the birds came back, — the eider-ducks, and the little auks, that I have told you of, and great flocks of geese and gulls, all looking out for places in which to make their nests; and they fairly kept the air alive with the flutter of their wings, and their 'quack, quack, quack,' and their gladsome screams, as they hurried to and fro.

"And then bright yellow butterflies and little bees came fluttering and buzzing about the little flowers, and all was life and happiness and brightness in the air about us; but there was no one there to look at us and see how heavy were our hearts at times, — no one but God.

"But not on our desert island alone was nature full of life and gayety. The seals, as if glad that summer had once more returned, crawled out upon the ice, and lay there on it, where it floated in the water, basking in the sun. There were hundreds and hundreds of them to be seen almost every day; and, besides the seals, the walruses, with their great long hideous-looking tusks and ugly and ungraceful bodies, came up too; and the narwhals, also, with their long ivory horns, and the white whales, were to be seen at almost any time, 'spouting' round about us in the sea. And besides all this life in the sea, and in the air, and on the land, we now and then saw a great white bear prowling about upon the floating ice-fields, seeking seals to feed upon; and, when tired of one ice-field, he would jump into the water, and swim away and crawl up on another.

"Thus you observe that, if we were upon a desert island in the Arctic Sea, it was not so barren as one would think who had never seen anything of such a place.

9   M

"It is not worth while for me to tell you how we lived through this second summer. Of course we had a much easier time of it than we had had the summer previous, for there was no hut to build, and we had now leisure to make ourselves more comfortable ; and indeed we used our time so well that we accumulated, in good season, everything we needed in the way of food and fuel, — catching the birds and other animals as before, which we stowed away in so many different places that we felt quite sure the bears would not be likely to discover all of them ; and then we made fresh suits of fine fur clothes, and fresh fur bedding, and carved new lamps and pots and cups out of soapstone, that we might be safe against all accidents.

"While we were thus working, and watching all the time for ships, without the hoped-for ship ever coming, the summer passed away, the birds flew off once more with the setting sun, the sea froze up all around the island, and we were left again alone, — all, all alone, in the cold and snow and darkness of another winter.

"O how heavy were our hearts now ! Bright had been our hopes of rescue ; great was our disappointment, and unhappy the prospect before us. For a time we were very despondent ; but the darkest hour, you know, is just before the break of day, and we were experiencing now only one more of our many periods of gloom with daybreak following ; for when the winter fairly sealed up the sea around us, and covered everything with snow, we felt the same spirit of resignation in our lives that had before carried us through so many trials and difficulties. And in this we were a great support to each other. If our hearts were more than commonly heavy at any time, we tried all we could to disguise it from each other, and tried always to be as cheerful as possible, If we had each always carried a gloomy face about with him, I am sure both of us must have died. Thus you see how important is the spirit of cheerfulness ; and, to tell the truth, I have n't much opinion of long-faced people anyway, whether they live on rocky islands or in big houses or in little huts, — whether they are old or young, rich or poor, civilized or savage, Christian or pagan. That 's my opinion.

"Well, this winter passed over just as the other had done ; — the same routine of work and hunting, the same cold and darkness, the same constant bearing up against our unhappy fortunes. It did not in any particular differ from the other in a manner worthy of mention, except that no bears came this time to disturb us. But there was the same aurora borealis, the same bright starlight and brighter moonlight, the same fierce snows and howling gales. We caught foxes and seals as we had done before, and wanted not for food or fuel. Our health was still always good.

"So you see there is no occasion for our halting over this period. I can tell you nothing new about it. The winter came to an end, as everything must, in time ; the sun came back ; the summer followed the winter ; and this, our third summer on the Rock of Good Hope, passed away like the others, with its bright sunshine, and its pretty butterflies and flowers, and myriads of birds, but still no ship, and still no rescue."

After the Captain had thus spoken, he paused as if to consider whether he had omitted anything, in connection with the long period they had passed on the island, that would make it worth his while to dwell longer upon any portion of his story up to this time. Satisfied always of the deep interest and close attention of his young auditors, he thought only of selecting such points of the narrative as seemed to him likely to convey most pleasure and instruction to the little people, who, ever eager to listen, were yet always curious to have something cleared up which the Captain had hastily passed over, thinking little of it. But still they had the good sense to see (to say nothing of the requirements of politeness) that they were not likely to be much benefited by interrupting the Captain; for if they asked questions in the midst of his story he would, in all probability, be put out, and lose the even thread of his narration. But a question, or perhaps a volley of them, was always sure to come if the Captain made a pause, or as he, in mariner phrase, expressed it, lay " hove to," for a little while.

So it was now. No sooner had the Captain stopped his speech, and got into the reflective mood, than William's tongue was loosened.

"O Captain Hardy!" said he, "don't go on until you have told us something more about those curious little flowers you have been speaking of. It is so odd to think of flowers growing in such a desert place!"

"O, do!" exclaimed little Alice, "O, do, do, Captain Hardy! they must be such pretty little things! But I don't see how they ever get any chance to grow, when it is so cold and dreary. How do they?"

"Pretty they are indeed, my dear," replied the kind-hearted Captain, pleased to have the question asked, as was evident, "and very wonderful. How they managed to grow is more than I can tell, and is just as astonishing to me as to yourselves.

The snow, however, in the spring went pretty quickly; and as soon as the earth was free in any place, then we saw the tini- est flowers you ever saw coming up, seemingly right out of the frozen earth, and almost underneath the very snow, — at least within a few inches of it. The Dean and I one day came across one of these little flowers, looking just like a buttercup, only the whole plant was — well, the littlest thing you ever did see. Why, it was so little that little Alice's little thimble, with which she is learning to sew so prettily, would have been quite large enough for a flower-pot to put the whole of it in! and it would have grown there, too, — and glad enough, no doubt. There was a great snow-bank hanging right over it, and there was ice all around it. But still it looked spunky, and happy, and well contented, and seemed quite able to take care of itself.

"As we walked on towards the hut, I noticed that the Dean grew very thoughtful.

"'What's the matter, Dean?' said I; 'what are you think-ing about?'

"'About that little flower,' replied the Dean.

"At this I laughed, asking the Dean what there was in the little flower to think about.

"'A great deal,' said he.

"I laughed again, and asked him what it was.

"'Why,' said he, very soberly, 'it is a lesson to us not to get the blues any more. If that poor flower can live and fight its way against such odds, I think we ought to!'

"Now there was more in that observation of the thoughtful little Dean than you would think for; and we talked a great deal about the little flower, — indeed, it came up between us very often; we went back many times to it, and watched it closely.

Once there came a snow-storm and buried it up ; but next day the snow was all melted, and the leaves came out as green, and the flower as yellow, and the whole plant as plucky, as ever. I should say the flower was about as large round as a very small pea, and it was just as yellow as gold; and the whole wee thing was not taller than a common-sized pin.

"We talked so much about this little flower that we got to making rhymes about it ; and, every time we made a new rhyme, we were much delighted, you may be sure. How we wished we had some way to write down what we thought! It would have been much easier, and a great satisfaction. But, for all that, we finally got quite a song of it, which I have not forgotten, even to this time. To be sure we did not know much about making verses, and nothing at all about what they call 'feet' in poetry ; yet we got some pretty good rhymes for all, though they might be called a little worm-fency, or like as if they had n't got their sea-legs on, you know. Now, would you like to hear this little song that the Dean and I made about the little Arctic flower?"

"O yes, yes, dear Captain Hardy ! — yes, yes, indeed!" said the children, in such a loud and universal chorus that nobody could have told who "deared" the Captain, or who said " O," or who, " indeed "; but you may be sure they all said "yes !" and so the Captain, being thus encouraged, cleared his throat, and said he would repeat it.

"My impression is," he continued, "that it is n't exactly a song ; in fact, I don't know what it is. I should hardly venture on calling it a ' poem,' you see ; but still, for all that, we must give it a name, you know, and ' song,' ' poem,' or what not, its right title anyhow is : —

THE ARCTIC FLOWER.

O tiny, tiny Arctic flower
 Where have you kept yourself so long?
Deep buried in a snowy bower?
  And did the winter treat you wrong?
  You little, smiling, gladsome thing!
  You pretty, pretty flower of spring!
  You little, little, wee, wee thing!
So bright, so cheery in the sun,
So everything that every one
  Would wish a flower to bring.
  You tiny, tiny little thing!
I'm so afraid the frosts will nip
  Your little feet, you tenderling,
  You crazy, crazy little thing!
What e'er possessed you to come up
  And nestle there beside the snow,
  As if you'd warm it with a glow
Of golden light from your bright face,
On which there is no single trace
  Of anything like sorrow?
Cheery, cheery, always cheery,
Always cheery, never weary,
  E'en with frozen sod close bound,
  E'en with snow all piled around,
  E'en with the frosts upon the ground,
Your little tender roots to chill!
O, what a royal little will
  You have, you little gladsome thing,
  You pretty, pretty flower of spring,
·You little, little weesome mite, ·
You tiny, tiny little sprite!
  E'en now the snows are at your feet,
And piled a hundred times your height,
  Close, close beside your face so sweet!
And yet you smile, you pretty thing,
You pretty, pretty flower of spring,
You little, little, wee, wee thing!

> And do not seem to care a bit,
> And look as happy, every whit,
> As any other flower of spring.
> And what a lesson, too, you bring
> To all of us, you little thing !
> You show us how to persevere,
> You show us how a happy cheer
> May always on the face appear,
> If God we trust and God we fear ;
> For God is every, every where,
> And this the flower doth declare, —
> The tiny, tiny little flower,
> The weesome, weesome little flower,
> The little, smiling, gladsome thing,
> The pretty, pretty flower of spring,
> The little, little, wee, wee thing.

" There, now you have it ! " exclaimed the Captain, drawing a very long breath, and looking around, no doubt to see the impression he had produced, — " there you have it, my dears ! "

The children all expressed themselves highly delighted with this effort of the Captain's in the poetical way, and they all declared if that was n't a song they " would like to see one."

Thus greatly flattered by the pleasure the children received from his recitation of what had become old to him, and deeply rooted in his memory, the Captain resumed once more the thread of his narrative, or, rather, " once more picked up the broken yarn, and spun away," as he would have more graphically expressed it.

" Well, well," continued the Captain, " You see our little flower died after a while, and all the other little flowers died ; and this brought us to the end of our third summer on the island and into the third winter.

"This winter passed away as the previous ones had done, and we felt still greater resignation.

"'Here we are forever,' said the Dean, 'and that we must make up our minds to. It is God's will, and we must bow before it and be reconciled.'

"'I fear, Dean, that is so,' I answered, solemnly.

"This was in the month of February, and the sunlight was coming back, and, to see if we could not catch a glimpse of the god of day, we had gone out together, wading through the snow.

"The Dean felt it when he said 'we must be reconciled'; but he had hardly spoken when our attention was quickly called away from such reflections (and from the sun too) by seeing something dark upon the frozen sea, not far away from us. It was moving.

"We were not long in doubt as to what it was, for we had seen too many polar bears to be cheated this time, — a bear, without any doubt at all.

"He was running very fast, and was making directly towards the island. He soon ran behind a large iceberg, and for a little while was out of sight; but he appeared again soon afterwards, and held on in the same course. Then we lost him once more among rough ice, and then again he came in view. He appeared so dark at first, that less-experienced persons might have been uncertain about what it was; for although the polar bear is usually called the white bear, yet in truth he has a yellowish hue, and is quite dark, at least in comparison with the pure white snow.

"'It's another bear, I do believe!' exclaimed the Dean, and at once we made for the hut. But the bear was running much faster than we were, and was moreover coming in right to-

9*

wards the place for which we were bound. So we grew much alarmed, and quickened our speed, not however without difficulty ; for the snow was, in places, very deep.

"By and by the bear, which proved to be a very large one, caught sight of us ; and, as you know already that the polar bear is rather a cowardly beast than otherwise, you will not be much surprised to learn that, when he saw us, he altered his course, and turned off from the island as fast as he could go. Seeing him do this (as you may be sure to our great delight), we halted to watch him ; and now we perceived, for the first time, that the animal was pursued. By what we could not imagine, but, clearly enough, by something ; for in the distance, and from the quarter whence the bear had come, there was plainly to be seen, winding among the bergs and rough masses of ice, something dark following on the very track which the bear had taken, sometimes lost to sight and sometimes in full view, and growing larger every moment, just as the bear had done.

"Nearer and nearer came this object, and our wonder increased. Presently we heard a cry.

"'Hark !' said the Dean.

"The cry was repeated.

"'A dog !' exclaimed the Dean.

"'A dog !' said I, in answer, for I heard it distinctly.

"'Hark !' said the Dean again, for there was another sound.

"'A man,' said I.

"'A man !' repeated the Dean, excitedly.

"And a man it was.

"Dogs and men ! what could they be doing there ? was the question that ran through both our minds at once.

" But dogs and a man (not men) there were, and whatever they might be doing there, or whence they might have cóme, it was certain that dogs and a man made the dark spot which we saw upon the white sea ; and it was, moreover, clear that they were pursuing the bear which had passed us and was now pretty far away.

" Nearer and nearer came the dogs and man, and the sounds became more and more distinct ; the dogs were upon the bear's tracks, the man was upon a sledge to which the dogs were fastened. At length they came so near that the dogs could be easily counted. They were seven, and all of different colors, and were fastened with long lines to the sledge, so that they were a great way in front of it, and they were running all abreast. They were straining and pressing into their collars, all the while crying impatiently, as they bounded over the snow at a rapid gallop. The man was encouraging them along all he could with a long whip, which he threw out with a lively snap, exclaiming, 'Ka-ka! ka-ka!' over and over again ; and then, ' Nen-ook, nen-ook, nen-ook !' — many times repeated ; for he was now so near that we could distinguish every word he said.

" It was a wild chase, and the Dean and I became much excited over it, running all the time to get nearer to the passing sledge and man and dogs.

"Very soon we should have met, but suddenly the bear came in full view of the dogs, evidently for the first time. Up to this moment the dogs had only been following the track.

" The dogs, now leaving the track, gave a wild, concerted howl, and dashed off after the bear in a straight line. Man, sledge, dogs, and all passed us quickly by, — the man shouting more excitedly than ever to his dogs, sometimes calling them by name, as it seemed to us, and sometimes crying ' Nen-

ook, nen-ook!' and sometimes, 'Ka-ka! ka-ka!' and so away
they went, rushing like the wind, — the whole scene more
strange than strangest dream, — the dogs and man like spectral
things, so quickly had they come and so unexpectedly ; or, at
the least, the dogs seemed like howling wolves, and the man
a wild man of the frozen ocean, clothed in wild beasts' skins.

A Race for Life.

"We called to the man to stop ; we shouted, 'Come here,
come here!' and then again, 'Come back, come back!' as
loud as we could shout, waving our caps, and throwing up
our arms, and running in a frantic way ; but not the slightest notice would he take of us, not one instant would he stop,
but upon his course and purpose he kept right on, pushing

after the running bear, without appearing to give us even a single thought. We could not doubt that he had seen us, we were so near to him.

"On went the bear, on after him went the dogs and sledge and man. More impatient grew the dogs, louder called the man to his excited team, and the Dean and I ran after, shouting still, as we had done in the beginning. We came soon upon the sledge track, and followed it at our greatest speed.

"At length the cries of the dogs grew indistinct, and then died away at last entirely, and the man's voice was no longer heard ; and that which had come so suddenly soon became but a dark moving speck upon the great white frozen sea, as it had first appeared ; but after it we still followed on.

"Then the moving speck faded out of sight, and everything around was still and cold and solemn and desolate as before. Yet still we ran and ran.

"I said as desolate as before. But O, it was a thousand times more desolate now than ever, — as the night is darker for the lightning flash that has died away, or a cloudy noon is colder for a single ray of sunshine that has broken through the vapors.

"Yet on and on we ran and ran, until we could run no more.

"And then we laid us down upon the snow and wept, and bemoaned our hard, hard fate ; but no word was spoken. The disappointment was too great for words ; and, after a short rest in the chilly air upon the frozen sea, we wandered slowly back to our poor hut ; and after many weary hours we reached it, not so much alive as dead, — for through miles and miles of heavy snow we had run after the sledge, and through these same miles we had trudged back again, with the cruel disappointment rankling in our hearts, and with no hope to buoy us up.

"Strange — was it not ? — that at no period of our life upon the desert island were we so unhappy as we were that day, — never so utterly cast down, never so broken-spirited, never looking on the future with such hopelessness.

"And in this state of mind we crawled beneath our furs, feeling too lonely and forsaken to have a thought to cook a meal, and so very, very weary with the labor we had done, in running and wading through the heavy snow, that we did not care for food ; and in deep sleep we buried up the heaviest sorrow that we had ever known, — the grievous sorrow of a dead, dead hope, — the hope of rescue that had come and gone from us, as the cloud-shadow flies across the summer field."

CHAPTER XVII.

A VERY PECULIAR PERSON APPEARS AND DISAPPEARS, AND THE CASTAWAYS
ARE FILLED ALTERNATELY WITH HOPE AND FEAR.

"HOW long we slept I have not the least idea. It may
have been a whole day, or it may have been two days.
It was not a twenty years' sleep, (how we wished it was!) like
that of Rip Van Winkle, yet it was a very long sleep ; and,
indeed, neither of us cared how long it lasted, we were so heart-
broken about what seemed to be the greatest misfortune that
had yet happened to us. If we woke up at any time, we went
to sleep again as quickly as possible, not caring at all to come
back any sooner than was necessary to the contemplation of
our miserable situation, — never reflecting for a moment that
the situation had not been changed in the least by the unknown man who had appeared and disappeared in such a mysterious way. But the sight of him had brought our thoughts
freshly back to the world from which we had been cut off, — a
world with human beings in it like ourselves ; and it was not
unnatural, therefore, that we should be made miserable by the
event. And so we slept on and on, and thus we drowned
everything but our dreams, which are everywhere very apt to
be most bright and cheering in the most gloomy and despondent times. Such, at least, was the case with me ; and if I
could have kept dreaming and dreaming on forever, about
pleasant things to eat, and pleasant people talking to me, I
should have been quite well satisfied.

"Thus you see what a great number of ups and downs we

had, — sometimes being cheerful and fully resigned, then again buried in the very depths of despair. Sometimes we felt real pleasure in the life to which we had become so well accustomed ; and it seemed to us, as we chatted together in our warm and well-lighted hut, that, since every necessary want was well supplied, and we were entirely free from care, we should be well satisfied to continue in that situation all our lives. We had, in truth, few troubles and few anxieties. Food, fuel, and clothing we possessed in abundance, and no fears crossed our minds that they would ever fail us.

"But this satisfactory state of mind, so natural at times, was apt to be broken up by a very slight occurrence, — unusual fatigue, a restless sleep, a severe storm confining us to the hut for many days together, or by the disappointment we so often experienced when an object which we had confidently believed to be a ship proved to be but an iceberg. Nor was this more unnatural than that we should at times be perfectly happy and well contented. Thus are we all made, and thus are we all, at times, inconsistent ; being often unhappy when there is no assignable cause, and often experiencing the sense of great happiness, under circumstances apparently the most distressing.

"You will see, therefore, that there is but one way for any of us to preserve an even temper and uniform disposition; that is, I mean, always to be cheerful, never despondent, ever hopeful ; and this can only be attained by always feeling the real presence of God with us ; when we meet with disappointment, to say in our hearts, 'Well, it was not the will of God,' or, if we meet with what seems great good fortune, 'It is the will of God that we do some good work, and therefore he has thus blessed us.' Thus only can we be truly happy. With this feeling there is always consolation in distress. It begets charity, and love, and confidence, and gentleness ; it makes the heart light and the face cheerful, and the life like a sunbeam gladdening where it goes. That 's what the love of God does.

"These thoughts are suggested to me by the experiences that the Dean and I were having at the time I speak of. How much more happy we should have been, had we felt always as I have last described! we should then never have been cast down, but should have been always hopeful, — never wishing to sleep on and on, and thus drown sorrow. We should not have felt as we did now when the strange man had come from the frozen sea and disappeared again.

"Well, to come back to the story, we were not allowed to sleep as long as we wanted to. Our sleep was indeed brought to an end very suddenly. I was first startled by a great noise, and then, springing up, much alarmed, I aroused the Dean, who was a sounder sleeper even than myself.

"'What 's the matter?' cried he.

"'Did n't you hear a noise?' I asked.

"'No!' answered the Dean ; 'nothing more, at least, than a church-bell, and that was in my sleep,' — which was clear enough.

"Presently I heard the noise again, and this time it seemed to proceed from something not far off. It was now the Dean's turn to be amazed.

"'Did you hear?' I asked again.

"'Yes,' said the Dean, holding his breath to listen.

"Again the strange sound was repeated.

"'Is it the wind?'

"'How can it be? the wind does not make a noise like that!'

N

" 'Can it be a bear ? '

" ' No ! it cannot be a bear ! '

" ' A fox ? perhaps it is a fox ! '

" ' No, listen ! there it is again.'

"The sound was louder now, and nearer to the hut. Again and again it was repeated, — nearer now and more constant ; then a footfall on the crusted snow.

" ' It is a man ! the bear-hunter has come back again !' spoke the Dean, throwing up his hands.

"Again the noise was heard ; again the footfall creaked upon the snow.

" ' The bear-hunter, it must be !' cried the Dean, again.

" ' O, I pray that it is so !' I added, earnestly.

"Again the voice was heard. I answered it. The answer was returned, and with the answer came a heavier and more rapid creaking of the footfalls on the snow.

"We rushed from the hut into the open air without another moment's loss of time, and without saying another word ; and there, not ten yards away, stood the very man who had passed us on the sledge, — the bear-hunter of the frozen sea.

"And a strange-looking creature he was, to be sure. There was not the least sign of alarm or fear about him ; but, on the contrary, he was looking mightily pleased, and was talking very fast in a language of which the Dean and I could neither of us understand a single word. When he was not talking he was laughing, and his enormous mouth was stretched almost from ear to ear. '*Yeh, yeh !*' he went, and I went that way too, by way of answer, which seemed greatly to delight him. He was dressed all over in furs, and looked very wild ; but, as he kept *yeh-yeh*-ing all the time, we were not afraid. As he came up to us, we greeted him very cordially ; but he could no more understand what we said than we could understand him. He talked very much, and gesticulated a great deal, pointing very often in one particular direction with his right hand. Then he cried, 'Mick-ee, mick-ee!' and pointed to the beach below, towards which we followed him. There we found a sledge and seven dogs ; and now we understood very certainly, if we had any doubts before, that this was the man and these were the dogs that had passed us, following the bear.

"The man tried his best to explain to us the whole affair, talking very rapidly ; but we could not gather from what he said more than our eyes told us already, for on the sledge we soon discovered a large bear-skin, all bloody and folded up, and some large pieces of bear's meat. The dogs were tied some distance from the sledge, and were securely fastened by their traces to a heavy stone, which I was very glad of, for the wolfish-looking beasts were snarling at each other, and fighting, and howling at us continually, — seeming all the while to wish themselves loose, that they might fly upon us, and tear us to pieces.

"If we could not understand the hunter's words, we made out by his signs, after a while, that he had seen us when he passed in pursuit of the bear. After overtaking and capturing the animal, he turned about upon his track to look for us, and, finding our footmarks at last, he had followed us to the hut, calling loudly, as he neared us, to attract our attention, for he could not find us easily, — our hut was so buried up in snow.

"After being fully satisfied with the inspection of the dogs and sledge, and what there was upon it, we all three went up to the hut.

"It would be difficult to describe our visitor. I have said that he was wholly dressed in furs. His pantaloons were made of bear-skins reaching to the knees, where they met the boots, which were made of the same materials. His under-clothing was made of birds' skins, like our own, and he wore a coat of fox-skins, with a heavy hood covering up the head completely. On his hands he wore mittens made of seal-skins, with warm dog-skin for an inside lining, and his stockings were of the same. So you see no part of him was exposed but his face, which was quite dark, ·or, rather, copper-colored (something darker than a North American Indian), and it was very broad and very round. The nose was very small and very flat, and the eyes were small and narrow. His hair was jet black, long and tangled, and was cut straight across the forehead. He had but little beard, — only a few black, wiry-looking bristles growing on his upper lip and on the tip of his chin. You would hardly suppose that such a creature could be anything but savage and repulsive ; yet this he did not seem to be at all ; on the contrary he appeared like the most amiable fellow that ever was seen.

" He sat down before the fire on one of the big stones we used for stools, and the Dean and I sat one on either side of him ; and I can never tell you how strange it seemed to be sitting there with another human being besides ourselves, after all that time spent without ever seeing anybody but each other. It was like a dream. We could hardly realize that it was true, as there we sat, staring at the strange man in wonder and astonishment.

" And all this time we were speculating about him, — where he came from, where he was going to, what relation did he hold to the world from which we had come in the Blackbird, could he tell us where we were, would he take us from the island, would he rescue us from this dreary life.

"O, how much we would have given for a few words from him that we could understand! How rejoiced we would have been to have these questions answered! Answering them, however, he might be even then, for anything we knew to the contrary; for he scarcely left off talking a single instant, but away he rattled as lively as a magpie and just as intelligibly. We could make nothing at all out of what he said, any more than I could of the hieroglyphics I have since seen on the stones of Egypt, until he put his hand to his mouth, at the same time throwing his head back a little, and repeating, several times, '*Me drinkum, Me drinkum.*'

"This very much surprised us, as we knew that he was asking for water, which having been given him, he then said, '*Me catum,*' signifying that he was hungry. We lost no time, therefore, in preparing him a hearty meal of ducks and bear's meat, which he appeared to think very fine. Then he had a great deal to tell us about something that he called '*Oomcaksuak,*' the meaning of which we could not make out; but, as he pointed in a particular direction, we thought he meant the ·place where he lived. We could not understand from him what his name was; so, as we had to speak of him to each other constantly, we called him at once 'Eatum,' as that was the word he used most. He amused us very much with his frequent repetition of it, and with the enormous quantities of food he took into his stomach after he did repeat it; for he only had to say, '*Me catum,*' to get as much food as he wanted. It soon got to be quite a joke with us, and when he said, '*Me catum,*' we all three fell, not only to feeding, but to laughing besides.

"Finding himself in such good quarters, Eatum manifested no disposition to leave them; but, after he had taken a sound sleep, he had a great deal to say about '*mickce*,' as before; and since he made a great many motions, as if using a whip (pointing all the while towards the beach), we concluded that he must mean something about his dogs, which we found to be true, for '*mickce*' in his language means dog, as we afterwards discovered. As soon as we had settled this, we all went out of the hut again, and went down and brought the bear's meat and skin on the sledge up to the hut, and then we fastened the dogs near by. After being fed, they all lay down and went to sleep on the snow. These dogs were very large and strong animals; and the seven could draw a very heavy load, — I should think that the whole seven could draw as much as a small horse.

"Eatum seemed to have been quite exhausted with long hunting when he came to us, and he did very little but eat and sleep for several days. His nose had been a little touched by the frost, but he scorched some oil, and rubbed it on as we would ointment, and cured it very quickly.

"After he had eaten and slept to his entire satisfaction, he appeared to grow more lively, and showed a great deal of curiosity about our hut and furniture, and hunting implements, being highly pleased with every new thing he saw. It was very surprising to see how nearly like his own many of our things were, — our lamp and pot and cups, for instance, and also our clothing. Our harpoon (the 'Dean's Delight') was almost exactly a match for his.

"It was a great drawback to our satisfaction that we could not understand him or he us, but little by little we got over part of this difficulty; for, upon discovering that he used one particular word very often, I guessed that he must be asking a question. The word was '*Kina*'; so once when he used it he was pointing to our lamp, and I said 'lamp' at a venture, whereupon, after repeating it several times, he appeared to be much gratified, and then said, '*Kolipsut*,' and this I repeated after him, which pleased him again. Then I knew that '*Kina?*' meant 'What is it?' or 'What's this?' so after that we *kina*-ed everything, and got on finely. We, of course, learned more rapidly than Eatum, picking up a great many words from him; and, having both of us good memories, we got to be able to make him understand us a little in the course of time; and as fast as we learned we taught him, and he got to know some of our language, in which we encouraged him. 'Me speakum much bad,' he would say sometimes, which was very true; but so long as we understood him it made little matter.

"And now it was that we got to find out how he had picked up the few words such as *me drinkum, me eatum*, and so on, that he had used at first; for he gave us to know that we were not a long way from where ships came every year, and that some of his people saw the ships when they passed, and some-times went aboard of them. 'Ship' was what he meant by '*Oomeaksuak*,' which word he had at first used so often. He had frequently been aboard of an *Oomeaksuak*, he said.

"Now this was great news for us, and we began at once to devise means of escape from the island. We made Eatum understand as much of what we wanted as possible. All this time I must not neglect to mention, however, that Eatum was of the greatest service to us; for when the weather was good he would fasten his dogs to the sledge, and all three of us would go out together on the sea to hunt, — Eatum driving. It was very lively sport; and sometimes, when the ice was very smooth and the snow hard, we went very fast, almost as fast as a horse would run, even with the three of us upon the sledge. The sledge, by the way, I must tell you, was made out of bits of bones, all cunningly lashed together with seal-skin thongs. Once we were caught in a severe gale a good way from home, and had to make a little house to shelter ourselves from it out of snow; and in this, with our furs on, we managed to sleep quite comfortably, and remained there about twenty-four hours before the weather would permit us to go on again.

"While in the snow hut we had a lamp to give us light and warmth; and this lamp (which was Eatum's) was made like ours, and Eatum made a spark, and started a flame, and kept it burning just as we had done, — the tinder being the down of the willow blossom (which he carried wrapped up in several layers of seal-skin), with moss for wick and the blubber for fuel. The pot in which he melted snow for water, and cooked our supper, was made, like ours, of soapstone.

"When the storm broke, we left the snow hut, and set out for the island; catching two seals by the way, and in the very same manner, too, that the Dean and I had done long before we ever knew there was such a person as Eatum in the world. We were much disappointed at not discovering any bears, and so were the dogs.

"But not many days afterward, the weather being fine, we went out upon the sea a great way, and were rejoiced to come across a bear's track, which Eatum said was very fresh. No sooner had the dogs seen it than away they started upon it; and over the ice and snow — rough and smooth, right upon the track — they ran as fast as they could go.

"The bear had been sleeping behind an iceberg, and we had come upon him so suddenly that he had not time even to get out of sight, and we saw him almost as soon as we had discov-

ered the track. '*Nen-ook, nen-ook !*' cried Eatum, pointing towards the bear ; and there he was, sure enough, running as fast
as he could. But, no matter how fast he ran, we went still
faster ; and it could not have been an hour before we overtook
him. Then Eatum leaned forward and untied his dogs, letting
them run ahead while the sledge stopped. In a few minutes
the dogs had brought the bear to bay, — surrounding the huge
wild beast, and flying at his sides, and tormenting him in a
very fierce manner. But I always observed that they took
good care to keep away from his head, for if he should get a
chance at one of them, and hit him with his huge paws, he
would mash him flat enough, or knock him all into little bits.

"While the dogs were worrying the bear we got out our
weapons, — the Dean his 'Delight,' I 'Old Crumply,' and
Eatum a spear made of a narwhal horn, and looking, for all
the world, just like 'Old Crumply's' twin brother. Then we
rushed up to the bear, Eatum leading ; and fierce though the
animal looked, and awfully as he roared, we closed right in
upon him, and quickly made an end of him. Then we drove
off the dogs, and tied them to a hummock of ice, while we
butchered the dead animal and secured the skin and what
meat we wanted, after which we allowed the dogs to gorge
themselves. Being now too full to haul, we had to let them
lie down and sleep, while we built a snow hut, and, crawling
into it, got a good rest. Then we returned to the island,
mighty well satisfied with ourselves.

"After this we fell again into conversation about the *Oomeaksuaks*, or ships, as I have explained before ; and, having
learned more and more of the language which Eatum spoke,
we got to comprehend him better, so we fixed clearly in our
minds where the place was that the ships came to, and were

fully satisfied that Eatum told the truth about it. We now offered to give him everything we had if he would take us there, and stay with us until the ships should come along and take us off his hands. About this we had several conversations ; but just when we thought the treaty was complete, and Eatum was going to carry out the plan we had fixed upon, this singular savage disappeared very suddenly, — dogs, sledge, and all, — without saying a single word to us about it.

"When we made the discovery that he was gone, we were filled with astonishment and dismay. We hoped, at first, that he had gone off hunting ; but, finding that he did not return, we tried to follow the tracks of his sledge, but the wind had drifted snow over them, and we could not.

"We now made up our minds that Eatum was nothing more than a treacherous savage ; and we were afraid that he would come back with more savages and murder us, in order that he might get the furs and other things that we had ; so for a while we were much alarmed, and were more heart-broken I believe, than ever before, for our hopes of rescue had been raised very high by hearing of Eatum's people and the ships. The suddenness with which all our expectations were thus dashed to the ground quite overcame us, and we passed the next five days very miserably, hardly stirring out of the hut during all that time. But at length we saw the folly of giving way to despair.

"One thing we quickly determined upon, and that was to leave the island, one way or another ; for now we were so afraid of the savages coming to murder us, that we would suffer any risk and hardship rather than remain there longer. So once more we began to devise means for our safety.

"It was no longer what we should do for food and fuel, or

clothing, but how we should escape. The ships we had given up long ago, and with the ships had vanished every hope of rescue. But now a wild man had come to us out of the ice-desert, and had told us that ships came in the summer not far from where we were, and through this intelligence we had obtained a glimpse of home and our native country, as it were; and this too at the very time when we had become most reconciled to our condition, and had made up our minds to live as best we could on the Rock of Good Hope for the remainder of our days.

"But now our minds were wholly changed. 'We are worse off than ever,' said the Dean, 'for this little hope the savage gave us, and the fear, besides, that he has put into us,' — which was true enough.

"Stimulated now by the memory of that hope and the presence of that fear, we prepared to undertake the bold task of rescuing ourselves. The savage had pointed out to us the direction of the place where the ships passed, 'And now,' we thought, 'if we can only reach the land there before the summer comes we shall be all right.' But if we should not get to the proper place, or if the ships did not come along, then the chances were that we might starve or freeze to death. Nothing daunted, however, by the contemplation of that gloomy side of the picture, we went earnestly to work, and very soon had contrived a plan.

"Of course we must have a sledge, as we were obliged to travel a long distance, and must carry not only food to eat by the way, but blubber for a lamp with which to melt water from . the snow, and furs to keep us warm while we slept. Eatum had taught us how to construct a snow hut, so that we felt sure of being able to shelter ourselves from the storms.

"But the sledge was the great difficulty. How should we make a sledge? was the question which most occupied our thoughts, and taxed our ingenuity. Apparently we had nothing to make it of, nor tools to make it with. To fasten together pieces of bone in the manner that Eatum had done, and thus construct a runner, was not possible, as we had no drill to make holes with, — and besides, if we had, the work would have required too long a time for our present necessities. Our purpose was to get away from the island with all possible haste.

"We made a sledge, however, at last, and in a very ingenious way as we thought, though not a particularly good way as we afterwards discovered. First we cut two strips of seal-skin, and sewed them into tubes. Then we filled the tubes with hair, and pieces of meat chopped very fine, and also bits of moss. Then we poured water into the tubes, and flattened them down by stamping upon them. Very soon the whole froze together, solid as a board, and these we soon fashioned into the proper shape for runners. We found no difficulty in fastening the two together with cross-ties of bone, which we lashed firmly to the runners. Thus, in seven days from the time of beginning to work upon it, our sledge was complete.

"Very much rejoiced over this triumph, we put a load on the sledge, and set out to give it a trial. But one runner gave way before we had gone a dozen fathoms, and we were in a state of great perplexity. We resolved now to bundle up everything we needed in a bear-skin, and drag that over the snow after us, so great was our haste to get away. We would drag the bear-skin head-foremost, so that the fur would slip more easily over the snow. But when we had done this, we discovered that, to say nothing of dragging the load, we could not even start it. Our united efforts were wholly unequal to the task of moving it even so much as an inch ; and, like Robinson Crusoe with his boat, we had wholly miscalculated the means, thinking only of the end. And so it is sometimes, even with wiser heads than ours.

We were now in even greater trouble than ever ; but being at length fully satisfied of the utter hopelessness of proceeding in this manner, we went back next day to the sledge, and began to work upon it again ; all the while looking out for the savages, and expecting them every minute to come and murder us."

CHAPTER XVIII.

"WE worked away at the sledge as fast as possible, being
bent upon having it finished and getting off from the
island as quickly as we could.

"At last it was completed, and we dragged it down to
the beach and out upon the ice. Finding that it went
better than we had dared to expect, we returned to our
hut, and, bundling together such of our furs and other
things as we thought we should require on the long journey
before us, carried them down and stowed them on the sledge.
Among them were included one lamp, one pot, and one cup.
We could not drag a very heavy load, even if the sledge would
bear up under it, so we had to limit ourselves to the least
possible allowance of everything. Food was, of course, more
important to us than anything else, and of this we determined to take all that we could put upon the sledge with
safety.

"All this time we felt very sad, and we worked in a very
gloomy spirit. Everything appeared so uncertain before us;
the journey we were about to undertake, at first seeming to
promise so hopefully, had become a very doubtful undertaking;
and, since day after day passed by without bringing the savages
upon us, we got to be less afraid of them, and in this same
proportion was reduced our confidence in the propriety of

leaving the island in this manner for an unknown place, and in utter ignorance as to whether the savage had told us truth about the ships.

"However, as you have seen before, when the Dean and I got an idea in our heads we did not easily abandon it. Once determined to make the trial, we had persevered until we had obtained a sledge ; and now, as I have told you, it was already half loaded.

"But we might have saved ourselves all this trouble, as you will soon see.

"While in the very midst of our packing, we were suddenly startled by a loud noise. Looking up from our work, and turning in the direction whence the sound proceeded, there, to our horror and dismay, were the very savages we had been for so long a time expecting. They were just rounding a point of the island, and were nearing us at a rapid pace.

"We soon discovered them to be five in number, each riding upon a sledge, drawn by wild and fierce-looking dogs, that made a great outcry as soon as they saw us, as did also the savages on the sledges.

"'At last,' thought I, 'our time has come. We shall be murdered now for certain, and then be given to the dogs for food.'

"'Oh !' exclaimed the Dean, 'if our poor mothers only knew where we were !'

"Dangerous as appeared to be our situation, I could still not help asking the Dean whether he did not think it would be quite as much to the purpose if we only knew where we were ourselves, — to which, however, he made no reply, for the savages were almost upon us. Seizing our weapons, we prepared to defend ourselves, since there was no use trying to run away, as the dogs would be atop of us before we could reach the hut.

"But there was not the least use of our being so much alarmed, for the savages soon convinced us that they meant no harm. They would not let their dogs come near us, but kept them off, and, stopping, tied them fast. Then, without any weapons in their hands, they came up to us in a most friendly manner, all *ych-ych*-ing at a wonderful rate. So we took the five of them right off up to the hut, and now our fears were turned into rejoicing and our sorrow into joy. One of them was Eatum, and they all proved to be just as singular-looking people, and were as curious about us and about everything we had as Eatum had been. Their faces were on a broad grin all the while.

" Having learned something of their language from Eatum, as I told you before, we contrived to make them understand, with the aid of a great many signs, how the ship had been wrecked, and how we got first to the ice and then to the land, — for this they were most curious about, — and they were greatly puzzled to know how we came to be there at all. After this they treated us quite affectionately, patting us on the back, and exclaiming, *Tyma, tyma,* which we knew to mean 'Good, good,' as Eatum had told us. Then Eatum wanted to show himself off in our language, and, pointing to us, he said, ' Hunter plenty good, plenty eat get. All same,' (pointing to himself by way of illustration, and thus finishing it,) '*tyma? yeh-yeh, ych !*' which was the way he had of laughing, as I told you before, and all the rest *ych, ych*-ed just like him. One of them we called at once ' Old Grim,' because he *ych-ych*-ed with his insides ; but no laugh ever showed itself in his face.

"After their curiosity was satisfied, they imitated Eatum, and began to call loudly, *drinkum* and then *eatum*, — *yeh-yeh*-ing as before in a very lively manner ; so that, what with their *yeh-yeh*-ing and *eatum* and *drinkum*, there was quite a merry time of it.   Meanwhile, however, we were busying ourselves to satisfy their wants, and it was not long before the savages were as full as they could hold.   It was a curious sight to see them eat.   They would put one end of a great chunk of meat in the mouth, and, holding tight to the other end, they would cut it off close up to the lips.   Our seal-blubber they treated in the same way.   To this blubber they seemed to be very partial ; and, indeed, all people living in cold climates soon grow fond of fat of every kind.   It is such strong food, which people require there as much as they do warm clothing, and in great quantities too.   The people living in the Arctic regions have little desire for vegetable food ; and the savages there eat nothing but meat, fish, and fat.

"Our guests did not leave off eating until each had consumed a quantity of food equal at least to the size of his head ; · and then they grew drowsy, and wanted to *singikpok*, which we knew from Eatum meant sleep ; and in *singikpok* we were glad enough to indulge them, although greatly to our inconvenience, for they nearly filled our hut.

"But before this we went down to the sledge and brought up the furs and other things we had stowed upon it for our journey, as we needed them for the accommodation of our visitors.   The savages went with us, and when they saw what a sledge we had made, and understood what sort of journey we were going upon, they laughed.

"You must understand, however, that we did not give up the journey ; but, on the contrary, were more than ever disposed to make it. For, although we could see no harm in the savages, yet we put no trust in them, — they appeared to have no serious side to them at all, but treated everything with such levity that we could not tell what to make of them. Sometimes we wished they would go away ; and then again we wished they would stay ; and then we wished they would take us with them, and then again we were afraid to trust them. Thus did our hopes and fears alternately get the better of us.

"The savages slept very soundly for a while ; but one by one they woke up, and, as soon as their eyes were open, they fell to eating again until they were satisfied, and then in a minute afterwards they were fast asleep. This they kept up for about two days, and you may be sure they made way with a great deal of our provisions before they had finished.

"When they had thoroughly gorged themselves, and slept all they could, they were ready to start off again ; and now we found that they had come to take us away, — a discovery which was both agreeable and disagreeable ; for we could not tell what to make of the savages at all, we could understand so little of what they meant, or of what they said, or of what their designs might be respecting us.

"'However,' we thought, 'after all here is a possible chance of escape and rescue,' and, like a drowning man catching at a straw, we could not seriously think of allowing the opportunity to slip ; besides, there proved in the end to be little chance of our having our own will in the matter, since the savages never once asked us if we would go with them, but began to bundle up our furs, food, and blubber, and everything else we had, as if resolved to take us whether or no.

"At first we felt a little alarm, — without expressing it, however ; but, seeing how good-natured they were about it, and how considerate they appeared to be for us, we had no further fear, but trusted them entirely.

"The savages went to work with a hearty good-will to get us off. Not a thing escaped them, — not a piece of fur of any kind ; fox-skins, bird-skins, bear-skins, pots, lamps, and everything else, were picked up and carried off just as if we had no right to them at all ; and although there were, as I have said, five sledges, yet these were all quite heavily laden.

" As we passed down by our sledge, the savages set up another laugh at it. It seemed to amuse them very much, but they showed no disposition to take it along.

"At last we were all ready. The sledges were all stowed, everything was tightly lashed down, and off we started, — I riding on the sledge with Eatum, while the Dean was on the sledge of ' Old Grim.'

"The Dean carried his ' Delight,' of course, while I held on to ' Old Crumply.' Nor were our ' palm and needle,' and jack-knife, that had done such good service, forgotten. Indeed, we brought away everything.

"Of course we were very much rejoiced to get away from the Rock of Good Hope, even although our fortunes were yet very uncertain ; still, it had been our rock of refuge and safety, and, in our thankfulness, we could not fail to cast upon it a look of tender regret at parting from it. Together there the Dean and I had achieved many triumphs which were to us a source of great pride, and would always continue to be as long as we lived ; while, on the other hand, if we had suffered many discomforts and sorrows, these would not, we knew, linger long in the memory. Besides, on the Rock of Good Hope, and in the hut we were leaving, we had learned to know each other, and to love each other, and to be bound together by a strong bond of friendship, which, as it was formed in adversity, was not likely to be broken.

"But then, on the other hand, the prospect that loomed up ahead of us was not of a very encouraging description. 'Where were the savages taking us? what would they do with us?' were questions which kept haunting us all the time. We could see nothing clearly ; and no matter what might happen in the end for our advantage, we must, in any case, live among these wild people for an indefinite time, subject to their savage caprices and savage and lawless ways of life.

"But we soon had to give up speculating about the prospect ahead, and had to let the Rock of Good Hope, and the hut, and the life we had led there, with its struggles and trials and triumphs, pass away as some vaguely remembered dream ; for on we sped, with our caravan of sledges, over the frozen sea, — the dogs all lively, and galloping away with their bushy tails curled over their backs, and their heads up ; their savage drivers crying to them, now and then, '*Ka-ka ! ka-ka !*' and snapping their whips to keep them at a brisker run, and all the while talking to each other in a loud voice, — sometimes, as we could clearly understand, about ourselves, sometimes whether they should go off on a bear-hunt. Occasionally one of the teams would scent a seal-hole, and away the dogs would rush towards it as hard as they could go, all the other teams following after, pell-mell ; and, when they reached the hole, it was all the hunters could do, by whipping and shouting and scolding, to keep the teams from coming atop of each other, and getting into a snarl. Once this happened with two of the teams. The dogs all became tangled in each other's traces, the sledges got locked together, and the animals fell to fighting, one team against the other, in a most vicious manner,

"This was such a novel mode of travelling that we enjoyed it immensely, even although it was pretty cold and the journey was very long. It seemed strange to us to be thus wandering, without chart or compass, over the great ice-desert on the sea; for all around us was nothing but a great plain of whiteness, only broken here and there by an iceberg, which glittered like a great diamond in the bright sunshine.

"We must have gone at least sixty or seventy miles before we made a single halt; and then we came to the village where

The Children of the Frozen Sea.

these savages lived. It was not on the land, but out on the frozen sea over which we had travelled. As we approached, the dogs ran very fast. '*Igloo, igloo!*' exclaimed the savages, pointing, when we neared the village. As we had already learned that *igloo* meant hut, in their language, we were much rejoiced ; for we were very tired with the long journey, and cold besides. But still we fell to wondering what sort of place this was we were coming to, and what strange sight we were next going to see.

"Old Grim drove his sledge close up along side of Eatum's, trying to pass ; and we went into the village with a perfect rush, — the men shouting, the dogs barking, and everything in an uproar generally.

"While this race between Old Grim and Eatum was going on, the Dean and I were for a few moments side by side, and near together. The Dean called out to me, 'Hardy, this don't seem real, does it? These ain't dogs, they are wolves ; these ain't men, they're devils'; and, as I looked over at Old Grim, and saw him throwing his long whip to right and left, and heard him calling out to his dogs in a language which seemed like nothing human, and all the while preserving the same immovable expression of countenance, I must confess that there seemed to be a great deal of truth in what the Dean said.

"Thus it was we went rushing into the village. And a strange village, indeed, it proved to be, — nothing but a collection of huts made of frost-hardened snow. There were in all six of them.

"Many more savages were there, who came out to meet us ; and their dogs rushed out too, making a great noise ; and when we had halted, a number of women joined them, all dressed in furs just like the men, and also children dressed in the same way, and all very curious about us, and all *yeh-yeh-*

ing a great deal. Indeed, we made such a commotion in the village as never was seen before.

"But everybody appeared to be kindly disposed towards us, and into one of the huts we were both taken immediately, and down we sat on the floor of the hut, which was covered all over with bear-skins. There were two lamps in it, almost exactly like ours, and two pots were hanging over them. We had soon a good meal, and very quickly after that were sound asleep ; and even although it was a snow hut, and among savages, we were thankful in our very heart of hearts. And our thankfulness was because we were among human beings once more, and felt no longer as if we were wholly cast away from the world ; and we now felt hopeful that through these savages would come means of escape to our homes. We felt thankful, too, that they treated us so kindly, — the women especially ; for, savages though they were, they were possessed of much feeling and sympathy. One of the women made the Dean go to sleep with his head in her lap, which it was easy to see he did not like a bit ; and, before this, she had fed him with her own fingers, and, while he was sleeping, she stroked his bright hair away from his handsome face. Another of the women treated me very much in the same way ; but being older, and not handsome, like the Dean, I did not come in for so many favors.

"Then, besides that, the women took off our damp fur stockings, and gave us dry ones before we went to sleep ; and they seemed to want to do everything they could for us, so that we soon became convinced they meant us no harm. The woman who was particularly kind to me was the wife of Eatum ; and the Dean and I at once called her Mrs. Eatum, which made them all *yeh-yeh* very much ; and they got to calling

her that too, — as near, at least, as they could pronounce it,
which was, *Impsuseatum*. Her right name was *Serkut*, which
means 'little nose'; Eatum's right name was *Tuk-tuk*, that is,
reindeer, because he could run very fast. There were two
young Eatums; and when I began to play with them, I grew
in great favor with the Eatum family.

"The Dean was quite as well off for patrons as I, being
specially taken care of by a woman whose husband had been
one of our party. Her name I forget now, but it meant 'big
toes.' So what with nursing by 'Mrs. Little-nose' and 'Mrs.
Big-toes,' and with plenty of seal meat to eat, the Dean and I
got on famously. The name of Mrs. Big-toes' husband was
Awak, which means walrus. He was a fine hunter, and had
plenty of dogs. These dogs, I should mention, were always
allowed to run loose about the village; and, no matter how
cold it was, they slept on the snow. But their harness had to
be taken off, else they would eat it; and everything eatable
was buried out of sight in the snow, or brought inside the
hut.

"After we had been eating, and sleeping, and enjoying the
hospitality of these savages about three days, a young hunter
whose name was *Kossuit*, which meant that he was a little
dark-skinned fellow, came driving into the village (he had been
out prospecting for a hunt), proclaiming, in a very loud voice,
that there was a great crack in the ice, and that it was alive
with walrus and seal. There was immediately a great stir,
and a great harnessing of dogs, and hunting up of whips, and
getting together of harpoons and spears and lines. Everybody
was going on the hunt, that is, all the men and boys. Wher
all was ready, Eatum came to me, and said, 'Ketchum *awak*,
ketchum *pussay*, you go?' meaning, would we go with them,

and catch walrus and seals. Of course we said 'yes,' and off we started at a wild pace ; the Dean riding with Kossuit, while I rode with Eatum. We had to go I should think four miles before we came to the crack ; and, when we reached it, we found it to be as Kossuit had described it. As soon as the savages saw the crack, they stopped their dogs, which was done by crying, *Eigh, eigh, eigh!* to them, and whipping them fiercely if they did not mind soon enough. The dogs being now fastened by running the points of the runners into the snow, the hunters went forward with their lines and spears and harpoons ; and, by approaching the side of the crack very cautiously, they managed at length to get near enough to throw their harpoons into the animals when they came up to the surface to breathe. Their mode of capturing them was almost the same as that which we employed in catching seals, after finding it out for ourselves. Thus you see how all people in the same conditions of life will naturally be led to the same way of providing for their wants, — our senses being given to us all, whether savage or civilized, for the same purpose. I have showed you already how, in our mode of starting a fire, in our lamp, pot, and other domestic implements ; our clothing, harpoon, and the like, — we had imitated these savages unconsciously ; and the more I was with them, the more I saw how much we were like them.

"Knowing how we killed the seals, it is not necessary to tell you how the savages managed ; and catching the walrus was just the same, only more difficult, for a walrus is several times larger than a seal. You know the walrus are those huge marine animals, living in the Arctic seas, that have long white tusks, and look so fierce. They make a very loud and very hideous noise ; and in the summer, like the seals, they come up on the ice, or on the rocks along the shore, in great numbers, to bask and sleep in the sun.

"It is enough to say there was a great deal of sport, and a great deal of excitement, not unmixed with danger. One of the hunters got a line tangled about his legs, and was whipped over into the water, where he was not noticed, except to be laughed at, while all the hunters went on with what they were about, letting him shift for himself, — little caring, as it appeared, whether he drowned or not ; and I really believe he would have drowned, had it not been for the assistance of the Dean and myself. This was the first time I had observed how reckless these people were of their lives.

"There were in the party altogether nine sledges, with one good hunter to each sledge. Five of them were old men and four were young men, besides which there were six boys of various ages ; and these, with the Dean and myself, made seventeen. By helping each other all round, we caught seven seals and three walruses, — all of which we skinned and quartered, and put on the sledges ; and then we returned to the village, — walking back, however, as the load on the sledges was too heavy to allow us to ride.

"When we reached the village, the women came out to meet us, talking very much, and *yeh*, *yeh*-ing louder than ever ; and now I observed that they took all the game we had captured, and butchered it, the men doing nothing at all but look after their dogs. It was thought to be a disgrace for a man to do any work about his hut.

"The Dean and I had taken our full share in the hunt, and won much admiration. Before, they had treated us with a kind of pity, but now they had great respect for us. Eatum said, 'Much good hunter you.'

"Seeing that we were good hunters, they were now going to marry us right off, that we might have wives to cut up our seals when we brought them home, which proposition put us in a great embarrassment. If we refused, they might be offended, as was very natural; so I accepted their offer at once without a moment's hesitation, appearing as if I was very glad, and thought it a great compliment indeed ; but at the same time I told them, with a very grave face, that all our relations lived in a far-off country, to which we were obliged to go as soon as a ship came that way ; and, of course, when we did go, the wives they gave us would go along. As none of the young women were willing to take us on these conditions, although not very flattering to us, we got out of the difficulty without offending anybody. At first the Dean was quite indignant, but afterwards he laughed, and said, 'Why, just think of it ! Mrs. Hardy and Mrs. Dean in seal-skin breeches and long boots, — a jolly idea indeed!' But one of the girls was fond enough of the Dean for all, only she must n't show it ; for these people are mighty particular about that. When all is arranged by the parents, the girl is obliged, even then, to say she won't have her lover. So the lover has to steal up, and take her unawares, and run off with her bodily. Of course, if she really likes the fellow, and wants to get married to him, he has an easy time enough of it ; but if, on the other hand, she dislikes him, she can readily get away from him.

"Old Grim (whose right name was Metak, meaning eider-duck) had an adventure of this sort, as they told me, which resulted very differently from what usually happens. He was then quite a young man, but, having caught a seal, he thought it was time he had a wife. Meanwhile a wife had been provided for him by his father, who had made the bargain with the girl's father. The girl was told who her husband was to be, but it would have been against all rules to tell her when he was coming after her. Well, as I have said, having caught his first seal, Metak made up his mind to have a wife to butcher it for him ; so he set out for the snow hut of his lady-love's father, where the dusky-faced girl was lying fast asleep, all rolled up in furs.

"As it was contrary to custom for any girl to be captured in a hut, but must be taken on the wing, as it were, Metak had to wait for her to come out, which she finally did, and passed very near a deep bank of snow, behind which her lover was lying, shivering with cold, and crying with impatience. Quick as a fox to pounce upon an unsuspecting rabbit was Metak to pounce upon the unsuspecting girl. He seized her, and started for his sledge. She screamed, she pulled his hair, she tore his fur, she bit his fingers ; but the valiant Metak held manfully to his purpose, and would not let her go. He reached the sledge, and put her on it ; he tied her there, and, springing on himself, he whipped up his dogs, and started for his home. But the refractory damsel would not stay tied. She cut the lashings with her teeth, she seized the whip out of Metak's hands, she pushed Metak off the sledge, and sent him sprawling on the snow ; and then she wheeled the dogs around, and fairly made them fly again on the backward track to her father's hut, where she crawled once more into her nest of furs, and where the luckless Metak was ever afterwards content to let her stay, satisfied that he was no match for her.

"This story was told by Eatum one evening in the snow hut, while Old Grim was present, and it was evidently a standing joke against him. He did not seem to relish it at all, for he went out of the hut as if driven away by their shouts of laughter. I could not understand the language well enough to fully appreciate the story at the time, but afterward I got Eatum to repeat it to me.

"It proved that the name Old Grim, that the Dean and I had given Metak, was even more appropriate than we thought; for it seemed that he was generally known as the man who laughed with his insides without the help of his face.

"Altogether these savages were a most singular people. They seemed to be happy and cheerful all the time, never caring for anything, so long as they had enough to eat, and plenty of time to tell stories about each other and make each other laugh. But what struck the Dean and I most strangely was that they should be living in this happy state away out there on the sea, a long distance from land, really burrowing in the snow for shelter, and roaming about for food like beasts of prey, and yet enjoying themselves and amusing themselves after the fashion of civilized human beings, so far as their relations to one another were concerned.

"'Well, I do declare,' said the Dean, 'this is an odd party, to be sure. I'm going to christen them, Hardy.'

"'Christen them, or Christian them'? I asked.

"'Both, perhaps,' answered the Dean; 'but for the present I mean christen, — that is, give them a name.

"'That I understand; but what's the name?'

"'THE CHILDREN OF THE FROZEN SEA.'

"'Very good,' I said, 'capital! Children of the frozen sea! Sounds good, at any rate; and all the world is agreed that whatever sounds good must be good.'"

CHAPTER XIX.

THE PECULIAR PEOPLE PROVING TO BE SAVAGES, THE CASTAWAYS SEIZE THE
FIRST OPPORTUNITY TO LEAVE THEM, NOT RELISHING THEIR COMPANY.

" I HAVE not latterly said much about the Dean ; but you
may be very sure that such a fine fellow could not fail to
be greatly delighted with the change that had come about, as
it not only led us away from our desolate life on the desert isl-
and, but gave us a promise at least of the rescue which we
had so earnestly prayed for. 'We ought to be very thankful,'
said the Dean to me one day, 'very thankful indeed for this
deliverance.' But as I did not much relish the habits and customs of the savages, I did not find myself of the same thankful
disposition ; so I replied to the Dean, that the change looked
much like that of the fish who fell out of the frying-pan into
the fire. 'You should not say so,' replied the Dean. 'I see
the hand of God in it ; and he who has mercifully preserved
us through so many trials and dangers will not desert us now.'

" The Dean said no more at that time, but he became very
thoughtful, while, as for myself, I felt quite ashamed that I
had spoken so slightingly of the savages, and had shown so
much impatience with their rather disagreeable company ; for,
to tell the truth, their ways were somewhat offensive, as they
never washed their faces, and were altogether rather a filthy
set.

" The Dean, however, did not stop with preaching about
them, but, on the contrary, did everything he could for them.
One of the hunters had gone to catch seals, and, the ice break-

ing up, he was drifted out to sea, where he took refuge on an iceberg, upon which he managed to drag his dogs and sledge. Here he lived through terrible storms and cold for a whole moon (that being the way they reckon time), and he only escaped finally by the iceberg drifting in near the land, when the sea froze around it. After great trouble he got ashore, with both of his feet dreadfully frozen, which is easily accounted for when you know that the poor fellow had no shelter at all while on the iceberg, and had nothing to eat but his dogs, all of which died of starvation. This savage had no wife, and the Dean took care of him, and dressed his frost-bites, and was so good to him that the savages all called him '*Paw-weit*,' which means ' Little Good-heart.' So the Dean got on famously ; but the poor frozen savage that he had been so kind to died at last, and was buried in the snow.

" A child fell on the ice, and broke its arm, and the Dean set it, and made it all right ; and to other people he did many things to show his sympathy for them ; but, when he began to tell them about our religion, they did not understand him, and had no mind to listen. This very much grieved the Dean ; for he wanted to convert the whole of them, and thought, if he only knew their language better, he could persuade them all to be Christians, — which I think very likely, for nobody could resist him.

" We remained at the snow village three weeks, but we did not do much more hunting, as the savages seemed to think they had enough for their present wants ; and since they are almost constantly moving about from place to place in search of food, they never store up much for the future. Having enough to eat for the present, they let the future take care of itself; and, sure of a good meal, they amuse themselves mostly with telling stories, usually about each other, — that is, when they are not eating or sleeping, which I must say occupies most of their time.

"They had a singular custom in their story-telling which I have never seen among any other people. One person recites the story, and the listeners break in, every now and then, with a laughing chorus that is nothing more than a repetition of the meaningless words, ' *amna aya*,' which are sung over and over to any extent. The women generally enjoy it the most, and sing the loudest, especially when a man is concerned. I will give you a specimen of this kind of song, — translated, of course, as I have long ago forgotten how to speak their language.

"Eatum is telling the story of a bear-hunt, and as you will see that it is a kind of song, I will sing it for you, and you can join in the chorus just as well as if you were all little savages yourselves. We will call it

"THE SONG OF KARSUK'S BEAR-HUNT.

" A bear is seen upon the ice,
    Amna aya ;
Karsuk goes out to hunt the bear,
    Amna, amna aya.

" The dogs get quick upon the trail,
    Amna aya ;
The dogs are pulling all they can,
    Amna, amna aya.

" The bear is running all he can,
    Amna aya ;
The bear gets tired and cannot run,
    Amna, amna aya.

"He turns around to charge Karsuk
   Amna aya ;
Karsuk jumps off and runs away,
   Amna, amna aya.

"He runs away all full of fright,
   Amna aya ;
So full of fright he tumbles down,
   Amna, amna aya.

"Bear kills the dogs and breaks the sledge,
   Amna aya ;
What girl will marry such a man ?
   Amna, amna aya."

and so on, after that, they keep *aya*-ing, *aya*-ing, and *amna-aya*-ing uproariously, until they are entirely broken down with shouting and laughing, in the midst of which Karsuk is pretty sure to run away.

"In the same manner I have heard the story of Metak's love adventure sung, or rather recited, or *amna-aya*-ed as one might say.

"They use the same *amna-aya* chorus when they sing over the dead, or sing praises of the dead, only instead of being lively, then it is sung in a solemn tone. I will repeat one called

"THE GRAVE-SONG OF MERAKUT.

"Merakut, Merakut, Merakut dead !
   Amna aya ;
Merakut dead, her lamp is smoking,
   Amna, amna aya.

"Her children are crying, her baby is freezing,
   Amna aya ;
O, her hut and our hearts are all cold !
   Amna, amna aya."

and after that, as in the other song, they keep on *amna-aya*-ing
for a long while, but with a very doleful voice and manner.
Indeed, it is quite as distressing to hear them *amna-aya* the
dead as it is amusing to hear them *amna-aya* the living.

"The Dean and I very much wanted to go on another bear-
hunt, but the savages said it was too late in the season for that,
as the ice had many cracks in it, and there was no use chasing
a bear, as he would jump into the first crack he came to, and
swim over it to the other side, and there he would be safe
enough. And, indeed, when I climbed one day to the top of
a tall iceberg, and looked out in the direction of our solitary
island, I could see several cracks from a yard to a hundred
yards wide, so that it was very fortunate we escaped from the
island when we did.

" The savages now said it was time to be moving, or a crack
might come between us and the shore. Indeed, the season
was getting well advanced ; the snow was melting a little, and
in places it was quite sloppy ; so everything in and about the
snow huts was packed upon the sledges, and we went then
to the main-land, which was not more than ten miles distant.
Here we came upon a village of three huts, built in the hillside very near the sea, and were in many respects fitted up as
our own had been ; only they had regularly constructed walls
of stones and turf, which, tapering in from either side, joined
at the top, making a space large enough to accommodate two
or three families in each hut. Into these three huts were
crowded all the men, women, and children that had been in
the snow village.

"There we lived five days, after which we took up our
march again, keeping along near the shore, where the ice
was most solid and safe. Then we came to a deep, broad bay,

where the hillside, which was exposed to the south, was quite free of snow, — the snow having melted and run down to the sea. Here we halted, and the savages went to some great piles of stones, and brought out from under them a number of sealskins, which were spread over some narwhal horns that were just like 'Old Crumply,' and in a few hours they had pitched two tents, under which we all slept soundly, being very tired. The next day they got more sealskins, and pitched three more tents, and a few days afterward other people came along, and put up two other tents, making in all seven, — quite a little sealskin village, and a much more comfortable looking one than the snow village had been.

"Here it seemed to be the intention of the savages to remain for some time, as they went regularly to work to prepare for hunting various kinds of game, chiefly walruses and seals, and besides these, among others, an animal I had not seen before, — a beautiful rabbit, or hare rather, very large, and pure white. These were quite numerous, and fed upon the buds and bark of the willow-bushes, and were caught by stretching a very long line across the tops of a great number of stones, or piles of stones rather, which were placed about six feet apart, the line itself being about a foot from the ground. To this line they tied a great number of loops, and then all the people, going out, surrounded the rabbits and drove them under the line, and several of them found themselves noosed when they least expected it. I saw there also a beautiful white bird called a ptarmigan, which is a grouse, but it could not be caught.

"By this time we had become quite domesticated among the savages. They called me *Annorak*, which meant that I resembled the wind when I talked, — that is, I talked when I

liked and where I liked, and nothing could stop me, while the
Dean was much more sober.   Him they finally called *Aupad-*
leit, which means 'Little Red-head,' though the Dean's hair
was not exactly red, but very bright, and the savages admired
it very much ; so the Dean, to humor them, cut off great locks
of it, and gave it to them all round.

   " I took a great interest in Eatum's children, and this further inclined Mr. and Mrs. Eatum to have a good opinion of
me.   As they were people of much consequence in their tribe,
this was a matter of great importance ; and, in truth, the juve-
nile Eatums were quite an interesting pair of savages, and
were fond of play like any other children.   One was a boy and
the other a girl.   I cannot remember their right names, but
the Dean and I christened the boy *Mop-head*, because of the
great quantity of dirty black hair he had, and the girl we
called *Gimlet-eyes*.   Mop-head had a little sledge made of
bones, just like his father's ; and with this the two children
used to play at travelling and other games.   Gimlet-eyes had
little dolls carved out of bones, which she used to dress up in
furs and put on the sledge for Mop-head to drag when they
went on their journeys ; and he had little spears, and she had
little pots and lamps, and they used to make excursions over
the snow that you could hardly throw a stone to the end of ;
and then they would build little snow houses and put the dolls
in them, and, while Mop-head went off to hunt, Gimlet-eyes
would *amna-aya* them to sleep.   Thus you see little children
are much alike all the world over.

   "In these playful exercises we used to amuse ourselves with
the children ; and when we were travelling about in earnest,
the Dean and I sometimes pulled Mop-head's little sledge for
him, when we were going slow ; and he thought it great fun

to have the white-faced strangers drag his sister's lamps and pots and dolls along.

"And now the summer was fairly come. The snow was melting very rapidly, and first in small and then in large streams the water came rushing and roaring down into the sea. The birds soon afterward came back from the south, — the eider-ducks and the little auks, which we had caught in the summer time when upon the island; and then, as soon as the snow was all gone, the moss and stunted grass grew green, and plants sprouted up here and there, and the butter-flies with bright yellow wings went gathering the honey from flower to flower, and you cannot imagine how glad we were once more to come out of the dreary winter into this bright sunshine and this pleasant summer.

"It was apparent now why the savages had gone to this place. The little auks came in great numbers, and these birds I was told formed their principal subsistence in the summer season; indeed sometimes this is their only kind of food. There must have been millions on millions of them, swarming there like bees, and they made their nests among the stones on the hillside. The savages caught them as we had done, in nets. There were some reindeer, but these were not often caught. The reindeer here run wild, and are not as in Lapland tamed and taught to draw sledges. When the sav-ages went on this kind of hunting, two always went together, walking so close, one behind the other, as to appear like one man. As soon as the deer saw the hunters, the latter would turn round and go back the other way, and the deer, being very curious, would follow them. Thus a deer may sometimes be enticed a long distance, and if through a narrow defile, there is then a chance of catching him; for one of the hunters drops down suddenly behind a rock, while the other goes on as if nothing had happened. The deer, thus cheated, keeps following the single hunter, where he had before followed a double one all unknown to himself, and at length approaches very near to the hunter lying behind the rock. As soon as the deer comes within a few yards of him, this concealed hunter rises, and throws his harpoon, the line of which he has previously made fast to a heavy stone. If fortunate enough to hit the deer, and the harpoon to hold, the animal is easily killed by the two hunters, who attack it with their spears.

"Besides the birds that I have told you of, there came a great many snipes, and different varieties of sea-gulls, and ducks of various species, and gerfalcons, and ravens, — also some little sparrows.

" I was very desirous to know how they managed to make their harpoon and spear heads, as I observed that they were all tipped with iron. So one day they took us over to a place they call *Savisavick*, which means 'The Iron Place,' — the name being derived from a large block of meteoric iron, from which the savages chipped small scales ; and these were set in the edges and tips of their harpoon and spear heads, just as I had done with my brass buttons. They also made knives in the same way. Many of their spear-handles were nothing more than narwhal horns, just like 'Old Crumply' ; and so you see how the Lord provides for all his creatures, endowing them all, whether white or black or copper-colored, with the same instinct of self-preservation, which leads them to seek and obtain for the security of their lives the materials that He places within their reach. How beautiful are all His works ! and how constantly He watches over the rich and the poor, the savage and the Christian, the just and the unjust alike !

"Thus occupied, we drifted on into the final week of July. There was scarcely any snow left on the hillsides by this time ; the air was filled with the incessant cry of birds and the constant plash of falling waters. We could sleep well enough once more on the green grass in the open air ; and another period of watching now began, for here it was that the vessels passed every year, as the savages told us. Sometimes, however, they did not stop ; but, when the ships appeared, the savages always went to a valley facing the sea, from one side of which the snow never melted, and, running to and fro over the white snow, endeavored to attract the attention of the people on the ships.

"We were much alarmed to find the ice holding firmly along the shore ; and, as far away as the eye could reach, there was not much water to be seen.   At last, however, a strong wind came, and started the ice.   Some cracks were soon opened, and then a long lead or lane of water was seen stretching away to the south, and running close in by the land.

"The savages said that the *Oomeaksuaks* (big ships) would come very soon now, if at all ; so we watched very carefully for them.   The Dean and I did not hunt any more, as the savages, seeing how anxious we were, and how our hearts yearned for our own homes and kindred, provided us with food in abundance ; and, besides this, they sent some of their women and young lads to aid us in looking out for the ships.

"Thus the time wore on, and we were becoming very fearful that the ships would not come at all.   This was a dreadful thought to us, for, although the savages were very obliging, yet we looked forward with great dread to living long with them.   Besides this and our longing to get home, we had had quite enough of 'this cold, desolate part of the world, where the sun never sets in summer nor rises in winter.

"While reflecting in this way, we heard one of the savages cry out *'Oomcaksuak, Oomcaksuak!'* several times ; and, running a little higher up the hillside whence the cry proceeded, our eyes were gladdened by seeing far off, with the hull yet hidden below the horizon, a ship under full sail, steering northward. At first the Dean, who had been so often cheated, thought it might be an iceberg ; but it was clearly a ship that we saw this time. From fear that it might be an iceberg, we passed now to fear that it might hold off from the land, and not discover us, which would be even harder to bear.

"By and by the hull of the ship was plainly to be seen, and after a while we discovered that the ship was not alone, but that another was following only a few miles behind it ; and directly two more were seen, making four, and then a fifth hove in sight some hours afterward. We knew this must be part of a whaling fleet that annually visits the Arctic seas, and we rejoiced greatly at the prospect of our deliverance.

"You will see how fortunate it was for us that there were so many of these ships ; for, as we had feared, the first ship held so far away from the land that it was hopeless to think of being seen from her. But the lead through which this first ship had sailed off from the land was closed up before the others could enter it ; and now these other ships were forced to come nearer to us. Seeing this, we hastened to the white hillside I have spoken of before, all the savages accompanying us, and we all began running up and down ; but the next ship was still too far away to discover us. And the same with another and still another. Thus had four ships gone by without any soul on board being aware that two poor shipwrecked boys were so near, calling to them, and praying with all their might that they might see or hear.

"But there was yet a fifth ship, a long way behind all the others, and we still had hope. If this failed us, all was over, and we must be content to live with the savages. We had observed one thing which gave us great encouragement. Each ship that had passed us came a little nearer to the land; and this we saw was in consequence of the ice drifting steadily in before the wind. Indeed, by the time the last ship came along, the ice had pushed in ahead of her, and had touched the land, while the other ships had run through just in time.

"When the people on board saw what was ahead of them, and that they could not pass, they tacked ship, and stood away from us; but we saw clearly enough, from our elevated position on the hill, that they were not likely to get through in that direction, — which was, no doubt, a much more pleasant thing for us than for the people on board. This proved true; for presently they tacked again, and stood straight in towards where we were standing. Coming very near the shore, we did everything we could to attract their attention. We shouted as loud as we could, we threw up our caps and waved them round our heads, and we ran to and fro, all the savages doing the same.

"O how excited we became! almost frantic, indeed. A ship so near and yet so far away! Four ships gone by and out of sight! Those on board the fifth and last unconscious of our presence on the desolate shore; and how could we make the people see us? I cannot tell you what anxious moments these were during which we watched the ship as she came nearer and nearer to where we stood.

"At length she is so near that we can see the people on the deck; why can they not see us?

"The sails are shivering; the ship is coming to the wind!

11*

Have they seen us? are they heaving the vessel to? will they send a boat ashore to fetch us off?

"We hear the creaking of the blocks; the yards are swinging round; the braces are hauled taut; the other tack is aboard; they are *not* heaving to!

"The vessel fills away again; the sails are bulging out; the vessel drives ahead; they have not seen us!

"Shout again! Up and down, up and down, once more across the snow, — shout! shout all in chorus! but it is of no use.

"The bows fall off; the vessel turns back upon her course. Where is she going now? is she homeward bound?

"O no! she steers for the land; she nears it; she passes beyond a point below us, and is out of sight! Where has she gone?

"We follow after her, hurrying all we can. Miles of rough travelling over rocks and through deep gorges, — climbing down one side and up the other. The savages are with us.

"What is our hope? It is that the vessel, failing to get through the ice, has sought the land for shelter, and will find an anchorage and there remain until the ice opens ahead, and gives the ship once more a chance to go upon her course.

" Soon we round a lofty cliff that rises almost squarely from the sea, with only a narrow, rugged track between it and the water, and we come upon a narrow bay. A little farther, and there the vessel lies before us, — quietly at anchor, with her sails all furled.

"Again we see the men upon the deck, — faintly, but still we see them.

"Again we shout.

"We see a man halting by the bulwarks; something glitters in his hand. Is it a spyglass?

"No ; he moves away.

"Is that a man mounting to the mizen cross-trees ?

"Yes, it is a man.

"Is that a spyglass glittering in his hand ? Yes, surely it must be.

"He waves his cap ; he shouts to the people on deck ; he descends ; all is bustle in the ship ; a boat is lowered to the water ; men spring into it; the oars are dipped ; the men give way ; the boat heads for the spot where we are standing ; we are discovered ! O, God be praised ! at last, at last !

"The boat cuts through the water quickly ; it nears us ; again we see white human faces ; again we hear human speech in a familiar tongue.

"' In oars !' — the boat touches the rocks, and we are there to take the painter, and to make her fast.

"Two of the men spring out ; a man rises in the stern ; he shades his eyes with his hands, as if to protect them from the glaring sun, and stares at us, and then at the savages, who — of both sexes, and of every age and size — surround us. Then he calls out, ' Is there a white man in that crowd ?'

"' Yes, sir ; two of them.'

"' I thought so from the motions,' says the man. Then he stared at me again, and cried : ' Is that the lubber Hardy, of the *Blackbird* ?'

"' Yes, sir ; it is,' I answered.

"' Is that other chap the cabin-boy ? — him they called the Dean ?'

"' Yes, sir,' spoke up the Dean.

"In an instant the man was out upon the rocks, and he grasped us warmly by the hands. He had recognized us, now we recognized *him*. He was the master of a ship that lay alongside the *Blackbird* when we first went among the ice, catching seals. His ship was the *Rob Roy*, of Aberdeen.

"This much he said to quiet us, for he saw the state of agitation we were in. Then he went on to tell us that the *Blackbird*, not having been heard from in all this time, it was thought that she must have gone down somewhere among the ice, with all on board; and he told us further, that he was on a whaling voyage now, and then he said, 'The *Rob Roy* will give you a bonny welcome, lads.'

"Afterward he told us that the vessels were, as we had supposed, a part of the whaling fleet, and he said it was fortunate that he had discovered us, as this was our only chance, for all the other vessels that were following him would be very likely, on account of the state of the ice, to hold to the westward, and not come near the land.

"All this time the savages were *yeh-yeh*-ing round us, greatly to the amusement of the captain of the *Rob Roy* and his boat's crew. Then, when I told the captain how good they had been to us, he sent his boat back to the ship, and had fetched for them wood and knives and iron and needles, in such great abundance that they set up a *yeh, yeh*, in consequence, which, for anything I know to the contrary, may be going on even to this present time.

"But what was the happiness of the savages compared to ours? Our feelings cannot be described. It seemed almost as if we had come from death to life. We could hardly believe our eyes, — that this was the ship we had so long hoped for, this the rescue we had so often despaired of. We cried with very joy, and behaved like two crazy people. The captain of the *Rob Roy* laughed good-naturedly at us, and proposed at once to hurry us off aboard his ship.

"We kept our promise to give Eatum all our property; but the captain of the *Rob Roy* wanted 'Old Crumply' and 'The Dean's Delight,' and our pot and lamp, and some other things; so he gave Eatum other valuables in place of them. Then we took leave of our savage friends, which we of course did not do without some feelings of sorrow and regret at parting from them, remembering as we did how kind they had been to us, and how they had rescued us from our unhappy situation; and the savages seemed a little sorry too. First came Eatum and Mrs. Eatum, and then the two little Eatums (Mop-head and Gimlet-eyes) that I had so often played with; then Old Grim and Big-toes and Little-nose; and Awak, the walrus, and Kossuit; and the two young ladies who might have been our wives: and then all the rest of them, big and little, old and young.

"Then off we went to the *Rob Roy;* and a fair wind coming soon, the ice began to move away from the land, the *Rob Roy's* sails were unfurled to the fresh breeze, and now, with hearts turned thankfully to Heaven for our deliverance, we were again afloat upon the blue water, — whither bound we did not know, but *homeward* in the end."

"O, how glad you must have been!" said Fred.

"How splendidly the rescue and all that comes round." said William; "just like it does in all the printed books. Why, Captain Hardy, it could n't have been better if you 'd made the story up, it looks so *real!*"

While, as for little Alice, she never said a word, but only looked upon the old man wonderingly.

CHAPTER XX.

BRINGS THE HOLIDAYS OF THE LITTLE PEOPLE AND THE STORY OF THE
OLD MAN TO AN END.

A GAIN the Mariner's Rest receives the little people ;
again the Ancient Mariner is there to welcome them.
But a shade of sadness is upon the old man's face, and the
children are not so gay as is their wont ; for all things must
have an end, and holidays are no exception to the rule.

"Is'nt it too bad," said William, looking very sober, —
"is n't it too bad that this is to be the last of it ? "

"Not so bad for you as for me," replied the Ancient Mariner ; and the old man looked as gloomy and forsaken as if
he had been cast away in the cold again. But he soon cheered
up, and in a much livelier way he said, "Well now, my hearties, since this *is* to be the last of it, suppose we close the
story in the 'Crow's Nest,' where we first began it ; for you
see, if the Dean and I were rescued from the desolate island
and the savages, we were not home yet. Now, what do you
say to that, my dears ? "

"The Crow's Nest ! Yes, yes, the Crow's Nest !" cried the
children all at once ; and away they scampered to it, as light
and merry as if they had never for an instant been sad at
thought of the parting that was so soon to come.

And now once more our little party are together in the dear
old rustic vine-clad arbor, and, as on the first day of meeting
there, the old man takes his long clay pipe out of his mouth,

and sticks it in a rafter overhead ; then around little Alice he puts his great, big arm, and he draws the fair-haired, bright-eyed child close to his side, and thus "ballasted," as he says, he "bears away for port."

"Now, to bring our story to an end," ran on the Captain, "I must say first that the *Rob Roy* was a good, stout ship ; the master a bluff, good-hearted Scotchman ; the mate a kindly man, and altogether different from the red-faced mate that was on the *Blackbird;* and the people were all just as good and kind to us as the savages had been. But they gave us right away so much coffee and ship's biscuit and other things to eat and drink (none of which had we tasted for three years and more), that we got a dreadful colic, and had like to have died. But the next day we were quite well again, and then we related to the Captain and everybody on board the story of our adventures. The worst was, they would make us tell our story over and over again, as I have been telling it to you, until we almost wished we had never been rescued at all. It is, indeed, a fearful thing in anybody's life ever to have met with any adventure that is at all peculiar ; for to the end of his days people will never get done asking him about it ; and most likely their questions are of the most ridiculous kind, like, 'Hardy, was n't it cold there ?' just as if anybody could be cast away in the cold, and find it anything else ; or, 'How did you feel, Hardy ?' as if *feeling* has anything at all to do with you when you are trying to save your life.

"The captain of the *Rob Roy* took a great fancy to our odd-looking fur clothes, especially our underclothing, which was made of birds' skins ; and he gave us civilized garments out of the ship's stores. You may be sure that we were glad enough to get these nasty fur clothes off, and be rid of them forever. The captain offered to keep them for us, but we said ' No, no,' for we had had quite enough of them.

" So we went after whales, and made a ' good catch,' as the whale-fishers call a good shipload of oil, and then we bore away for Aberdeen, only stopping on the way at two or three half-savage places.

"When we reached Aberdeen, which occurred on the 29th of October, there was a great talk made about us, and, when we walked through the streets, people stuck out their fingers, and said, 'There they go! look!' so we were great lions there, and had to tell our story so often that we found out what they liked most to hear, and this we repeated over and over again ; and by this method we saved much time and talk.

" The very first thing the Dean did, after landing, was to write a letter to his mother, sending it off right away by post. It was just like the little fellow to do it, and what he wrote was like him too. It began thus : ' Through the mercy of Providence I have been saved, and am coming back to you, mother dear.'

" Then we were shipped on board an American vessel, by the American Consul, for New York, where we arrived after a prosperous voyage, in good health, and without anything happening to us worth mentioning. This was on the 22d day of December, which made just three years, nine months, and nineteen days since we sailed from New Bedford.

"As soon as we had landed, we set out for the hospital to find the Dean's mother. The Dean had directed his letter there, thinking that if she had got well and gone away, they would know where ; and this they did, so we took down the address and hurried on. It was in a little by-street, and we had much trouble to find it ; but by and by we came upon a tumble-down old house, and were shown into a little tumble-down old room, with a tumble-down old bed in it, and a tumble-

The Dean's Mother.

down box for a chair, and a small tumble-down table, and right in the middle of the floor stood a little woman that was more tumble-down than all. It was the Dean's poor mother. She stood beside a tub in which she had been washing clothes, and she held a scrap of paper in both her hands, which, bony

Q

and hard with work, work, work, and scrub, scrub, scrub, were trembling violently, while she tried to puzzle out the contents of the Dean's letter (for this it was), that she held up before a face the deep wrinkles on which told of many sorrows and much suffering. The letter had arrived only a few minutes before we did, and she had only just made out that it was from the Dean, and we could see that this had started great tears rolling down her cheeks.

"But there was no use to puzzle more now. There was her darling, bright-haired boy, whom she 'always felt sure,' she said, 'would come back again,' — never losing hope ; and now you can imagine how she was not long in recognizing him, and how she greeted him, and cried over him, and called him pretty names, and all that, — or, rather, I mean to say, you can't imagine it at all, for I never saw the like of it. It seemed to me as if she would never let him go out of her arms again, for fear she should lose him ; and, seeing how matters stood, I went outside, where after a while the Dean joined me, and having some money in our pockets, that we had earned on board the *Rob Roy* and the American packet-ship, we went right off and bought the best supper we could get, and had it brought into the tumble-down room and spread out upon the tumble-down table ; and never was any poor woman so glad in all the world as the Dean's mother, and never were any two boys so happy as the Dean and I. The Dean's mother would sometimes laugh for joy, and sometimes cry for the same excellent reason ; and, when neither of these would do, nor both together even, she would fly at the Dean with open arms, and hug and kiss him until she was quite exhausted, and temporarily quieted down. Meanwhile the Dean, besides eating his supper, was trying to tell his mother what he had been doing all the time, — to neither of which purposes were these maternal interruptions peculiarly favorable.

"So now you see we were at home at last, safe in body and thankful in spirit. Transported with delight, we could hardly believe our senses. After so many years' absence, and such hardships and dangers as we had passed through, New York seemed like another world. So accustomed had we been to exposure that we could hardly sleep in-doors. The confined air of the house greatly troubled us. Everything we saw seemed new, and we were in a constant state of wonder. We did not, however, forget the obligation we owed to our Heavenly Father for our deliverance; and we lost no time in going to a church, and there, in secret, we poured out our hearts to Him who rules the winds and the waves, and never forgets any of the creatures he has made.

"'And now,' said the Dean, 'I am going to further show my gratitude by making my mother comfortable for the rest of her days,' — which he did by getting her into a better house, where she did not have to work any more, — the Dean declaring that he would hereafter make all the money that was necessary for her support ; and he kept his word, too.

"As for the money the Dean had when we came home, that was soon all gone, and mine too, for that matter, since I helped the Dean, of course. Then we looked about us for a good ship to go to sea in, as we felt that we should make better sailors now than anything else ; indeed, neither of us knew what else to do.

"The story of our remarkable adventures getting abroad, we found many friends, so you may be sure, when we shipped again, it was not in such a crazy old hulk as the *Blackbird*, nor did we go any more whale or seal fishing, having got enough of that to last us during the remainder of our lives. Still, I have been back to the Arctic regions once since then; but it was not with a red-faced mate to torment me.

"I did not feel like coming up to Rockdale yet, being very much ashamed, not having made anything, as I could see, by running away. Besides, I learned that my father had given me up for dead long ago, and had moved with all my brothers and sisters to Ohio, where I wrote to him, telling all about my voyage and shipwreck, — the best I could, that is ; for, having neglected my studies when at school, I could not write very well.

" So now I came to be a regular sailor, going away first with the Dean on a voyage to the Mediterranean in a fine bark, where we got moderately good wages, and, being both rather ambitious, we grew in favor and saved our money. When we returned, I proposed to the Dean that we should make a common stock of our earnings, and get ourselves a nice little home, which we did ; and remembering the Rock of Good Hope, we called it Good Hope Cottage, of which the Dean's mother took possession, of course, while off we went to sea again, this time to Rio de Janeiro, in the same bark ; then afterwards we went to the Mediterranean twice more, and on the last voyage I got to be mate ; and, afterward, when we stopped at Barcelona, the Dean was made second mate. Then, in course of time, the Dean got to be a Captain, and prospered greatly, while his mother lived at Good Hope Cottage, and the Dean and I were always happy to come back and have a home like that to go to. After a while we were separated, for I was a Captain as well as the Dean, and we could no longer be together in the same ship ; but still we both had a home together, and a place always to hail from, you see.

" But I go too fast and too far. I must stop now, for I have given you the story that I promised, of how I was *cast away in the cold*, — and it is high time too ; for, as you have said, the holidays are at an end, and see there! the sun is sinking down behind the trees, and once more, as on the first day we met and parted in this pleasant little arbor, the shadows trail their ghostly length across the fields. But to me the shadows have another meaning now. They will lie there heavy on the ground until you come to lift them, and I shall be very, very sad and lonely now without my little friends. The night is closing in, my dears, as if it were a curtain dropped purposely to hide what we would gladly see again ; and the dew is falling heavy on the grass, my dears, and so 'good by' is the word."

The Captain paused and bent his eyes upon the golden light that lay far-off behind the trees, as if he would divine something of the future that was before himself and the little children by his side, and which he thought the golden sunlight held ; but, while he looked, it seemed as if some tender chord within his gentle heart had snapped asunder and had been badly tied again, for he said quite hurriedly, " Well, well, my hearties, we must pass the word, and get it over. Good by, — there it is ! God bless you, and good by !"

" Good by, dear Captain Hardy," said William, putting out his hand, — a hand that promised to be a very manly one indeed some day, — " good by, and thank you for all your goodness to us," and the little fellow could not keep a tear from coming out upon his plump and rosy cheek.

" Good by," said Fred, and, as he said it, there were two tears at the very least on his.

"Good by," dear little Alice would have said, though she did n't ; but instead she threw her arms about the old man's neck and kissed his sunburnt cheek.

"Good by," the Captain was about to say again, but (he was always good at getting out of scrapes) at that very moment he contracted a suspicion that something moist was getting up into his own big hazel eyes ; and so he began to whistle briskly, and then to cry out, loud enough to call all hands to close reef the topsails in a gale of wind : " Port and Starboard ! Port and Starboard ! come here, old curs and landlubbers that you are, — come, bear a hand and be lively there, and say 'good by.' "

And along Port and Starboard came, bounding at a tremendous rate, barking "good by " at every bound, and with their great bushy tails wagging " good by " besides.

The foreign ducks stopped shovelling and spattering mud, and quacked "good by."

The chickens stopped stuffing themselves with grasshoppers, and, while the hens cackled "good by," the roosters crowed it.

And, lastly, Main Brace came waddling along on his sausage legs, and from his plum-duff head let off " good by " at intervals, as a revolving gun lets off its balls, without appearing to have any more idea of what it was all about than the gun itself, until he reached the arbor, when he broke out into a loud " boo-hoo," which was the only " good by " he was now equal to ; and as the first "boo-hoo " let loose a second, and the second a third, and the third a deluge and an earthquake all in one, there is no knowing what might have happened, had not the children scampered off and stopped the outburst, — Fred running on ahead, and William following after, leading his sister Alice by the hand, while the gentle little girl turned every dozen steps to throw back through the tender evening air, from her dainty little finger-tips, a loving kiss (there was no laughing now) to the Ancient Mariner, whose face beamed brightly on her from the arbor door, and whose lips were saying plainly, " Good by, and God bless you till you come again ! "

THE END.

YOUNG AMERICA ABROAD.

FIRST SERIES.

**A Library of Travel and Adventure in Foreign Lands. 16mo.
Illustrated by Nast, Stevens, Perkins, and others.
Per volume, $1.50.**

1. OUTWARD BOUND;
Or, Young America Afloat.

2. SHAMROCK AND THISTLE;
Or, Young America in Ireland and Scotland.

3. RED CROSS;
Or. Young America in England and Wales.

4. DIKES AND DITCHES;
Or, Young America in Holland and Belgium.

5. PALACE AND COTTAGE;
Or, Young America in France and Switzerland.

6. DOWN THE RHINE;
Or, Young America in Germany.

The story from its inception and through the twelve vol
umes (see *Second Series*), is a bewitching one, while the information imparted, concerning the countries of Europe and
the isles of the sea, is not only correct in every particular, but
is told in a captivating style. " Oliver Optic " will continue
to be the boy's friend, and his pleasant books will continue to
he read by thousands of American boys. What a fine holiday
present either or both series of " Young America Abroad "
would be for a young friend! It would make a little library
highly prized by the recipient, and would not be an expensive
one. — *Providence Press.*

YOUNG AMERICA ABROAD.

SECOND SERIES.

**A Library of Travel and Adventure in Foreign Lands. 16mo.
Illustrated by Nast, Stevens, Perkins, and others.
Per volume, $1.50.**

1. UP THE BALTIC;
Or, Young America in Norway, Sweden, and
Denmark.

2. NORTHERN LANDS;
Or, Young America in Russia and Prussia.

3. CROSS AND CRESCENT;
Or, Young America in Turkey and Greece.

4. SUNNY SHORES;
Or, Young America in Italy and Austria.

5. VINE AND OLIVE;
Or, Young America in Spain and Portugal.

6. ISLES OF THE SEA;
Or, Young America Homeward Bound.

" Oliver Optic " is a *nom de plume* that is known and loved by almost every boy of intelligence in the land. We have seen a highly intellectual and world-weary man, a cynic whose heart was somewhat imbittered by its large experience of human nature, take up one of Oliver Optic's books and read it at a sitting, neglecting his work in yielding to the fascination of the pages. When a mature and exceedingly well-informed mind, long despoiled of all its freshness, can thus find pleasure in a book for boys, no additional words of recommendation are needed. — *Sunday Times.*

THE GREAT WESTERN

SERIES.

Six Volumes. Illustrated. Per vol., $1.50.

1. **GOING WEST;**
   Or, The Perils of a Poor Boy.

2. **OUT WEST;**
   Or, Roughing it on the Great Lakes.

3. **LAKE BREEZES;**
   Or, The Cruise of the Sylvania.

4. **GOING SOUTH;**
   Or, Yachting on the Atlantic Coast.

5. **DOWN SOUTH;**
   Or, Yacht Adventures in Florida.

6. **UP THE RIVER;**
   Or, Yachting on the Mississippi.

This is the latest series of books issued by this popular writer, and deals with Life on the Great Lakes, for which a careful study was made by the author in a summer tour of the immense water sources of America. The story, which carries the same hero through the six books of the series, is always entertaining, novel scenes and varied incidents giving a constantly changing, yet always attractive aspect to the narrative. "Oliver Optic" has written nothing better.

YACHT CLUB SERIES.

Uniform with the ever popular "Boat Club," Series, Completed in six vols. 16mo. Illustrated. Per vol., $1.50.

1. LITTLE BOBTAIL;
Or, The Wreck of the Penobscot

2. THE YACHT CLUB;
Or, The Young Boat-Builders.

8. MONEY-MAKER;
Or, The Victory of the Basilisk.

4. THE COMING WAVE;
Or, The Treasure of High Rock.

6. THE DORCAS CLUB;
Or, Our Girls Afloat.

6. OCEAN BORN;
Or, The Cruise of the Clubs.

The series has this peculiarity, that all of its constituent volumes are independent of one another, and therefore each story is complete in itself. "Oliver Optic" is perhaps the favorite author of the boys and girls of this country, and he seems destined to enjoy an endless popularity. He deserves his success, for he makes very interesting stories, and inculcates none but the best sentiments; and the "Yacht Club" is no exception to this rule. — *New Haven Jour. and Courier*.

THE BOAT-BUILDER SERIES.

**Completed in Six Volumes. Illustrated.
Per Vol., $1.25.**

1. **ALL ADRIFT;**
   Or, The Goldwing Club.

2. **SNUG HARBOR;**
   Or, The Champlain Mechanics.

3. **SQUARE AND COMPASS;**
   Or, Building the House.

4. **STEM TO STERN;**
   Or Building the Boat.

5. **ALL TAUT;**
   Or, Rigging the Boat.

6. **READY ABOUT;**
   Or, Sailing the Boat.

The series includes in six successive volumes the whole art of boat-building, boat-rigging, boat managing, and practical hints to make the ownership of a boat pay. A great deal of useful information will be given in this Boat-Building series, and in each book a very interesting story is sure to be interwoven with the information. Every reader will be interested at once in " Dory," the hero of "All Adrift," and one of the characters to be retained in the future volumes of the series, at least there are already several of his recently made friends who do not want to lose sight of him, and this will be the case of pretty much every boy who makes his acquaintance in "All Adrift."

FAMOUS "BOAT-CLUB" SERIES.

Library for Young People. Six volumes, handsomely illustrated
Per volume, $1.25.

1. THE BOAT CLUB;
Or, The Bunkers of Rippleton.

2. ALL ABOARD;
Or, Life on the Lake.

3. NOW OR NEVER;
Or, The Adventures of Bobby Bright.

4. TRY AGAIN;
Or, The Trials and Triumphs of Harry West.

5. POOR AND PROUD;
Or, The Fortunes of Katy Redburn.

6. LITTLE BY LITTLE;
Or, The Cruise of the Flyaway.

This is the first series of books written for the young by " Oliver Optic." It laid the foundation for his fame as the first of authors in which the young delight, and gained for him the title of the Prince of Story-Tellers. The six books are varied in incident and plot, but all are entertaining and original.

THE LAKE SHORE SERIES.

Six volumes. Illustrated. In neat box. Per vol., $1.25.

1. THROUGH BY DAYLIGHT;
Or, The Young Engineer of the Lake Shore Railroad.

2. LIGHTNING EXPRESS;
Or, The Rival Academies.

3. ON TIME;
Or, The Young Captain of the Ucayga Steamer

4. SWITCH OFF;
Or, The War of the Students.

5. BRAKE-UP;
Or, The Young Peacemakers.

6. BEAR AND FORBEAR;
Or, The Young Skipper of Lake Ucayga.

"Oliver Optic" is one of the most fascinating writers for youth, and withal one of the best to be found in this or any past age. Troops of young people hang over his vivid pages, and not one of them ever learned to be mean, ignoble, cowardly, selfish, or to yield to any vice from anything they ever read from his pen. — *Providence Press.*

THE ONWARD AND UPWARD
SERIES.

Complete in six volumes. Illustrated. In neat box,
Per volume, $1.25.

1. FIELD AND FOREST;
Or, The Fortunes of a Farmer.

2. PLANE AND PLANK;
Or, The Mishaps of a Mechanic.

3. DESK AND DEBIT;
Or, The Catastrophes of a Clerk.

4. CRINGLE AND CROSS-TREE;
Or, The Sea Swashes of a Sailor.

5. BIVOUAC AND BATTLE;
Or, The Struggles of a Soldier.

6. SEA AND SHORE;
Or, The Tramps of a Traveller.

Paul Farringford, the hero of these tales, is, like most of this author's heroes, a young man of high spirit, and of high aims and correct principles, appearing in the different volumes as a farmer, a captain, a bookkeeper, a soldier, a sailor, and a traveller. In all of them the hero meets with very exciting adventures, told in the graphic style for which the author is famous. — *Native.*

WOODVILLE STORIES.

Uniform with Library for Young People. Six vols. 16mo. Illustrated. Per vol., $1.25.

1. **RICH AND HUMBLE;**
   Or, The Mission of Bertha Grant.

2. **IN SCHOOL AND OUT;**
   Or, The Conquest of Richard Grant.

3. **WATCH AND WAIT;**
   Or, The Young Fugitives.

4. **WORK AND WIN;**
   Or, Noddy Newman on a Cruise.

5. **HOPE AND HAVE;**
   Or, Fanny Grant among the Indians.

6 **HASTE AND WASTE;**
   Or, The Young Pilot of Lake Champlain.

Though we are not so young as we once were, we relished these stories almost as much as the boys and girls for whom they were written. They were really refreshing even to us. There is much in them which is calculated to inspire a generous, healthy ambition, and to make distasteful all reading tending to stimulate base desires. — *Fitchburg Reveille.*

RIVERDALE STORY-BOOKS.

Twelve volumes, profusely illustrated. A new edition. Illuminated Paper
Covers, per set, $2.00; Cloth, in neat box, per set, $3.60.

1. LITTLE MERCHANT.
2. YOUNG VOYAGERS.
3. CHRISTMAS GIFT.
4. DOLLY AND I.
5. UNCLE BEN.
6. BIRTHDAY PARTY.
7. PROUD AND LAZY.
8. CARELESS KATE.
9. ROBINSOE CRUSOE, JR.
10. THE PICNIC PARTY.
11. THE GOLD THIMBLE.
12. THE DO-SOMETHINGS.

The "Riverdale Stories" are a series of short bright stories for younger children than those who are able to comprehend "The Starry Flag Series," "The Woodville Stories,"
"Army and Navy Stories," &c. But they all display the
author's talent for pleasing "Little Folks" as well as the
older children. They are all fresh, taking stories, preaching
no sermons but inculcating good lessons.

YOUNG FOLKS' .... :
.... BOOKS OF TRAVEL

DRIFTING ROUND THE WORLD; A Boy's Adventures by Sea and Land

By Capt. CHARLES W. HALL, author of "Adrift in the Ice-Fields," "The Great Bonanza," etc. With numerous full-page and letter-press illustrations. Royal 8vo. Handsome cover. $1.75. Cloth, gilt, $2.50.
"Out of the beaten track" in its course of travel, record of adventures, and descriptions of life in Greenland, Labrador, Ireland, Scotland, England, France, Holland, Russia, Asia, Siberia, and Alaska. Its hero is young, bold, and adventurous; and the book is in every way interesting and attractive.

EDWARD GREEY'S JAPANESE SERIES

YOUNG AMERICANS IN JAPAN; or, The Adventures of the Jewett Family and their Friend Oto Nambo

With 170 full-page and letter-press illustrations. Royal 8vo, 7 x 9½ inches. Handsomely illuminated cover. $1.75. Cloth, black and gold, $2.50.
This story, though essentially a work of fiction, is filled with interesting and truthful descriptions of the curious ways of living of the good people of the land of the rising sun.

THE WONDERFUL CITY OF TOKIO; or, The Further Adventures of the Jewett Family and their Friend Oto Nambo

With 169 illustrations. Royal 8vo, 7 x 9½ inches. With cover in gold and colors, designed by the author. $1.75. Cloth, black and gold, $2.50.
"A book full of delightful information. The author has the happy gift of permitting the reader to view things as he saw them. The illustrations are mostly drawn by a Japanese artist, and are very unique." —*Chicago Herald.*

THE BEAR WORSHIPPERS OF YEZO AND THE ISLAND OF KARAFUTO; being the further Adventures of the Jewett Family and their Friend Oto Nambo

180 illustrations. Boards, $1.75. Cloth, $2.50.
Graphic pen and pencil pictures of the remarkable bearded people who live in the north of Japan. The illustrations are by native Japanese artists, and give queer pictures of a queer people, who have been seldom visited.

HARRY W. FRENCH'S BOOKS

OUR BOYS IN INDIA

The wanderings of two young Americans in Hindustan, with their exciting adventures on the sacred rivers and wild mountains. With 145 illustrations. Royal 8vo, 7 x 9½ inches. Bound in emblematic covers of Oriental design, $1.75. Cloth, black and gold, $2.50.
While it has all the exciting interest of a romance, it is remarkably vivid in its pictures of manners and customs in the land of the Hindu. The illustrations are many and excellent.

OUR BOYS IN CHINA

The adventures of two young Americans, wrecked in the China Sea on their return from India, with their strange wanderings through the Chinese Empire. 188 illustrations. Boards, ornamental covers in colors and gold, $1.75. Cloth, $2.50.
This gives the further adventures of "Our Boys" of India fame in the land of Tea and Queues.

Sold by all booksellers, and sent by mail, postpaid, on receipt of price

LEE AND SHEPARD Publishers Boston